# Pine Grove

## A Journey of Love, Loss, and Light

### ANNA VANDENBROUCKE

PARK PLACE PUBLICATIONS
Pacific Grove, California

*Pine Grove*
*A Journey Of Love, Loss, And Light*
by Anna Vandenbroucke



ISBN 978-1-953120-67-0
Printed in U.S.A.
First U.S. Edition: November 2023

Disclaimer: This is a work of fiction. Any resemblance of characters to
actual persons, living or dead, is purely coincidental.
The Author holds exclusive rights to this work.

Cover photo by Frank Geisler and Paint Snap
Published by Park Place Publications
Pacific Grove, California

**In honor of my Angel …**

*Annabelle Abby Vandenbroucke*

*February 13, 2002 – July 18, 2018*

Praise for

## *Thirty-Seven Houses*

by Anna Vandenbroucke

*A riveting tale that brims with surprises ...
I couldn't put it down.*

**Kedron Bryson**

*Thirty-Seven Houses is an incredible story of
a woman's success against all odds...inspiring.*

**Regina Ryan, Regina Ryan Books**

*I was so moved by this story ...*

**Eve Bridburg, Zachary, Shuster, Harsworth**

# *Pine Grove*

# 1998

# ONE

Lola Ingram had scheduled Romey to clean her windows on what her husband said was the hottest day of the year. Sam Ingram had already gone outside three times to ask Romey if he could steady his ladder while the window cleaner climbed on the roof. Three times, Romey politely declined, so Sam gave up and came inside.

"I don't know why you keep asking him if you can hold his ladder," said Lola. "He always says no."

"Damn fool's gonna break his neck one of these days crawling up there on the roof with nothing to protect himself if he were to fall. Why does he have to go on the roof anyway if he's washing the windows?"

"Now, Sam. He's a professional and knows what he's doing. He's up there checking the gutters and cleaning out pine needles. Those dried needles are a fire hazard plus they clog up the drains. Romey's so good about clearing them out and he doesn't even charge us extra for it."

"Did you see those shoes he's wearing?"

"No, Sam, I haven't noticed his shoes."

"They're some sort of cloggy-looking things. They don't look very safe for climbing a ladder." He shook his head and sank into his recliner as he had done almost every day for the last twenty years.

Ordinarily, Sam would look out the large front window at his manicured lawn and to the street beyond lined with pine trees. But his eyes fixed on a fly stirring on the window's ledge. Something about watching that spry window cleaner scale up the ladder so nimble and quick, struck Sam with a presentiment that was deeply disturbing—he had crossed over the line of old age. Although he was a well preserved sixty-nine years old and still had his hair, his faculties, and his dignity, questions creeped into the forefront of his mind; Who is in charge of this concept of time and why are there suddenly more years behind me then there are ahead? Is it too much to ask to salvage what's left of my virility, my acute hearing, and my winning golf swing?

The annoying sound of the fly's wings and the buzzing was overtaken by a gnawing tension in his jaw. He clenched his teeth as the tightness slowly traveled down his neck and into his shoulder. He focused on the spinning fly and tried to ignore the increasing weight of his arm. With effort, he put his hand below his collarbone and fingered a sharp sensation near his shirt pocket. His head began to ache and he inhaled sharply and held his breath. *Zizzzz.* The fly stopped flapping and lay silent.

"Lemonade?" asked Lola.

He exhaled slowly. "Nah. I don't feel so good."

"What do you mean? Did you get overheated out there?" He shook his head again.

"I'll get you some water," she said, and went into the kitchen. It was a little too early for happy hour and too hot for cheese and crackers. Seemed like a good day for something cold and refreshing, like peppermint ice cream, the kind with the real peppermint chips that crunch and crackle and get stuck in your molars. She would have to remember to pick some up at Stein's grocery store the next time she was in town.

Outside the kitchen window a bumblebee floated lazily in and out of a cardinal flower. Lola saw the delicate blossoms curled at the edges taking a beating from the heat. Maybe Sam was actually showing signs of heatstroke. He sure seemed crabby, and Lola knew about taking someone seriously when they said they don't feel so well, especially if they're older. She had, after all, married a man twenty-one years her senior.

A swooshing sound came from the rooftop and Lola saw a flurry of dried leaves and pine needles fall to the ground. That Romey is such a hard worker, she thought. He was just a boy the first time he washed their windows, a sincere kid who could sell you an apple for a nickel and you would give him a quarter. Always cheerful, never complains, and now here he is out there in the scorching sun. He probably needs some water and if his little dog is here, he most certainly needs a drink too.

Lola reached for a glass from the cupboard and heard a loud snort come from the living room, followed by a deafening silence. Lola ran into the living room where Sam was sprawled in his chair, arms splayed at his side, head back, eyes half shut, mouth wide open.

"Sam!" she yelled, "Sam!"

She leaned over and put her face near his, her eyes peering right into his gaping mouth. "Sam! Please wake up!" She shook his shoulders hard and his head wobbled lifelessly. She patted his cheek quickly and then slapped him with such power tears began to cloud her vision. His face was ashen. Somehow, through the fear and confusion she found the wherewithal to check for a pulse. None. She jumped on his lap and straddled her lanky legs over his.

"Don't leave me, Sam!" she screamed. "Please wake up!" She curled her fists and double-slugged him in the chest. "Don't you dare leave me! Sam! Sam! God damn you! Do not leave me!" She threw her arms up and with the weight of her whole body, slammed both fists into his chest. He jerked forward, his eyes popped open and stared into Lola's face. Her cheeks were flushed and wet. He smacked his lips, swallowed slowly, rubbed his chest, and tentatively drew in a slow, deep breath.

"What's the matter, Lola, honey? Why are you crying? And what are you doing on my lap?"

"You weren't breathing," she murmured. "I was so scared, Sam." She put her ear on his chest and listened to the slow thud of his heart.

"Well, I'll be damned," he said, and Lola noticed a bit of color returning to his cheeks.

She crawled off him, keeping a hand on his shoulder. She kissed him softly on the cheek. "You rest here. Don't move. I'll bring you some water."

Just then they heard a loud crack outside the window. The ladder had bounced back against the house when Romey dropped from a low rung to the ground. Romey smiled and waved at them, lifted the ladder over his head and walked to his truck.

"Damn fool," Sam said.

Lola was worried sick. Her hands trembled as she attempted to make dinner. She made broth but spilled it while pouring it into a cup. She made toast but burned it black. Sam seemed a bit cheerier, saying he liked burnt toast, but Lola knew better. Sam had convinced her he did not need a doctor. They owned a hospital, after all, and having a strong medical background, they both knew that Lola's fists had revived his old heart with a precordial thump. It was a skill every paramedic used before the advent of the automatic defibrillator.

Between Lola's nervous inability to cook and Sam's loss of appetite, they skipped dinner altogether that night. Sitting in the kitchen, Lola drummed her fingers on the tabletop and stared at Sam. He told her a story of when he was a boy on a hunting trip with a neighbor he called Uncle Ray. Like today, he said, it was a record-breaking heat wave and after drinking from his silver flask at high elevation, Uncle Ray fell asleep by a boulder. When he woke up, he saw a streak of blood on his index finger. Uncle Ray figured it was a rattlesnake bite so he took out his pocket knife and cut off his finger. Later he realized it was merely a nose bleed he had swiped with the now missing digit.

"Oh Lordy," said Lola. They had a good chuckle and with the lightness of the mood, Sam went to have one last sit in his chair, while Lola went to the bedroom. For the first time ever, she decided to leave the bedroom curtain open. She had always insisted it be closed in case a peeping tom came, but tonight, she thought, it would be nice to look out at the stars.

Thirty minutes later, she heard a low, guttural groan. She ran to the recliner, but this time her fists didn't work. Her screams went unheard as the ring of fire seared across Sam's sternum and through his weary heart. Even the night sky did not bear witness as his body quivered, and with one final jerk, Samuel T. Ingram III was gone.

# TWO

The village of Pine Grove, Idaho was settled by the Ingrams in 1873. The entire Ingram family is buried in the two cemeteries at the west entrance. It is recorded in *Ripley's Believe It or Not* that Pine Grove is the only village in the country whose elevation is the same as its population, which is fourteen hundred forty-five, and the only place with a main street flanked by cemeteries.

Running through the center of Pine Grove is a wide lane specifically for big rigs and logging trucks that pass through from US forest territory. The village is home to Stein's Family Grocery, a bank, a florist, and two churches. There is a gas station with a coffee hut called Drip 'n Sip. Next to the Hometown Cafe is the local paper, the *Pine Tree News*. There is a Super 8 motel, a liquor store, and Mel's Bar and Grill. A large brick school borders the park, which has a pool in the summer and an ice rink in the winter. There is a hair salon/barber next to the post office. The Samuel T. Ingram Community Hospital, also known as STICH, services the village and the outlying region with its six beds and two operating rooms.

It was Samuel T. Ingram's grandfather who built the hospital and his grandmother who was responsible for the now massive trees in the park. The huge pines are lit up year-round. Pine Grove has a reputation of having zero crime and a fair amount of gossip. Although there is no police department, the highway patrol or the sheriff cruise through two times a week because they are hired out of Lincoln County to do so. Anticipation among the villagers is growing because next year Pine Grove will celebrate its one hundred twenty-fifth birthday and the coming of the new millennium.

Lola stood in the kitchen wrapped in gloom and confusion. The counter was scattered with all the things she needed to bake cinnamon rolls, but everything was in such disarray. She looked at the stack of pots and pans and knew something was missing and she couldn't figure out what it was. Why does it all have to be so complicated, she thought. She pawed through the cannisters of flour, sugar, salt, and granola. She stared blankly at the spices, nuts, and powdered milk. She picked up a box of baking soda and remembered it was yeast she needed. But the last time she checked, Stein's was out of yeast and she would now have to drive thirty-five miles to the nearest metropolis to buy it. For a moment, she considered making the trip even though it had begun to snow and the roads would soon become slick.

She had grown accustomed to procrastination, but actually, as she thought about it, driving that far in this weather really did seem excessive. She just wasn't thinking straight these days. She looked out the window at the gentle snow flurry and decided she wasn't in the mood to bake anyway.

Absorbed by grief, she had sunk deeper into the stark reality that she would live alone for the rest of her life and had been wandering around the house aimlessly for five weeks now, breathless, and weak. After *it* happened, her chest felt tight, like her lungs had shrunk and she couldn't get enough oxygen into them. Unfillable. When she was able to nod off, she would surface from a deep sleep gasping for breath. She had come to know that grieving has its own way of drowning you, yet not killing you. It only keeps you submerged for so long you forget what air and sunshine feel like.

She had gotten in the car twice, started the ignition, turned it off, and gone back into the house. *Maybe tomorrow will be a better day.* She had not washed her hair in eight days. Water didn't sound good. Getting wet at all sounded awful. Nothing appealed to her. She had a bounding heart and thought maybe she should get her thyroid checked. There was a constant nagging in the pit of her stomach, but she couldn't eat or sleep or listen to music. She found herself sighing constantly—big, deep, shaky sighs. The grief was something she could not go around or put off for another day, for the only way out was *through*. How many times had Evie said that? Lola knew she was right. Cry and cry some more, question, doubt, get mad, be sad, feel sick, and then lie down and cry again.

Exhausted, she went to the downstairs bathroom and looked in the mirror. She had aged a lot since Sam's death, like the sadness had weighted down her jowls in a droopy cascade of skin. The bags under her red-rimmed eyes had a dusky purple cast, and her milky skin and caramel-colored hair had lost its sheen. Oddly enough she didn't care what she looked like, as if it were her mourner's right to neglect herself and actually find comfort in looking her worst.

She opened the drawer and saw Sam's hairbrush. It still had hair in it. What a head of curls that man had. She tenderly picked out the gray hair and balled it in her palm. "I miss you, Sam," she said to the mirror. She dropped the brush in the sink, folded her arms on the counter and laid her face down. A soft whimper slipped from her throat. It hurt deep in the center of her being, as if there were a jagged crack through her heart. A black hole. Nothingness. Yet, when every cell in her body hurt, she was numb to emotion. Sometimes, for a fleeting second, she forgot what caused the emptiness. Then she would snap back into a hot panic where no one or no thing could save her. She shook her head, uncurled herself and looked in the mirror again. "You'd think a forty-nine-year-old woman who has seen the world and shared in the sorrow this planet has to offer could get a hold of herself. He's not coming back."

The doorbell rang and Lola jumped. She patted her eyes with her sleeve and slapped her cheeks. She stood staring in the mirror. She was torn between answering the door or ignoring it. The doorbell rang a second time. She turned and shuffled slowly toward the door in Sam's big slippers with his socks stuffed in the toes.

Evie stood on Lola's porch holding a card and gift with every intention of reminding her friend Lola that she was not alone. Evie rang the doorbell again and suddenly her heart began to race. She thought of being at her friend Lori's house when they were teenagers so many years ago watching Billy Idol on MTV. They were rolling on the bedroom floor, laughing uncontrollably because Billy Idol was wearing more makeup than they were. Then they heard Lori's doorbell ring. Once. Twice. Three times.

After the third ring, Evie set the gift on Lola's doorstep, put her hand over her mouth and backed away. *Lola needs to be alone right now.*

By the time Lola got to the door, there was no one there. At her feet was a small clay pot filled with flowering succulents, moss, and a little porcelain frog sitting on a rock reading a book. A small card with neat cursive handwriting said, *Thinking of you Lola, Love Evie.*

Lola brought the pot inside and set it on the kitchen counter searching the sweet frog's face for something that might bring her even a speck of joy on this dreary day. She sighed again as her eyes drifted toward the window. She ought to give her dear friend a call and thank her again. Evie had helped Lola with all those unthinkable things: arranging the funeral, choosing the best photo for the memory card and going clear to Lincoln County to get it printed, driving to the cemetery while Lola stared a hole in the back of the hearse feeling like she was the one who had died. Lola was ashamed and feared the devil himself would grab her for her thoughts of lying on top of Sam in the coffin, breathing life back into him to the point of arousal. Evie had submitted a touching sentiment with Sam's picture to the *Pine Tree News* in lieu of an obituary. Lola had refused to see, in print, that Samuel Ingram was survived by his wife when Lola considered herself anything but a survivor. Evie also put fresh water in countless flower arrangements and cleaned out the refrigerator when Lola would have let every baked lasagna and casserole sit until it rotted.

Already, six years had passed since Evie had first walked by the Ingram's house to see Lola struggling with a wheelbarrow overflowing with weeds. Evie stopped when the wheelbarrow tipped onto its side, the contents dumped in a heap on the walkway. Evie approached Lola, offered to help, and introduced herself as the new gardener/landscaper in the area. Lola had taken an instant liking to the girl, who stood before her, holding the hand of a little boy less than three years old. Lola admired their golden-blonde hair and eager faces and smiled when Evie set the wheelbarrow straight and said she could also decorate if Lola was having a party. This amused Lola. *Sam's gonna get a kick out of this.* Lola figured Evie was ambitious and in need of work, but in a self-assured, not desperate, way.

Lola looked at the pot of succulents again. It's a shame Evie doesn't meet a nice guy, Lola thought. Someone who would appreciate what a good soul she is. Raising that boy on her own, working as hard as she does, running two businesses. My, the gardening and party planning she does. Sam used to call it "Eviescaping" when she would take such good care of the flower beds out front and then create the most beautiful table settings for their dinner parties. How she ever came up with the idea of being a table setting designer. Of course, Evie acted like it was nothing to transform a dining room table into a masterpiece or turn a plot of weeds into an oasis. How she wished Evie could transform her life the way she transformed her dinner parties. I'll call her later, Lola thought.

Lola went into the living room and stared at Sam's chair. She could clearly see him napping there, the newspaper spread across his lap. He called it circadian rhythm, but she knew that it was purely routine when he awoke each day at exactly five o'clock just in time for happy hour. They would have cheese and crackers, nuts, and sometimes olives or grapes, he with gin and tonic and she with vodka and soda. They seldom ran out of the appetite for conversation or for each other.

Lola put her hands to her chest and shook her head. She could feel the cockles of her heart, as if there were two separate sides. One side held a fond and familiar memory while the other blue-gray side barely pulsed.

I am beyond exhaustion, she thought, and slid into the chair. She could still smell him. She put her hands on the two dark places where he rested his elbows. Looking at her left hand, she saw her wedding ring was getting looser. A few sighs later she slipped into a deep sleep.

It was evening when Lola awoke with drool at the corner of her mouth. She opened her eyes to find she was still clutching the little ball of Sam's hair.

# THREE

Evie knew she was blessed, and every day she opened her arms and inhaled the clear, fresh air. She so gratefully embraced her plot of land and all that surrounded it. From her front yard she could see a blue sky so vast and deep that one could fall into it forever. The two-bedroom, one-hundred-year-old farmhouse she had inherited from her great aunt was one mile out of the village. It sat on three acres overlooking eighty miles of Camus Valley and Lake Camus. At the back of the property a pine forest led to a rock butte that rose to seven-hundred feet. Along with the old house, Evie had a garage and a well-organized shop, a stable with a pine-stake corral, and a charming henhouse. Her garden was large and bountiful, and the flower beds thrived as they did when her auntie had cared for them years ago.

Evie, now twenty-nine, had met her husband, Jon, in a college psychology class in California. She sat behind him the entire semester, observing his behavior through the back of his head and wondering why he acted so bored. He was very good looking in a lofty sort of way. She noted his neat brown hair and the turned-up collar covering the nape of his neck. During lecture she discovered that his left earlobe was two millimeters longer than the right, which proved he truly wasn't a superior being. Once when his pencil rolled off his desk and he bent down to retrieve it, she saw he had a premature white streak at the base of his hairline. This made her think of the story she used to tell her little sister, Ellie, about the kid who saw a ghost and was so scared it turned a strip of his hair white.

She observed the fine, tawny fuzz on Jon's forearms as he rested his chin on his fist. The sight of his graceful hands stirred something foreign and feral inside her. She was both intrigued and put off by his arrogance and general aloofness. He bestowed special notice of no one, yet had a fake smile for some, and appeared disengaged and unaware of the world around him. She secretly wanted that unawareness. *I've never been unaware, have I?*

One day she and Jon were appointed to be partners in a psychoanalysis exercise. They had to first answer ten questions from the Myers and Briggs personality test, followed by a short but detailed evaluation from their class partner. After reading her answers, Jon looked at Evie and said, "You have special interests in disorders that plague deeply disturbed and possibly brilliant people."

"You don't know the first thing about me," she retorted.

"Remember," said the professor to the class. "You must refrain from responding until your partner has completed the analysis. Examiners are allowed only ninety seconds."

Jon smiled with his teeth clenched. "So, Evie, I'm not deeply disturbed, but I am possibly brilliant enough to know you understand such deviants but hang onto your own sanity very efficiently."

She felt her cheeks burn and didn't know why she had the urge to either slap him or have the floor open up and swallow her, the same feeling she frequently had when her own psychotherapist had forced her to sit quietly and listen to him without speaking.

Jon looked at his watch. "You like order and logic and that's what sustains you—that's why you aren't married. Yet. Undoubtedly you were just waiting for me."

Her vision turned splotchy and she, who second-guessed and analyzed every second of her life, was overcome by the prickling instincts women develop about men. Thinking about marriage, she suddenly wanted desperately to fill a void so deep, to have a family, a ring on her finger, and a husband to protect her from all the bad things in the world. Her inner dialogue was so loud she thought the class may hear it. Before she could speak, Jon said. "I must exceed my ninety seconds to say that I don't need Myers and Briggs to prove that you and I are compatible. I'm astute enough to know you've been burning a hole in the back of my head for five weeks now and you leave me no choice but to make you my wife."

Later she would not regret that they were married just long enough to have a son, Jack. Then she got off the emotional roller coaster, took the baby and ran, knowing what she had suspected all along—Jon was too selfish to be a father or a husband, and she was too impatient to put up with it.

To this day she spoke no bad words to Jack about his father. The boy simply believed he was born without a dad. Evie knew the time would come when she would explain it all to Jack. Every child deserves to know who their parents are and the circumstances that brought them into this world. For now, she vowed she would refrain from telling him the truth—that after a grueling twenty-eight hours of labor, bursting a blood vessel across her face and squeezing out a throbbing hemorrhoid and a baby boy at the same time, Jon walked into the family birthing room holding a cheeseburger. Jon and Evie had agreed that Jon would name their firstborn child and Evie would name their second. Jon looked at his son for the first time and said, "Oh my God, his head is pointed."

"Where have you been?" Evie barely breathed out the question.

"You've been in here for almost two days. I was starving. You know I can't eat stuff like this, but you left me no choice. There's no decent restaurant around here so I had to go to Jack in the Box and get a 'Jumbo Jack' of all things. Hey, that could be his name—'Jumbo!'" He saw Evie's expression and laughed. "How about 'Jack?' It's better than if I had gone to McDonalds. Then it might be 'Mac.'"

"That's your Dad's name. I like it." She looked down at the baby's pointy little head, smiled, and said, "Welcome to the world, Jack."

Evie quickly learned that Jon's sense of humor wasn't

enough to overcome his arrogance, and it wasn't long before she decided that she and the baby would be better off raising each other. In her studies she had learned that his narcissism would never change, and so she chose to leave him. Evie was independent, resilient, and confident enough to fall apart at the seams on her own. She had already survived hardships in her youth and knew her biggest blessings were her own strength and her healthy baby boy. She was stubborn and driven and would do what was needed without the help of a man, selfish or not.

Evie had earned degrees in psychology and literature but abandoned the idea of counseling or teaching high school English. She opted for self-employment, with motherhood, of course, being the priority. She would protect him and teach only love and nurture Jack to become an honorable and respectful young man. She believed it is a mother's duty to bring good men into the world, and it was her goal to harbor no resentment for Jon. She believed that, for the most part, we are all doing our best in this life.

Before leaving her marriage, she gave her mother-in-law a birthday party. Evie shopped around, procuring everything it took to make a beautiful table setting. After the birthday cake was served, she gave the entire table setting to Jon's mom, who in return, told Evie she was very talented and should start her own business. Then she added that Evie would never be the number one woman in their family.

Hurtful as her comment was, it provided the catalyst that drove Evie to buy twelve black square plates from Pier One Imports and put an ad in the paper stating, "I will set your table. Call this number." When the phone rang a week later, a woman named Penny said she was a corporate event planner and wanted to meet for a consultation. Evie wasn't sure what a corporate event planner was or what she needed for a consultation.

She nursed the baby, put him in his car seat and drove thirty-five miles to meet Penny at an art gallery in Newton Falls.

Penny met Evie with a stoic air and showed her around the gallery. As they stood looking at the artwork and the event space, Penny crossed her arms and said, "So, what do you think?"

Evie stopped herself from biting her fingernails, prayed her breast milk wouldn't leak through her sweater, and said, "Because of the nature of the art exhibit and the black wrought iron railings, I envision something contemporary, like black square plates."

Penny curled up one side of her lip and squinted. Evie stood still and held her breath. After a moment, Penny put her hand on her hip and let out a quick breath, which blew her bangs off her fake eyelashes. She tapped her navy pumps on the stone floor and pointed her finger at Evie.

"Get me a proposal based on fifty guests. And, by the way, I'll need that tomorrow because the event is Saturday. "

Evie excused herself from the gallery, ran to her truck to check on the sleeping baby and hyperventilated, not knowing how she was going to pull this one off.

The next day she began calling around to many Pier One Imports stores. She went into debt five hundred dollars and had thirty-eight plates shipped just in time to remove the bar codes and rent the other things she needed for the event. Saturday morning as she loaded the last box of plates into her pickup, her "business line" rang. She ran into the house and grabbed the phone.

"Hello, this is Evie of Evie's Tablescapes. How can I help you?"

"It's Penny."

"Hi Penny, I'm loaded up and ready to leave."

"Good thing I caught you. Why are you leaving so early?"

"I know we agreed on three o'clock to begin setting up, but with traffic it will probably take me an hour to get to the gallery."

"Don't bother."

"Excuse me?" Evie said.

"The client canceled."

In the silence that followed, Evie felt shock, brief panic, then anger. She hung up the phone, or rather, Penny hung up on her. She took a deep breath and went out to remove Jack from his car seat. He puckered his lips, stuck out his little pink tongue and blew a slobbery bubble. She kissed him and said, "We've got fifty plates little man, I guess we've got a business!" Jack stuck a fist in his mouth and kicked his legs.

The experience taught her to ask for a retainer for each new job and to have a written document with her terms. For the next several years she used her black plates repeatedly until she made enough money to expand her inventory.

As time passed and Jack grew, so did her collection of tableware. She currently could provide table settings for as many as two hundred guests, although parties of that size were rare in Pine Grove.

Jack was now eight years old. Like his mom, he was tall and long-limbed with straight blonde hair and eyes a darting light-filled blue flecked with gold. He was fiery, wild, and constantly on the verge of getting in trouble.

It was late winter, and Evie was in the yard checking the iris bulbs. Jack was making a trap to catch a fox. The fox had killed two chickens already and Jack was going to put an end to it. The previous evening, they were coming home and Jack spotted the fox with a fat hen in its mouth. The hen was screeching, so Jack jumped out of the moving pickup, miraculously landed on his feet, and ran after it. The fox slammed into the fence and Jack kicked it until it dropped the bloody hen and ran. Evie screamed for him to stop, but the kid was fearless. Jack picked up the hen and held her to his chest and asked Evie for a needle and thread to sew its gashed neck. He stroked her breast feathers and told his mom it was like a lobster, that by petting her feathers in the opposite direction of the way they lay, he would put her in a trance while he stitched her up.

Secretly, because the chicken was such a mess, Evie had decided to bury it while Jack was sleeping, but when she went out to the coop that night, the hen was perched up on its roost with four SpongeBob band-aids around its neck.

Evie smiled at the thought of Jack's determination. He continually surprised her. At two years old, he had thrown up after eating a bowl of cooked carrots and announced that he was "emergent to carrots." He never ate a carrot after that.

Evie remembered potty training Jack. Her neighbor, Chrissy, who also had a young boy, told her to throw a Froot Loop in the toilet and have him aim at it so he would learn to pee in the potty. Evie bought a whole box just for one bright orange Froot Loop. As they stood at the toilet, Evie pretending to hold her imaginary penis and Jack holding his, she said, "Okay, aim for the Froot Loop." He looked up at her and said, "Wait, Mom. Where's *your* weenie?" Evie stood there and cried knowing that, as hard as she tried, she couldn't be his father too.

Then there was the brief potty training when she set him on the toilet and told him to push. He dropped a little hunk and said, "There." Evie was so excited she danced in the bathroom. She clapped and squealed, turned on the faucet, wiped his butt and told him he was an absolute miracle of nature. The following morning Chrissy and Evie took the boys to the Hometown Cafe. Both boys were strapped in highchairs and Evie said, "Be right back. I'm going to wash my hands." When she came out of the bathroom, crossing the packed cafe she spotted Jack. He had slipped out of the strap, stood up in the highchair and yelled, "Mama! Did you poop?"

Now, Chrissy pulled up in her Honda Civic and her boy, Dillon, jumped out and ran over to Jack. His black German shepherd, Rex, followed with a giant chew-bone in his mouth.

Dillon was six-and-a-half years old, and he and Jack were next-door neighbors and best friends. Dillon, unlike his mom, had a mop of unruly dark curls, and big green eyes.

"Hey," said Chrissy. She rolled out of the front seat wearing black sweatpants and an over-sized flannel shirt, chomping on a Snickers bar. She wore a necklace with a plastic mermaid hanging from a strand of painted clay beads. She was short and plump with a round, child-like face and kinky, pink-dyed hair. She was outspoken, honest to a fault and, unlike Evie, rarely bothered to be polite. Chrissy was indeed rough around the edges, but Evie secretly admired her boldness.

"Can Dill hang with you for a bit? I'm on call 'til eight."

"Sure, I'll feed them," said Evie. Rex dropped down by Evie's feet and gnawed the bone. "Where'd you get this big chew-bone?"

"Oh, we saw Romey, the window washer, by the market. Do you know him?"

"I've seen his truck, but I've never seen him."

"Well, one of his customers, Mr. Murphy, gave Romey's dog this bone that looks like a frickin' moose leg. Poor little Max couldn't even get it in his mouth so Romey gave it to Rex. He said that in Central America there would be ten dogs chewin' on this thing."

"That was nice of him. So, he's been to Central America?

"Yeah. I think he's been all over the place."

"Must be nice. How was your day as a scrub tech?"

"It was okay. I'm actually a surgical technologist." She did air quotes and rolled her eyes as she walked over and sat on the porch step. "We did three hemorrhoid surgeries, a couple of hernia repairs, and shot Botox into an anal sphincter."

"Gross," said Evie, but she had to admit she found Chrissy's profession intriguing. "I'm sure you've told me this before, but what's the difference between a surgical technologist and a nurse?"

"Well," said Chrissy. "A surg tech or scrub, as we call it, is the one who stays sterile and assists in the surgery. We handle all the instruments and give the surgeon what they need, which usually isn't what they ask for. The nurse, or the circulator, takes care of the patient, helps the anesthesiologist put the patient to sleep, and gets us what we need."

"Did you have to work with that anesthesia doctor you don't like?"

"Thank God, not today. I swear if I have to work with him again, I'm gonna quit and go work at Mel's. Being a bartender would be way better than having to look at his beady little eyes."

"Just your luck he'd come and hang out at your bar just so he could look at your big bootie and your pink hair."

"Shut up. He makes my skin crawl. He's just plain mean and super needy. He's really not nice to anyone, but neither am I. He's just extra assholian to me. It irks me big time when he's mean to little kids."

"How could anyone be mean to little kids? Especially a doctor."

"I know, right? Yesterday, he told a six-year-old to be quiet or he was gonna give him a shot. I almost kicked him in the shin. The poor nurse was practically crying right along with the kid. Then the jerk presses a mask over the kid's face and says, 'There'll be no negotiating!' That boy's gonna be messed up for the rest of his life."

"That's so sad. Hopefully the little boy'll grow up and become a pediatrician and treat children with great kindness."

"Not. He'll be freaked out every time he gets near a doctor."

"Or he'll become a high-powered attorney known for his negotiation skills."

"You've always gotta put a little sugar on it," said Chrissy.

"Well," said Evie. "That doctor is either sorely misunderstood or has major control issues. It's probably best you didn't kick him in the shin."

"Yeah, whatever. I'll be back later. Thanks for havin' Dill."

"No worries."

Chrissy headed to the car then turned around. "Oh yeah, I just saw that STICH housekeeping guy. The one with the snake tattoo on his neck. He's sitting in his car at the end of Main Street by the cemeteries."

"What's he doing?" Evie wrinkled her nose.

"He's gettin' stoned with the windows up. The smoke's so thick I could barely see him. I'm tellin' you, the guy's trouble. He cleans the ORs and the break room at night. Today I went in early and when I turned on our big computer screen in the OR there was a porn site on."

"That's disgusting. Why don't they fire him?"

"Because he hasn't been caught doing anything illegal yet and because they can't find another housekeeper. Plenty of people can't stand the sight of blood."

Chrissy bounced over to her Honda. Evie noticed she was wearing two different colored shoes. She reached in the front seat and grabbed a paper grocery bag.

"I almost forgot. Here's some Ritz crackers for the boys." She handed Evie the bag. Evie looked in. "Jeez, why do you have so many?"

Chrissy put her finger to her lips. "I stole them from the break room."

"What do you mean, you stole them. What's going on with you?"

"Hey, it ain't no big thing. They got tons a crackers. It's not like I took the coffee pot or jacked the microwave."

Evie and Chrissy had been neighbors for over five years and, as they became closer friends, Evie had begun to see Chrissy change. Although they were complete opposites in so many ways, the chip on Chrissy's shoulder was getting bigger, and she was becoming more defensive. *Now she's stealing crackers?* Perhaps it was because Chrissy's husband Rob had come and gone three times in the last year and this time, he hadn't come back. They had a lot of turbulence in their marriage, and when things got heavy, Evie kept Dillon at her house. Collectively, she'd probably spared Dillon a hundred hours of watching his parents fight. After all, thought Evie, there's nothing more frightening to a child than to see their parents arguing, or worse yet, hurting one another both emotionally and physically. Well, it could always be worse. Evie shook her head. At least Dillon had parents.

Chrissy revved the engine, cranked the radio, and drove away. Evie waved and then looked at Rex, who had moved under a pine tree where he was digging a hole to bury the rest of the bone. *If our old dog, Turbo, was in Central America, there's no way he would share that bone with nine other dogs.*

# FOUR

Romey and Jean Paul were twelve and thirteen years old when they knocked on Sam and Lola Ingram's door and offered to wash all the windows in their house for one dollar. Lola accepted and the boys did an excellent job. She paid them each two dollars for the fine work and the good manners. She knew they were from a large family and, at this age, boys always needed money for something.

Lola told her neighbor about the window washers and that neighbor told the next. It was the youngest brother, Romey, who implemented the business plan of increasing their prices one dollar at a time.

When the boys were of driving age, they had saved enough money to buy their own trucks. Romey named the company Shine On Window Cleaning. Now the Shine On brothers had a thriving business, and all of Pine Grove knew them for their hard work and their bright yellow smiley-face logo, the size of a dinner plate.

With their hoses, buckets, ladders, and squeegees, they perfected their craft and eventually expanded their services to include Christmas light installation. They hung lights for all the downtown storefronts and many of Pine Grove's residents. They had the year-round job of changing the lights on the giant pine trees. After the Christmas season, they switched the lights to red for Valentine's Day, then green for Saint Patrick's Day. The trees twinkled with spring colors for Easter, red, white, and blue for the Fourth of July, and fall colors for Halloween and Thanksgiving. The brothers were so busy they hired three more washer-installers to keep up with the demand.

There was no need for an office because Romey met his workers daily to give them their job assignments. He was one of the few people who had a car phone and did his billing in his truck. With all the money he saved from not renting office space, he was able to buy his first house outright at the age of twenty-three.

Each winter when the snow was its deepest, he left his dog with his brother and for a month traveled to other places in the world. He could speak several languages and had friends in thirteen countries. He had special interest in beach volleyball, art, and astrology.

Romey believed that we are all doing our best here on planet Earth and to do good each day is our basic purpose in life. He always returned to Pine Grove at the end of February with a different perspective and a renewed appreciation for life and hard work. He could be seen almost every morning at Drip 'n Sip getting himself a cup of coffee and a pepperoni stick for his little white terrier, Maxwell Smart, also known as Max.

It was almost Spring, and Evie was pruning a sterling rosebush in Lola's front yard while Jack and Dillon rode their bikes around the block, calling out a number each time they passed Evie. The goal was to ride around one hundred times. Rex ran behind them with his tongue hanging out the side of his mouth. They were on loop number eight.

A Shine On truck pulled up and two guys got out. They wore black tee shirts with their names, Romey and Josh, printed above a smiley-face logo. In the front seat sat Max. He was little and white with tufts on the tip of his ears, black eyes, a black nose, and a snaggle tooth smile.

Lola had mentioned that she was automatically scheduled to have her windows cleaned every four months and that Romey and Lola were the last two people to see Sam alive.

The window cleaners carried their buckets and ladders and went around the side of the house. Evie watched through the bushes as they attached a hose to a spigot and filled their buckets with water. Evie squinted. *Is that Dawn dishwashing liquid?*

They each had a towel over their shoulder, and the taller guy with the Romey shirt had a scrub brush and a squeegee hanging off his belt. He was wearing Levi 501s and leather shoes that looked like clogs. He had a major head of hair and a half smile on his face as if he were listening to a good song. The other guy with the Josh shirt was wearing cargo shorts that hung below his knees, a baseball cap, and sneakers. He wore headphones, and Evie wondered what he was listening to. In a way, she thought, window cleaning seemed like a stress-free job, although she could never crawl way up there or clean a window without leaving a bunch of streaks. She struggled even trying to clean her windshield. These guys seemed content with what they were doing. Kind of like gardening or table setting, where you could work at your own pace, in your own time—where you could create beauty and be appreciated for it and, of course, be your own boss.

"Nine!" yelled Jack as they raced by. Evie waved at them, took off her gloves and set them by the pruning shears. She went to the front door and knocked softly.

"Come in, Evie," Lola called.

She kicked off her garden clogs and went inside. The house smelled spicy, sweet, and nutty.

"Do I smell banana bread?

"Yes," said Lola, wiping her hands on a kitchen towel. "The bananas get overripe before I can eat them. Sam never would have let that happen. He loved fruit." She smiled and said, "One time he ate the entire bucket of plums you brought us. Poor guy paid for that for two days."

"That's actually very sweet," said Evie

Lola pulled out a chair and plopped down.

"I'm tuckered out. Have a seat, Evie. Are the boys still riding around the block?"

"Yes. Let's see who gets tired first, the boys or the dog."

Lola stared at her hand resting on the table. "I miss him so much Evie."

"I know you do Lola." Evie sat down.

Lola shook her head. "I feel like a crazy person. I mean it's been four months and twelve days and I'm not getting any better. I forget things constantly and I'm so distracted, it's frightening."

"Yeah." Evie put her hand on Lola's. "I understand." Evie's thoughts went back to a time when she had nothing but fear coursing through her veins. She knew the true meaning of frightening and that if you can get through it, you would discover that fear is a great motivator for change.

"I shouldn't be baking," said Lola. "The banana bread was in the oven for over an hour before it dawned on me to turn the oven on." She shook her head. "Yesterday I wanted to go to Stein's to get eggs after looking all morning for the car keys. I finally found them in the pantry, of all places. They were sitting *in* the flour sack, which I must have opened and dropped the keys into, and I didn't even remember being in the pantry."

"I'm sorry. It's understandable you're distracted."

"And, I have no right trying to drive, either. It's dangerous."

"I told you I'll drive for you, Lola."

"I know you did, and I appreciate it, but I've got to be able to fend for myself. It's taking forever." She rubbed her forehead.

"Lola, please be gentle on yourself. You've only got one job right now, and that's to take care of Lola. You're still raw. Grief sets its own timeline, not you. Or me. Or anyone."

"It's like I'm listening, but I can't hear you. Does that make any sense at all? Probably not."

"Of course, it does. You're doing and feeling what you need to right now."

"Well, anyway, after I found the keys in the flour sack, I sat in the car, totally blank as to how to start it. I feel so lost."

Evie nodded slowly, knowing the lost feeling.

"I finally drove into the village and pulled right into the log truck lane. An eighteen-wheeler had to lock up his brakes to avoid hitting me. I just sat there staring up at him with a stupid look on my face, I'm sure. He was leaning out the window yelling at me, and I just smiled and then put my head on the steering wheel and cried."

"That must've been so scary."

"I don't know how long I sat in the middle of Main Street like that but when I looked up the truck was gone and I thought to myself, I guess I'm not afraid to die anymore."

"Lola, please. You must be easy on yourself. Nothing else matters right now except you. There's no time limit or rule that says you must be *better*."

"I suppose, but I feel like I can't stop dwelling on the horror of it all. Watching him take his last breath, feeling so helpless and screaming for help. If only I'd fought harder to get him to a doctor."

Evie moved toward her shaking her head and put her hand on Lola's shoulder. But she didn't seem to register the touch.

"I never should have listened to him when he said we didn't need medical help. I mean, he was only sixty-nine. It wasn't like he was ninety-nine. How could I have been so stupid? We could have had another thirty years together. Sam was perfectly healthy! I should have done more, Evie."

"Lola, no."

"If I would've just tried harder, he'd probably still be alive. It's all my fault."

"That simply isn't true. You did the best you could. Guilt's a normal emotion in grieving but there is absolutely no one to blame. And it's fruitless to use 'couldas' and 'shouldas.'"

"I just can't get the scene out of my mind. I want to erase it all, get it out of my body." She shook her hands in front of her.

"Lola, you can't erase Sam. And the experience doesn't leave your body, it integrates into who you are. You're still very raw. I know it doesn't seem like it, but very little time has passed, hardly more than a hundred days, so naturally you're hurting so badly."

"In a way I'm grateful I didn't conceive because I couldn't bear the thought of having our children or grandchildren feel this loss."

"We all feel the loss, Lola, but not the way you do now. I'm here for you, every step of the way." Evie got up and filled a glass of water from the tap. She felt a lump rising in the back of her throat. She looked at the pot of succulents sitting on the sill and wondered what book the porcelain frog was reading. *Maybe I'm the one who's going crazy around here.* She looked out the window, then turned back to Lola. "Grieving is hard work. It's exhausting and unpredictable and will take all your energy and all your patience." She set the glass in front of Lola. "And just when you may feel slightly better, the grief will smack you on the head again and you'll feel like you're right back where you started." Evie put her fingertips to her temples. *And it never goes away. Grief is a dark and dreary journey, a long and painful path that you'll trudge day after day, dragging with you an unbelievable emptiness.*

Lola shook her head. "Yesterday I went out on the porch to get the newspaper but stopped because I knew I wouldn't read it anyway. I was never like this before. I don't care about anybody else's stories."

Evie thought back to the day she was finally able to read again. It had taken more than a year. Even then, it was as if she had to retrain her brain to process the letters on the page.

Lola sighed. "I can't stand the idea of reading something sad, and worse yet, I don't want to read how happy someone is because their kid scored the most points in a softball game. I don't want to read about the magic of Pine Grove and how a lucky nurse had a new baby boy the minute Sam died."

"I know."

"I just looked at the rolled-up newspaper and sat on the step and watched an ant carrying a tiny piece of a leaf. I bet I stared at that ant for an hour because I couldn't look up. It's as if I hate the sky and resent that it's got the nerve to be blue. I've never felt anger like this. I don't expect you to really understand."

"I do understand, Lola. There are so many emotions that come with grief, and anger's one of them. You have every right to be mad at the sky. You'll be angry with yourself and it's also a valid feeling to be mad at Sam for leaving."

"You're right, angry, exhausted, also jittery and these crying spells come out of nowhere. Sometimes I wake up crying. That's if I get to sleep in the first place."

"As terrible as it is, it's good that you're talking about it. You shouldn't isolate yourself and it's good to tell your story over and over until you don't need to talk about it anymore."

"When will these crying spells stop? They just keep coming out of nowhere. See? Here I am repeating myself again. It's like I'm detached from reality and can't focus enough to connect the dots or remember things or . . ." She started to cry.

"I know it feels like it'll never stop, but trust me, it will gradually lessen. Crying spells, depression, fatigue, they're all part of grieving. And, like I said before, these are all normal emotions." Evie remembered when she wanted to take the word *normal* and pulverize it. She despised the word and wanted to snuff out whoever had the gall to use it around her. "It's the price we pay for love."

"I guess that's why it hurts so much. I loved that man with . . ." She covered her face with her hands.

"I don't expect you to believe this right now, Lola, but I promise this misery will eventually fade and be replaced with beautiful memories. Sadly, it'll never completely stop hurting, but it'll, I don't know, become more tolerable?"

"I don't know how you know all this, but I hope you're right."

"The time will come when you'll find comfort."

"Comfort in what?"

"Sam's your angel now. You have an angel to watch over you." She looked out the window at the cumulus clouds high in the sky and thought of Ellie.

Right then, they heard screaming and barking. Evie

jumped up and bolted out the front door. Dillon, Jack, and the bikes were lying in a heap in the rose bushes. Max was springing up and down in the front seat barking out the truck window.

"Oh my God! Boys! Are you okay?"

Romey came running out from behind the house. Dillon was bawling, his arms and face bleeding from the thorns. Romey reached out with both hands and pulled the boys up at the same time. "Shake it off," he said. Dillon stopped crying and the dogs stopped barking. Jack straightened his helmet and picked up his bike. Romey smiled and said, "See? I knew you weren't a couple of wusses."

Jack smiled and Dillon stood his bike up. "Thanks," he said, wiping blood off his arm.

"Yeah, thanks. Romey, right?" said Evie.

"Yeah, that's why I wear this shirt every day. So I remember my name." He winked. "Evie, right?"

"Yes. I'm Evie, and this is my son Jack and his friends, Dillon and Rex."

"You guys alright?" asked Romey.

"Yep," they said in unison.

"I appreciate your help Romey," said Evie, noticing for the first time his dark blue eyes and disarming smile. "I'm not sure what happened, but they were in the process of riding around the block a hundred times."

Jack looked at Romey. "Yeah, we were on loop number thirty-nine, and Rex ran in front of Dillon's tire and I crashed into the back of him."

"Well," said Romey, "You guys are real troopers. No time to be crying like a couple of babies, right? Now, get back in the saddle and get on to loop number forty! Every other crybaby's home watching Gilligan's Island."

"We don't have a TV," said Jack.

"Well, what a coinky dink," said Romey. "Neither do I."

Evie blew out a long slow breath as she bent down and picked up her gloves. Josh came walking around the corner, balancing a ladder on his shoulder. She was slipping her feet back into her garden clogs when Romey said, "Okay, enough fun for now. On to the next job!"

# FIVE

Evie was kneeling on a towel, staining her front porch. She had just received a call from Lola about what to do with Sam's things. His clothes. His golf clubs. His car. Lola was also panicking about all the cards she was afraid to open. Evie told her, "Let's just take it slow. I'm here for you."

Chrissy pulled up and slammed on the brakes. The car shook, blaring '90s rap. Dillon crawled out of the back seat holding a grocery bag, and Rex jumped out after him. "Is Jack inside?" he asked.

"Hi, Dill. Yes, he's in the kitchen getting a snack. You'll have to go through the back door, but don't slam it or the doorknob'll get stuck. And don't let Rex on these steps, it'll stain his paws."

Chrissy killed the engine and got out holding a large bottle of screw-cap white wine. She was wearing scrubs and a lime green headband with a cardboard starfish on it.

"Uh oh," said Evie. "It must be a weekday."

"Hell, yes. I need to do some serious drinking." She panted, grunted like a big man, and lowered herself onto the lawn.

"I thought you weren't allowed to wear scrubs outside of work," said Evie.

"Oh, that's a bunch of bull. Apparently, now they have to monitor every scrub because they say they're getting more expensive and employees are taking them home and not bringing them back to STICH."

"That sounds reasonable."

"They say if scrubs keep disappearing, they're gonna charge us for the laundry service. It's ridiculous. Little do they know, I have about ten sets of scrubs that I wash myself. I refuse to be controlled by management."

"Jeez, Chrissy. What if you get caught?"

"So what? I don't give a shit."

"Dare I ask, how was your day?"

"It sucked as usual. I had to scrub a nine-hour plastics case with a surgeon who calls himself a master skin-grafter." She rolled her eyes.

"Wait. You did skin grafts for nine hours on the same person?"

"Yep. And a scar revision. It's not that it took so long that I hate, it's that the surgeon talks the entire time, telling stupid stories and then asking everyone in the operating room what they think about it. It's so annoying. And he never likes what I have to say anyway, so I don't know why he keeps asking."

"So why don't you let someone else answer him first, then

when it's your turn just say, 'Same.' That will diffuse him and eventually he'll see that Chrissy doesn't want to play anymore. It's basic psychology."

Chrissy unscrewed the cap and took a slug. "I mean he went on for two solid hours, talking about a friend of his whose wife is leaving him because he won't go through all his old boxes and clean out the garage. How ridiculous is that? I was so pissed off when he said, 'What do you think is in those boxes, Chrissy? Don't you think the wife should just look in there and decide for herself if it's important to keep all that stuff, or do you think that's probably his own personal stuff that really isn't anybody else's business?'

"Maybe some of that stuff is super important to him, like college photo albums and trophies and maybe love letters from an old flame. They say the first cut is the deepest. 'What do you think Chrissy? Do you believe the first one is the one we wished we would have stuck with? Do you think the wife might know there's things in there she doesn't want to see? What do you think Chrissy? Do you think she secretly wishes she could read those love letters if there are any? Do you think he should get another chance or should she divorce him?'

"It's obvious that he's talking about himself, so, I said, 'Half of that shit is probably old Playboy magazines, so why don't you just clean out your garage instead of talking about it all day?' That shut him up for a little while, anyway."

"I can't believe you don't get in trouble for that."

"So, fire me, I don't care."

"Have you ever considered changing your attitude? I

mean, it's staggering how you have the gall to be as rude as you are and get away with it."

Chrissy tipped the bottle back and took a long pull. "Then the next two hours are spent on the lifelong discussion of relationships in general. He says, 'What do you think, Chrissy? Do you think there is one special person for each of us, or do you think we can be with anyone we want? My brother says you can find a mate on any corner of the street and make it work. Do you believe that's true?' Makes me wanna flip my lid because he knows Rob and I have been separated for six months, and he's just hoping to make me squirm."

"Jeez, Chrissy. Your attitude is unbelievable. I think it's nice that he engages everyone in the room and that he's sincerely interested in your opinion. There aren't a lot of men like that. You're always complaining about that anesthesia doctor you can't stand because he's either mean or won't give you the time of day. And now, here's someone who's actively talking to you because, in his mind, he has a real concern for a real-life situation. If you were a little less defensive and realized he may not be judging you like you think he is and be a little more sensitive to what he's saying, it might make your work environment a bit more pleasant."

"But it's so annoying."

"And think about this possibility. Maybe he has no one at home he can talk to about this stuff and considers you all like family."

Chrissy rolled her eyes again.

"I have a lot of respect for someone who can do something

as complex as a skin graft and talk at the same time. I could never do that. By the way, what is plastic about plastic surgery?"

"You'd be surprised how many people ask that question. The word plastic means it can be molded, not that it's actually plastic. Basically, they change the shape of a patient. Our lady plastic surgeon calls it a 'cosmetic encounter.'"

"It sounds horrendous."

"Hey, it makes the patients happy. Most of them come from out of town, get a makeover, stay at the Super 8 motel until they heal enough to get their drains and staples out, then go home. If it wasn't so expensive, I'd do it myself. I wouldn't mind getting this whole gut whacked off and having a six pack."

Evie put her hand on her own side and felt her ribcage.

"We can make boobs bigger or smaller and perkier. We do liposuction where the fat gets sucked out and put back in somewhere else." She took another swig. "We cut skin off and sew it onto another body part. And there are facelifts and brow lifts, where we slice a hunk of scalp out of the top of the head."

Evie touched the top of her head and shuddered.

"Oh, and don't forget we do butt lifts, eyelids, nose jobs and chin implants. We're on the cutting edge of the nineties. No pun intended."

"You haven't quite rendered me speechless, but you have made me nauseous." Evie put the lid on the can of stain and tapped it with a hammer. "Let's go in and pretend we're classy enough to drink out of a wine glass."

They went around the house and through the back door. The boys were munching on crackers. The grocery bag was on the floor, the table piled with Nutri-Grain breakfast bars of every flavor. There were two boxes of Graham crackers, four packs of Ritz crackers and two huge jars of peanut butter.

"Where did all this come from?" Evie asked.

Dillon smacked his lips and said, "My mom got it from her work."

Evie raised her eyebrows. "What the heck, Chrissy!"

Chrissy shrugged and got two wine glasses from the cupboard. "Boy's gotta eat."

"Hey Jack," said Evie, "Did you tell Dill about the fox?"

"Oh yeah! We caught him in the cage last night. This morning he was snarling and trying to chew through the wire. His teeth were super sharp."

"What did you do with him?" asked Chrissy.

Evie said, "We took him down by the lake and let him go. He ran so fast. He was a red fox, according to Jack. Beautiful coat and a fluffy tail, and boy was he mad. He spent all night in a trap surrounded by chickens. Oh, and guess who else was at the lake? Your hospital housekeeping guy with the snake tattoo on his neck. Doesn't that tattoo mean something, like someone died or he murdered somebody?"

"No, Mom," said Jack. "You're thinking of the spider tattoo that people get when they survive a bite from a violin spider or maybe a black widow. A violin spider can kill you, but not a black widow."

"Thanks for that, Jack," Evie smiled. "Anyway, he was sitting on his car hood drinking out of a paper bag."

"What a loser," said Chrissy. She filled the glasses and pulled up a chair. "Why don't you boys go outside and play?"

"Mom," said Jack. "Do you know where my helmet is?"

"Walk backwards Jack," said Evie.

Jack opened the door and stepped backwards on to the lawn and toward the shed. Dillon copied him. Evie had taught Jack to retrace his steps whenever he misplaced something. Jack called it walking backwards. He also called a lawn mower a mow-lawner and an elevator a levitator. After analyzing him, Evie concluded that he wasn't dyslexic. He was adorable.

"So, Chrissy, tell me about all this food. Did you steal it from the surgery center?"

"Well, yes and no. I mean, they owe me big time. When I first started there, we got lunch every day and great benefits. Little by little they started taking stuff away. They stopped buying us lunch, and they cut the Christmas bonus and the cost-of-living increase, which is so messed up. We used to have at least two company parties a year and they stopped those too. Now we get coffee, crackers, and peanut butter."

"I think that's nice they provide you with coffee and snacks."

"Bullcrap! I'm basically a single mom. Rob can't afford to help and I can't afford to always bring my own lunch. Last week before payday all I had was a can of tuna. I couldn't even put mayo in it because they took all the condiments out of the fridge."

"But you're stealing, Chrissy. That's not right. You don't want to raise Dill to believe that it's acceptable to take what isn't yours, do you? My God, if I caught Jack stealing, I'd have his hide. We're single moms, yes. You know what that means? It means it's our responsibility to raise good men. We were given the gift of healthy, smart, kind, vibrant boys and as I always tell Jack, 'My job is to love you, feed you, protect you, and teach you right from wrong.'" Evie was trying to understand what had gotten into Chrissy and suspected she was about to spiral out of control.

Evie still hadn't touched the wine when Chrissy downed her glass. "Okay, it's revenge or taking the law into my own hands, call it what you want, but here's the deal. Last night, as you know, I left work late. In fact, I was almost the last to leave except for the recovery room staff, which was that sweet nurse Beth and Arlene with the incredible hair. I told them both goodnight and went to the women's locker room. It was close to eight o'clock. When I opened the door, I saw that dirtbag housekeeper guy rifling through the lockers. He had headphones on so he didn't hear me. I got creeped out and thought maybe I should call out to Arlene and Beth, but instead I backed out and went and hid in the front office until I heard him leave. When I went back and looked in my locker, I knew for sure he had been in my backpack. You know that feeling you get when someone creepy is messing with your shit?"

"Fortunately, no," said Evie.

Evie adjusted herself on the chair and smoothed down the goosebumps on her legs. She took a sip of wine. "Then what happened?"

"Well, I saw the slimeball had taken my last five-dollar bill and my mermaid necklace my niece made me for my birthday, like three years ago."

"Oh no! You always wear that necklace."

"No joke! It's my favorite necklace. I wear it all the time, except when I'm in the OR because the beads could fall into the sterile field. I love it so much and, as you know, I don't love a lot of things. I was pissed, Evie, I mean, so friggin' pissed I literally saw the lockers turn red. I went into the break room and got a big black trash bag and started stuffing shit into it. I took a jumbo can of Folgers coffee, a box of creamers, Ziplock bags and all this stuff here. I couldn't stop. I thought, if I see that mothereffer again, I'll kill him."

"Holy smokes."

"Then I went into the bathroom and saw all the toilet paper individually wrapped that he stacked up all nice. I crammed it in the bag and put six more rolls in my backpack and hauled it all out to my car. I was so freaked I didn't even clock out."

"Well, it seems to me that you could approach the guy and tell him how important the necklace is to you. I think when someone steals, it's an act of control or desperation."

"There's no frickin' way that guy's gonna admit that he took my money or my necklace. I feel like I got the revenge I needed by grabbing this stuff and making sure he gets blamed for it." She finished her wine and screwed the cap back on the bottle. "Guess I better get going."

"Okay, thanks for the wine and, I guess, the snacks. It's a bit strange to be eating stolen food."

"Well," said Chrissy. "Take a look around Evie. Life is strange!"

"Yeah, it is." Evie took a sip of wine. *You don't have to tell me about strange. I've lived and breathed the strangeness of life and inhaled the shocking, unfamiliar, and harsh reality of this strange world.* "Hey, remember tomorrow I have a party to set up. You still okay to watch Jack for a bit?"

"Yeah."

"It won't take me long."

"Where's the party?"

"It's for the Eastons up on the ridge, so most of it's driving time. I'll be back before dinner."

"Okay. Drop him off whenever you want."

# SIX

Mrs. Easton was doing a thousand-piece puzzle, and her husband was in his office on a conference call when Romey arrived to clean the windows. It had taken him forty-five minutes to drive up their nine-mile road. The stone and glass estate stood high on a hill overlooking the Camus Valley. Below, the vast land was covered with the deep-violet color of Springtime Camus blossoms.

Max was curled up on the front seat of the truck as Romey removed the sectionals from the ladder rack. He spread them out on the pavers and began assembling them when Patricia Easton opened the front door. Max jumped up and started barking.

"Hush, Max," said Romey.

"Hello, Max!" she said. "Hello, Romey. Thanks for coming on such short notice. I know you must be busy so close to

Easter. We're having a dinner party tonight, and I thought Don had called you last week, but he forgot. He's been so busy with his work.

"Gotta love a man who works that hard, right? And no problem, Pat. It's always a pleasure. You know, it's an opportunity to serve." He grinned.

"Just yesterday, Don was in the middle of a stressful business crisis and was fit to be tied. I told him he better watch his blood pressure. He said, 'I should have been a window washer. Those guys are always relaxed and happy.'"

"Well, you tell Mr. Easton that he's not dead yet, so if he wants to clean windows, it's not too late!" Romey gave her a thumbs up.

"Are you going to do all this by yourself?" she asked.

"Yep. Jake's truck broke down again, and Ron cut his thumb on a window blade, so he's out for a few more days."

"I'm sorry to hear that. I recall last time you came, Ron had an injury. Was it his foot?"

"Probably. I don't pay that much attention. He's always got something going on, but hey, don't we all? It's life here on planet Earth." He winked.

"Can I hold the ladder for you to keep it steady? It scares me to death every time I see you climb way up there."

"No thanks. It's nice of you to offer, but I've managed to make it this far without needing anyone to hold my ladder. You just keep puzzling. I'll take care of the windows. Ins and outs today, right?"

"Yes, please. Can you also clean the sculpture by the pool?

I know you did it four months ago right after it arrived from Italy. We still can't believe you climbed up thirty feet."

Romey smiled. "It's what we do, Pat. You know, making the world a better place, one window at a time. I better get some new material. Making the world a better place one sculpture at a time!"


Evie was loading her Chevy pickup for the Eastons dinner party. Her shed was well organized with cases of china and racks of glassware, flatware, props and tablecloths. Of all her clients, the Easton's were the only ones with a dining table made from a giant mango tree. It had been shipped from Hawaii, and Evie knew she would have to protect it. She chose a chenille tablecloth in a deep cranberry color, her Royal Gold china with gold flatware, and Imperial Gold etched crystal. Since there were only sixteen guests, she would do one of her more intricate napkin folds—the flowing lotus. The guests would have gold leaf base plates and individual cranberry glass salt dips with crystal salt spoons. The chef would be preparing a five-course meal paired with wine. Evie made the menus herself, printed on Italian cotton paper and tied with hand-dyed silk ribbon. She had been doing parties for Mrs. Easton for four years now and knew the woman had impeccable taste.

Evie went over the packing list in her head. She would pick up the centerpiece at Trina Adams' floral shop after she dropped Jack off at Chrissy's. She removed her magnetic landscaping sign from the truck door and replaced it with her *Evie's Tablescapes* sign.

"Jack," she called. "Come on, buddy, it's time to go. You

can jump in the back, or I can follow you on your bike. It's not that far." She heard the back door slam.

"Try not to slam the back door, Jack. Now we're locked out. Again. I've got to get that knob fixed."

"Sorry, Mom. I'll crawl through the bathroom window when we get home. Again." He ran out the driveway and down the road.

"Or you can run," Evie said to herself as she got into the truck and followed him. Leave it to Jack to come up with his own option. Evie tapped the horn, and he ran faster. When she pulled into the next driveway, Jack was petting Rex and they were both panting.

"You're a marvel, my little man. You and Dill be good. I'm going to do this job at the Eastons' and then I'll be back to make dinner. I love you up to the sky and back again." Jack grinned and she saw he had a knot on his forehead.

"What happened to your head, Buddy?"

"Me and Dillon dug a really deep hole and covered it with pine branches and peanut butter to see if we could catch a ground squirrel. Then Dillon pushed me in and I hit my head on a rock."

"Oh, my goodness."

"It's alright. It didn't even hurt that much. Love you, Mom."

Chrissy stood on the porch, wearing scrubs, holding a can of Bud Light. Evie honked the horn and yelled, "Really, Chrissy? Four pigtails?"

"Really, Evie? Your dress matches your tablecloths?"

Evie drove slowly down Main Street so as not to rattle the crystal and china. There were three Shine On trucks parked by the school. She saw the guys up on ladders pulling down long strands of lights, getting ready for Easter. She pulled up in front of Trina's Floral Shop behind a dirty gray Subaru Outback with an empty bike rack and a Washington state license plate.

When Evie entered the flower shop, the door chimed, "You're All I've Got Tonight."

"Hi Katie," said Evie. "How are you?"

"I'm good. Just helping Mom while I'm on spring break."

"Awesome. Is she here?"

"No, but your centerpiece is ready. Mom's over at the school library updating the Dewey Decimal System. She's also doing tons for the Easter egg hunt."

"Yes, and later she'll be preparing for the Fourth of July parade and organizing the changing of the lights, right?"

"Yep. That's my mama!"

"Of course. She's an amazing woman, your mom."

"I know." Katie smiled. "I love her sooooo much!" Katie went in the back of the shop and brought out the centerpiece, an array of Casa Blanca lilies, corrugated Callas, Maidenhair fern, and sprays of Rosehip berries, artfully arranged in a gold leaf Italian urn.

"Oh, this is perfect. Your mom is the best floral artist in all the land."

"I know. I'll tell her you said so. Do you need a receipt?"

"Yes, please. I'll pay cash now. Oh, and remind your mom that we need to plan the wedding flowers for the Eastons' event in October. Their daughter's getting married on their property, and I think it's about a hundred guests so that will be twelve or thirteen tables. Tell her we can meet later this month. I know she's very busy."

Katie wrote up a receipt and handed it to Evie. "For sure, I'll remind her."

"And we also have to think about the new millennium celebration and Pine Grove's birthday party." Evie set the money on the counter.

"Yeah, I can hardly believe it's going to be the year two thousand. Oh, and Mom said that from now on we're going to call the party the Big Blast. She's planning on having like a billion lights that all turn on at the same time."

"Wow, that's going to be dazzling. I can't wait!" Evie picked up the centerpiece. "Hey, Katie, do you know whose car is out front with the Washington plates?"

"No, I don't. It's weird. You never see an out-of-state plate in Pine Grove."

"Right," Evie said. "Take care. I hope to see you again."

"Oh, you will. For sure I'll be back for the summer to be in the parade with Mom. Daddy and Willy are making us a rolling cart for our flower basket."

"Wow! How are they gonna do that?"

"They're making it out of grandma's old oxygen tank holder."

"Those guys are brilliant."

"I know, right? I love them so so so much."

"Tell your mama hello for me." Evie carried the flower

arrangement out and set it on the floor of the truck. When she got into the driver's seat, she saw that the Subaru was gone.

The long drive up to the Eastons' was one of Evie's favorites. It was beautiful and quite stunning with the wild Camus in full bloom. An arrow of starlings shot across the sky as the lake below glinted far off in the afternoon sun.

Mid-way up the winding road, the Murphy farm came into view. It was from this angle and at this time of day that Evie loved the most. On a knoll, well settled into the landscape, sat the old white milkhouse illuminated by sunlight. Beyond the big red barn a llama, goats and horses grazed in the emerald-green meadow. There were Spring calves and lambs nursing and chickens free ranging. There were ducks bobbing in the pond and two white swans gliding across the glassy water. Evie rolled down the window and heard bullfrogs croaking and a peacock screech.

It was common knowledge that Mr. Murphy lived alone and sadly had a son he hadn't spoken to in ten years. They had a falling out and were both too stubborn to admit they were wrong, so to compensate for his loneliness, Mr. Murphy rescued every animal he could find. Evie considered him a kind man, as he often let Jack and Dillon ride his donkey and visit his potbellied pig named Oreo and his rabbits and chinchillas that played together. Jack was most intrigued with Sydney, the bug-eyed emu, the giant tortoise named Sir Freudian, and the iguana that did push-ups on a tilted fence post.

Evie was thinking she should make the old guy a pie when she saw something run across the road. It looked like a white rabbit. Maybe it belonged to Mr. Murphy. If Jack were here, he would tie his shoelaces together, lasso the rabbit, and return it to the animal farm. That kid could catch anything. Once she saw him capture a corn snake with a snare made from a willow branch. Her heart ached to think of him in the yard at three years old with a baby quail he had found. He was watching it pick at the grass, and Evie was beside him, pulling weeds. Suddenly a Steller's jay swooped down, impaled the tiny bird with its razor-sharp beak and carried it away. Jack was mortified, and they both sat on the grass and cried. Evie gently explained about the beauty and the cruelty of nature. Jack stopped crying and said, "I'm gonna kill that big bully bird." Not long after that, he figured out how to make a slingshot.

As Evie got closer, she saw a Chevy truck like hers, but with ladders, parked on the roadside and realized it was a Shine On window cleaning truck. The doors were open. *These guys are everywhere.* Beside the truck was the little dog, Max. Romey was standing, but he was bent over with his head by his knees. Her chest thudded, thinking he was throwing up, or worse yet, having a heart attack. She pulled over and jumped out. Max came to her, wagging his tail.

"Hey! Are you okay? Do you need help?" Although she wouldn't know what to do if he did. He raised up and shook his head hard. His face was red and puffy, and he was holding a pair of scissors with long blades and orange handles. *Oh my God! He's come up here to commit suicide! I knew nobody could be that happy. Always smiling, when deep down inside he can't live another day in agony. Mr. Shine On. I'll talk him off the ledge. I'll tell him I understand and maybe even tell him about when I was placed in a psychological trauma center and put on suicide watch.*

"Oh, no, I'm fine," he said.

"Whew. I saw your dog run across the road, and I thought it was one of Mr. Murphy's rabbits. I'm glad you're okay." She noticed an empty bowl and a spoon sitting on the dashboard above the steering wheel. Why did it look so familiar? Oh, it was the same white bowl and silverware pattern she had at home. The same empty cereal bowl Jack and Dillon left on the table, the bathroom counter, or the porch.

"Wow, I can't believe Max isn't barking at you. He barks at everybody."

Evie bent down and patted Max's head. "I like his tufts," she said.

"I like your dress," he said.

Evie felt her cheeks flush. "Thanks."

"What color would you call that? Cranberry?"

"That's right. Good guess. I'm going to the Eastons." She refrained from telling him about the ridiculous thing she did— wearing the same color as the tablecloths she chose.

"Yeah? I just cleaned their windows. Good people, they are. They have great taste, and Pat is a master puzzler."

"Yeah, I've seen her collection. She has hundreds of puzzles."

"I always try to bring her one back from a place I've traveled."

"Right, she mentioned that. Last time she was working on a scene of Patagonia. She said you had just returned from there last February. That must've been beautiful."

"Yep, it's beautiful and interesting. Especially if you're a penguin," he smiled. "You can almost reach up and pluck a star from the sky down there in the southern hemisphere."

"Wow," said Evie. *How poetic.*

"Anyway, I just did their windows because they're having a party tonight."

"Yes, I know. I'm going to help with the decor."

"Decor, you say? Sounds fancy. I'm obviously not that sophisticated. After all, you caught me cutting my own hair."

"Oh, that explains the scissors. Well, even if you don't consider yourself sophisticated, you're certainly resourceful."

"Yeah, I go to Drip 'n Sip every day, but I don't go to the Clip 'n Snip because it takes too much time. I can cut my own hair in less than three minutes, and then on to the next job."

Evie looked at the dark curly clippings lying by Romey's feet.

"Making the world a better place, one mediocre haircut and one clean window at a time." He grinned and brushed the hair off the front of his black tee shirt. "Well, have fun at the Eastons'. I'm off to the park to give Trina a hand. Maybe I'll see you tomorrow at the Easter egg hunt?"

"Thanks. Yeah, we'll be there. Oh, and thank you again for being so nice to the boys when they crashed their bikes at Lola's house."

"No problem. I like the little punks, and it's good they didn't get hurt. A few small bumps and bruises along the road of life is good for the soul."

Evie looked at him, nodded and smiled. *That's actually a really good haircut.*

He opened his truck door. "Up, Maxwell Smart!" Max jumped into the front seat and Romey got in and started the truck. "Stay young and happy!" he said and drove away.

When Evie pulled into the Eastons' driveway, Patricia Easton came out. "Hi Evie, I thought you were Romey. I didn't realize you two have the same truck." Evie thought that they not only had matching trucks, but the same dishes and silverware pattern. And what were the chances of meeting someone else who didn't have a television? She had read that only two percent of Idaho's residents didn't have a TV. She smiled inside at the vision of him standing out in the afternoon sun, way above the valley floor, holding a pair of scissors. *What color would you call that? Cranberry?*

"Hello Mrs. Easton. Yes, but different signs, and his truck is newer. This one's a '92."

"Well, he left a section of his ladder out by the pool, so I thought he was coming back to get it."

"After I unload and set up, I can put it in the back of my truck and drop it off to him tomorrow at the park. He said he'll be at the Easter egg hunt."

"That would be great Evie. Thank you. I'm going into town for a few things. Help yourself to anything you want. You know where everything is. The caterers will arrive at 5:30. We're doing cocktails at 7:00."

"Okay. I'll be done by 5:00. I'll be back Monday after Easter to pick up. They can just put everything in the garage."

Evie brought the linens in and began covering the table. Thoughts of Lola came to mind as they often did these days. She smiled, thinking of Lola's latest shared memories of Sam.

He was not a new man, Lola had said. He was a very old man, in the best possible way. He knew how to make her feel like a million bucks. She was his greatest pleasure, his most valued treasure. There had been no groping and probing like the college boys she once knew. No "How's that? There? Here? Ouch, move your elbow. Does that feel good?"

Sam had remembered a time when girls wore garter belts and girdles, when their dresses had low hems, tight, wide belts, and complicated buttons, and to undo a Cross-Your-Heart bra was a man's biggest dating challenge. He was a true gentleman whose patience was a virtue, for whom it was natural to have a six-month courtship as foreplay. Then he meets Lola, who gives him fair warning that she loves sex. Young, sassy Lola, with a voluptuous body and flowing caramel-colored hair. Breath-stopping Lola, half his age, whose apartment had posters of The Beatles and Led Zeppelin, and before he could register what color the couch was, her tee-shirt slips up and her lacey bra is flung across the room. Her jeans slide down and he's traipsing behind her, mesmerized, wading through a trail of panties and hair ties.

The first time he saw her naked and for years afterwards, he wore the expression of a kid faced with a giant ice cream cone. Once he got over the shock, Sam wedded the hunger of a man long denied to the happiness of a man suddenly fulfilled. When Lola had confided these memories with a slight smile, Evie noticed her breathing more deeply and hoped that these memories offered some solace in her deep grief.

As Evie placed the salt dips, her sweet baby sister Ellie came to mind. Ellie would have loved this table setting because cranberry or "Berry Jelly" was her favorite color. Evie had taught Ellie to read by memorizing the names of the colors in the Crayola sixty-four pack. Evie remembered walking into the kitchen to see Ellie there at five years old, scribbling on the wall with a crayon. She gasped when Ellie so proudly pointed to the wall and said, "Look! Berry Jelly!"

Evie placed the last fork, set the centerpiece on the table, and took a photo. She went out and put the ladder extension in her truck. As she drove slowly toward the low-lying sun, she felt a sense of accomplishment. And the warm memories of her baby sister, Ellie, and Lola's love story accompanied her toward the upcoming tangerine sky.

# SEVEN

The next morning was the Pine Grove annual Easter egg hunt in the park. Romey had offered to help hide the eggs. There were nine dozen hard boiled eggs, all dyed by Trina and Katie Adams. The church ladies filled another two hundred plastic eggs with candy, and Romey donated a golden egg, which held a five-dollar bill.

Chrissy and Evie brought the boys to the park and sat on the tailgate to watch. Chrissy was drinking Kahlua and coffee, and Evie was eating some early harvest snap peas from her garden. Dillon had a Ninja Turtle Easter basket, and Jack refused to carry a basket like all the little kids. He said he was only interested in finding the golden egg.

When Trina Adams stood on the park stage and rang her choir bells, the hunt began. Eager boys in vests and bowties and little girls in frilly dresses with satin sashes ran into the park.

Toddlers held their parents' hands, and a teenage girl tugged on the leash of a chocolate lab in a purple tutu.

Netty and Letty Gabilan, eighty-eight-year-old identical twins with dementia, participated every year in the Easter egg hunt and the Fourth of July parade. Today they wore matching yellow dresses, teal slippers, and pink bunny ears. Their grandkids pushed their wheelchairs and stopped to pick up an egg when the sisters spotted one. They pointed and screeched, "There's a green one! I see a blue one!"

"Those two are so darn cute," said Evie. "It would be awesome if they found the golden egg."

"Yeah, but they'd probably tear the five-dollar bill in half because they have to share everything." Chrissy took a gulp.

"I know. It's incredible that they were born and raised here and have never been away from Pine Grove, or each other." Evie put her hand on her heart. "So sweet."

"Which one has the messed-up leg?" asked Chrissy.

"Netty. It's the only way most people can tell them apart. I feel badly for her, how her leg's stuck underneath her. Seems like with modern medicine they could do something to help her."

"It's called a contracture. In surgery, they'd just amputate it."

"That's terrible."

"But even if they cut her leg off, it doesn't always help because then she could be left with a phantom limb and that can hurt worse than a contracted limb." Chrissy belched.

Evie pushed her bottom lip out. "That's so sad."

"Mom! Mom! Look!" Jack came running up with both arms over his head, holding a shiny golden egg. Dillon followed on his heels with three cracked eggs in his basket. His eyes were wide with wonder as he looked up at the golden egg.

Evie chewed nervously, feeling sorry for Dillon. He surely, along with every other kid, wanted that golden egg, and knowing him, Jack probably felt a guilt-ridden pleasure. Before Evie could say anything, Jack turned to Dillon and dropped the golden egg in his Ninja basket. Dillon's face lit up.

"That was nice, Jack," said Evie.

"Dillon actually saw it first," he said.

"Did not," said Dillon.

"Did too. And Mom says if you have something special that somebody else likes, you could always give it to them and that'll make your heart happier than if you keep it all to yourself," said Jack.

"Oh for Pete's sake, Evie," said Chrissy. "Do you bathe this kid in honey?"

"That's right little man," said Evie.

A small girl came running by, crying, and holding an empty basket. Evie looked at her and thought of Ellie at three years old with her bangs cut off at the roots, a blonde sprig sticking straight up. *You're not supposed to play with scissors, baby girl.*

The sobbing girl's dad came over with one hand behind his back and picked her up. She dropped the basket and wrapped her arms around his neck. "What's this?" he said. He held her on his big arm and she squealed when he handed her a fuzzy stuffed duck. "Where do you suppose this came from?" He bounced her up and down.

"The Easto bunny!"

"Yes indeed. And you know why?"

She wiped her nose on his chin. "Why?"

"Because you've been a good little girl. Now we're gonna go say our prayers and you're gonna take a nap." They walked away with her clutching the duck to her cheek.

Evie thought back to the times when she and Ellie said their prayers. Ellie was born when Evie was eleven, so they were more like mother and daughter than sisters. It wasn't that their mom was neglectful, just busy. *Now I lay me down to sleep. I pray the Lord my soul to keep. If I die before I wake, I pray the Lord my soul to take.* Then Ellie would say, "That's not how it goes. You don't die before you wake. It goes, *Angels watch me through the night and wake me up with morning light.*

Evie looked across the park and saw a Shine On truck by the school. "Look, there's Romey's truck. I have this ladder thing I have to get back to him. Jack, can you help me get it onto his truck and then we can go to the Hometown Café and have pancakes."

"Yay!" said Dillon. He popped the golden egg open and picked out the folded bill. "I can pay!"

"Aw, Chrissy. Look who's talking. You've got yourself a little cube of sugar right here."

Jack jumped into the back and got the ladder piece and handed it to Evie.

"You guys wait here. We'll be right back," said Evie. They carried it over to the truck and dropped it in the bed.

Romey walked up to them. "Hey now," he said. "That's mighty nice of you. Did you bring that from the Eastons'?"

"Yes. Mrs. Easton wanted you to get it back as soon as possible."

"We found the golden egg," said Jack.

"No way," Romey smiled and put his hand up. "High five!" Evie noticed he was wearing a tee shirt that said *Belize*, which gave her a little thrill.

Jack jumped up and slapped his hand. "Way."

# EIGHT

Evie and Jack were standing in the kitchen. "Happy Mother's Day!" said Jack. He handed her a present wrapped in hand-painted butcher paper.

"Thank you, Baby. This is so pretty. Did you do this yourself?"

"Yeah. I made it for you at school."

Evie unwrapped the gift. It was a photo of Jack coming down a slide with his arms flung out and his mouth wide open like he was screaming for joy. It was in a frame made of gold-painted elbow macaroni.

"I love it! Thank you." She hugged him and kissed him on the cheek.

They heard Rex barking outside. "Can me and Dillon go ride bikes?"

"Yep. Make sure you both wear your helmets. I'm gonna find the perfect place to hang my beautiful picture."

Jack grabbed his helmet and ran out the door. Evie took the picture and walked slowly to her room. She sat on the bed and turned the delicate frame over. On the back it said, "I Love You Every Day." She held it to her chest, closed her eyes and curled up on her side. It started deep in her stomach, a murky feeling like mud that bubbled and oozed through her body until a sob exploded out her mouth. She trembled and cried from the depths of her core until she was completely spent and her pillow was soaked with tears. *Mother's Day is always hard.*

On the last day of school there was a swim party in the park with games, pizza, and ice cream. As Chrissy packed Dillon's inflatable arm float bands, she couldn't help but being mad at Rob. He was the father after all and it was his job to teach Dillon how to swim, yet he just blew it off and now she had to be the one to worry about it. She put the bands in a plastic grocery bag, stuffed in a towel and dropped in an over-ripe banana and a peanut butter and honey sandwich, forgetting that there would be pizza.

After school let out that day, summer had officially begun. The pool was open seven days a week from morning to dusk. The Shine On crew began changing the lights on the great pines around the park and the town bustled with skateboards, bicycles, and Hula Hoops.

One week into summer, Chrissy woke up with a splitting headache. Dillon had spent the night with Jack, so she decided to treat herself to a bottle of brandy. Now her joints were burning, and she felt like throwing up, but her head hurt too badly to get out of bed and make it to the bathroom. She knew better than to drink brandy because all the sugar made her sick. It happened the last time she drank a whole bottle of port and barfed for an entire day. It seemed worth it last night when she was staying up late with the house all to herself, no one to fight with and no one to judge her. It was her special reward for being a single, hard-working mom. Thank God she didn't have to go to work today. Summer was finally here, and she didn't have to worry about making lunches every day, getting Dillon to school on time, taking care of the dog, and then going to work.

She rolled slowly off the bed, and her foot landed in something squishy. She groaned and looked down to see that Rex had gutted Dillon's backpack, pulling out the week-old plastic bag that held a wet, moldy towel and a rotten banana. The dog had chewed through the baggie and the float bands, and the floor was covered with the remains of old peanut butter and honey. She gagged and bent over, grabbed the wet towel and scraped up the sticky mess. She stumbled over to the kitchen and stuffed it in the trash. "That's it," she said. "New season. New day. Get your shit together Chrissy."


The first of July was sweltering. The Camus had dried up, leaving the valley floor parched and pale. Overhead, stark white clouds streaked the windless sky. Evie decided to take Rex and the boys to the lake. The community pool was packed, and the village was teeming with parade volunteers and preparations.

Evie put on a bikini and a white sundress and packed a bag of snacks, sunscreen, a blanket, towels, and her book, *The Agony and the Ecstasy*. She secretly wanted to, one day, visit Italy, and was looking forward to reading at the lake, absorbed in the passionate life of Michelangelo.

She put the bag in the front seat, watered the flowers by the porch, and called Jack to get in the truck. He ran out of the house, jumped off the steps and landed in the wet flower bed. He was wearing swimming trunks and one Batman sock.

"Don't get mud in the truck, Jack. Take that sock off."

They pulled into Chrissy's driveway, and Dillon and Rex jumped in. Chrissy yelled from the porch. "Dill, you got your arm floaty things?"

"Yeah," Dillon yelled back. She walked to the truck. "Thanks for taking 'em, Evie. It pisses me off that I have to go to work, and you all get to go have fun. I've got a staff meeting and hopefully a short day. Damn, it's hotter than hell out here."

"Language. Sorry you can't join us. It should be really nice at the lake. If you get off early, come on down."

"I'm working in urology today, and there'll be water splashing everywhere, so it's almost like being at the lake." She rolled her eyes.

"Urology?"

"Yeah, we're doin' prostate surgery and bladder tumors. It's actually kinda cool, like you would never know a bladder tumor is really pretty."

"Hmm."

"We fill the bladder with water and put a scope with a

camera inside. The picture comes up on a big screen. The tumors look like something you'd see out in a reef, like kelp beds or jellyfish."

"Yuck. Have fun."

Evie backed out and headed down the road. "We have to stop at Stein's and get some stuff for Lola, then we'll go to the lake."

"What do we have to get?" asked Jack.

"Just a few things so she can make a spinach quiche."

"Yuck," said Dillon. They stuck their tongues out and made gagging gestures in the backseat. Evie smiled.

After they got the items from the market, they drove to Lola's.

"You guys stay out here for a minute. I'm going to give this to Lola and check on her. You can go around by the kitchen window and see if you can find my little frog friend who lives by the vine. He's speckled."

"Is he a tree frog?" asked Jack.

"Yes. Be gentle with him and no, you can't keep him. He lives here."

The boys jumped out and ran around to the side of the house and Evie went to the front door.

"Lola?" she called from the porch. "Knock, knock. Are you there? It's Evie and the boys. Lola?" She heard a high whining sound as she opened the door and stepped in. She set the bag on the entryway table.

Lola was in the living room on her knees, her face in a pillow, with her upper body slumped on the couch. The vacuum cleaner hose was wrapped around her legs and she was screaming into the pillow. One hand scrunched the pillow and the other held a vacuum cleaning brush. She was wailing and beating the brush on the cushion, moaning, "Nooooo." She reared her head and slammed repeatedly into the wet fabric, screaming, and coughing.

Evie stood quietly and let her be. Lola eventually raised her head and inhaled several sharp, spastic breaths. She swiped her swollen eyes and dabbed her nose with her hand. "Oh, Evie. I'm so sorry. I didn't want you to see this. I'm such a mess. I wanna die. I really do. Life isn't worth living alone without my Sam. He was the very current that kept my blood flowing. He's gone, and he took me with him. I'm an empty shell. Empty. Useless. Worthless." She turned and tried to kick the hose free of her legs.

"Here, let me help you, Lola. It's okay. Let's sit up. You're all tangled. Let me unwrap you, here." Evie knelt by the couch and began to untangle the hose.

"Oh, Evie, I think I'm going crazy. I thought I was doing so well. I thought I could live one good day without plunging."

"Lola, can you remember, was there a trigger? It's okay. It's normal, well, your new normal."

"Nothing is NORMAL!" she screamed as the hose fell away. She turned to face Evie. "I'm going crazy, I'm telling you!"

"I promise you're not crazy," said Evie as she helped Lola up and sat her on the couch. Evie knew it would be inappropriate to share with Lola that the therapists of Evie's youth had told her that wanting to die was a normal reaction. Evie had spewed fire at the word, *normal,* and demanded that no one ever use that word around her again. Eventually they slipped in the term *new normal.*

Lola ran her hands through her hair. "Did you bring kids with you? I don't want to frighten the poor children. Look at me, I would scare them to death."

"They're okay. They're out in your garden, looking for a frog. I brought you the groceries you wanted." Evie took the brush from Lola's hand and dropped it on the carpet. She sat next to her and placed both hands on Lola's knees.

Lola stared, trancelike at the brush. "No one would ever believe how close Sam and I were. We were very, very lucky to have found one another, and I know that now more than ever. We really couldn't keep our hands off each other or our hearts away from each other, if that makes any sense at all."

Evie nodded. "What were you doing before this happened?"

"Well, I was feeling okay earlier today, even a little more energized than I have in a long time. I remembered you would be bringing the things I needed to make a spinach quiche, like he used to make for me. I was really looking forward to it, and as my morning brightened, I guess I bit off more than I could chew when I decided to clean the whole house."

"Yeah, that's a lot."

"Then I got triggered. You see, when I vacuumed the couch, he would sometimes take me by surprise, you know, come up behind me when I was bent over. I would feel his hand on the small of my back, and he would unplug the cord and the room would go quiet. That's when I dropped the cleaning brush and well, you know. We never had to say a word and even years later we still called those times our sofa serenade." She smiled. "One time the window cleaner appeared right out the front window when we were completely naked, *making love right here*. I jumped up and ran into the bathroom, and Sam told me the window washer smiled and waved and carried on as if he saw that every day."

Evie felt her face flush at the thought of Romey seeing them in the nude. "I love that you and Sam had so much passion."

Lola pulled back, drew a deep breath and looked at Evie.

"Are you okay, Evie? You look flushed."

"Yes, I'm good, Thank you. It's really hot out, so we're gonna go to the lake and cool off. You're welcome to come with us if you want."

"No. No, thank you."

"I can check on you later if you want. I can even finish vacuuming."

"You're such a dear. I think I'll just rest for a bit."

"Okay. Call if you need anything." *One step forward, two steps back.*

When Evie stepped out the door, there stood the boys and Rex. Jack had a big grin on his face with a speckled frog sitting on top of his head.

At the lake, Evie parked between a truck with a jet ski trailer and the gray Subaru. She read the Washington license plate—1BKR629. One banker, one baker, one biker without a bike? *That's strange*, she thought. *I keep seeing that car. The* boys jumped out and ran to the water. Rex trotted after them, stopping to squirt on a log. Evie grabbed the bag and saw Jack had thrown his muddy sock on top. She hung the sock on the side mirror to dry. Scanning the lakeshore, she was happy to see very few people—sunbathers, a family with three bare-butt babies, and a guy taking pictures with a Polaroid camera.

She spread out the blanket, took off her dress, and got out her book. "Come and get sunscreen you guys," she called. As she began tying the bikini string tighter around her neck, Rex bounded toward her and knocked the bag over, flipping the book off the blanket.

"Darn it Rex. You knocked my bookmark out, and now I don't know what page I'm on." Rex pricked his ears up and cocked his head to one side. She picked up the laminated bookmark Jack had made her in first grade and kissed the picture of him holding a cat they once had. Kitty had lived a good long life and was the only cat she knew that stood on its hind legs and did a pirouette. Jack had taught her to dance with him and had rigged up a little bell that Kitty would ring by swatting it with her paw when she wanted to go outside. Evie reached in the bag and pulled out a can of Pringles, popped the lid, and stuck a stack in her mouth. She gave one to Rex, who bobbed his head up and down and smacked his lips.

"You're such a good boy Rex." She took his big head in her hands and looked into his brown eyes. "I love you." He flung his head back and sneezed, spraying pieces of soggy potato all over the blanket. "Bless you."

She heard water lapping on the shore, the high-pitched whining of jet skis and looked out at the lake. Jack was swimming and Dillon was standing chest deep with his arms over his head, no floaties. Two neon-green jet skis were approaching at full speed, leaning on their sides, white water blasting out the back. The engines revved as they sped by, making a huge wake that slapped Dillon on the head and he disappeared. Evie jumped up and ran into the water. Dillon popped up, floundering and choking and sunk out of sight again. "Get out, Jack! Now! Get on the blanket!" Jack did as he was told. Dillon's hand shot up in the churning swirl and she grabbed his arm, yanked him onto her back and stumbled to the blanket. He tore at her suit and her hair, gagging and spitting.

"Where are your floaties?" she cried. She dropped him on his back and fell to her knees.

"I dunno," he blubbered.

"It's alright, buddy, you're safe now. Let's get you dried off." She was shaking all over. "You *have* to wear your floaties Dillon, until you learn to swim. Remember sweetheart, you're not as old as Jack and can't do everything he does." She put a towel over his head and scrubbed hard, then tucked it around him and kissed his cheek. "I would just roll over and die if I lost you on my watch. Let's just lie here for a while and catch our breath. Rex, get off the blanket, your feet are sandy!"

"I'm hungry," said Jack.

"Here, have a Pringle." She handed him the can. "Let me get you a Juicy box. Do you want apple or berry?"

"I want berry," said Dillon. She rubbed Dillon's feet to still his shakes. She pulled her long hair back, squeezing the water out. A low growl came from Rex's throat as a shadow came over her. Jack put his hand on Rex to quiet him. Evie looked up to see a guy, dripping with sweat. He had a Polaroid camera around his neck and was holding a shabby sandal in each hand. He was wearing cut-offs and a tattered Jack Daniels tee shirt. His face was stubbled, his hair sticking out in all directions. He knelt on the sand in front of her, smiling with his mouth open. He had a big space between his front teeth. He said, "I saw what happened. Is everything under control?"

The sight of him was disturbing. Who was this whacko? She stood up nearly pushing him backwards. Rex started whining and Jack held him by the collar. Evie threw her arms out to her sides, "Doesn't it look like everything is under control?" She wanted to tell him he was an idiot for watching the whole thing and making no effort to help. Obviously, nothing was in her control; she felt the anger and fear rise inside and wanted to puke, visualizing pulling out Dillon's limp body and trying to revive him because she wasn't paying enough attention to see he had no floaties. He could be lying here, his little lungs filled with water, the last words he ever heard his mama say being, "Do you have your floaty things, Dillon?" She wanted to throw rocks at the jet skiers for being so rude, but they were already halfway across the lake. They didn't need to come that close to shore or that close to the boys. If Chrissy were here, she would scrape a sharp rock all over their shiny green paint and slash their truck tires.

The guy gawked at her feet, and she saw his eyes traveling up her body. For a second she stopped breathing as goose bumps sprang up her legs.

He stood up, unsteady on his feet and staggered away, slapping the sandals against his temples and making a hoarse, hissing sound. He looked to the sky and yelled, "Stop it! Get out of my ears, hornets! No more buzzing!"

Evie watched him stumble. *Oh my God, what a weirdo. Where did he come from? Was he actually standing there watching Dillon almost drown? And he's walking like he's drunk and obviously mentally ill.* Wanting to protect the boys, she fell to her knees on the blanket.

With Pringles stuck to his face, Jack said, "Um, Mom?"

"What, honey?

He pointed his juice at her. She looked down and saw her bikini top was around her waist and her breasts were completely exposed.

"Ohhh!" She slapped her hands over her front. Shaking, she grabbed her dress and slipped it back on. Dillon looked out at the water and slurped his juicy box dry.

They stayed the rest of the afternoon. Evie was on edge. The jet skis droned on, and she thought of what she would say to the jerks when they finally came ashore. She kept glancing toward the parking lot and down the beach. It seemed the boys had recovered from the earlier trauma and were skipping rocks and playing fetch with Rex. When Evie packed up, the Pringles lid and her bookmark were missing. She emptied out the bag but didn't find them. She crawled around on the blanket, then got up and shook it out, but no Pringle lid or bookmark. She looked at Rex and said, "Did you eat them, Rex?" He cocked his head and smiled, showing all his teeth.

On the ride home, Evie decided to keep quiet about the wake incident and the creepy guy. If Chrissy was hammered by now, she might not notice the floaties were left behind. But then again, honesty was always the best policy. Evie decided if it came up, she would tell.

When they brought Dillon home, Chrissy came out wearing an orange muumuu and drinking out of Dillon's old sippy cup.

"Let me guess, tequila?" said Evie.

"Yep. Guess who got fired?"

"Oh no, Chrissy, I'm so sorry. What are you going to do?"

"Not me. I didn't get fired. That guy—the dirtbag housekeeper—got fired for stealing. Our manager, Alice, told us at the staff meeting that he stole a bunch of food. She said he even took Ziplock baggies, a big container of coffee, two big jars of peanut butter, and they are missing a case of toilet paper. I could hardly contain myself. I kept my mask on so they couldn't see me smiling."

Evie shook her head. "Unbelievable. How do you sleep at night?"

"Great. He got what he deserved." She took a sip. "And, booze and Tylenol PM."

The subject of floaties never came up.

# NINE

Evie was by the garage loading her truck with golf clubs, shoes, and clothes when Lola came out, holding a coat on a hanger. It was a long black pea coat with red lapels. "I guess you can donate this, too." Lola's lip quivered. "I didn't want to let it go."

"Then don't," said Evie. "Remember what we talked about, Lola. It's about you. Only get rid of what you can and what feels right to you. I know it's hard, but you must remember not to put pressure on yourself."

Lola pressed her face into the fabric and inhaled deeply. "I can still smell him."

Yes, thought Evie. *It's remarkable how their scent can linger and resurface at any given time. It's because their essence lives inside you now.* "I know you can, Lola, and it's a beautiful thing. And remember, you have every right to keep all his things if that's what you need to do right now. That's a very nice coat."

Lola held the coat to her cheek and closed her eyes, reflecting.

"We got it in Ireland years ago. I remember Sam was so persistent about buying me a wool sweater, although I'm allergic to wool. Every shop we went in, he picked up a sweater or scarf and said, 'What about this one?' and I told him it was lovely but I was allergic. It was as if he didn't hear me. That was something I just couldn't change about him. He was stubborn. He'd get his mind set on something and that was it." Evie thought about her dad. Her mom used to say that stubborn was her dad's middle name.

"Well, we can't change anyone else, only ourselves," said Evie

"Finally, after three days of telling him I couldn't wear wool, I turned the tables and suggested we buy something for *him*. We both spotted this gorgeous coat in a store window in Dingle. He tried it on, and it looked so good, fit like a glove. I told him how handsome he looked, and the shop owner winked at me and said, 'Looks dern good on yer pappy.' Sam winked at her and said, 'I'm not her pappy.' He kept the coat on, paid for it, and she cut the tag off the sleeve. He wore it for the rest of the trip. I told him again how nice the coat looked on him and he said, 'Lola, honey, it's like wearing a tuxedo. It can even make an unattractive man look good.'"

"Did you ever get your sweater?"

"No, but he bought me a beautiful emerald ring in Dublin. We drove all along the wild Atlantic coast of Ireland where the landscape is the greenest you'll ever see. The emerald island.

The ring was stunning. I worried about traveling with it on, but Sam said it would bring us good luck, like the Irish pea coat did. He was right; we had a cosmic beam over our heads everywhere we went." She paused, lost in the memory.

"Gosh Evie, it seems like yesterday he wrapped me up in this coat in the pouring rain and all we could do was laugh and kiss, and dance. It was magic."

Lola handed the coat to Evie, and she put it on the front seat.

"In a way I want to know who gets the coat," said Lola.

"Lola, it's okay if you aren't ready to let it go. If it brings you comfort, then we can certainly put it back in the closet."

Lola shook her head. "Chances are good, since it's the church rummage sale, that we'll know who buys it, and when winter comes, we'll see who's wearing it out Christmas caroling, but no matter what, they could never look as dapper as Sam."

"It's all okay. It's whatever you want."

"I don't know what I want. I feel like I can't make a decision, and if I do, it might not be right. As sentimental as the coat is, with Sam dead I've lost my greatest treasure, and nothing else will ever be that important to me."

Evie knew exactly what she meant. A fleeting thought came to her of her parents, Ellie, and Turbo, their golden retriever.

"I'm sorry," said Lola. "There I go again, being so wishy-washy."

"How about if we pin a note to the lapel that says *Please call if you buy this coat and care to learn about its history,* and leave your number. Does that feel alright?"

"Yes, Evie, thank you. I like that. But I'm so overwhelmed. Can we leave your number instead? You would be able to tell the story if someone really did call?"

"Of course."

When everything was packed up, Evie drove around to the two church donation sites, dividing Sam's things evenly. Seemed silly they had separate places when it would all end up at the community rummage sale the following week. Evie jotted her number on a scrap of paper and wrote, "If you are interested in the true love story behind this Irish pea coat, please call." She slipped it into the pocket.

When she hung the coat at the white chapel, the last site, a chill slid through her. She felt like she was being watched.


Evie now stood in Lola's kitchen holding a basket. "Okay," she said, "Let's take it slowly. It's not easy and if you cry, it's okay. It just affirms how much you're loved and supported." Evie set the basket full of cards on the table and sat next to Lola. "Pick one," she said.

Lola nibbled on her lip and picked up an envelope. She opened it slowly and regarded the picture of an autumn forest with filtered sunlight through the leaves. It said, *Gone, but not forgotten.*

Her hands began to tremble, and her eyes stung. She opened the card and silently read.

*May tomorrow and each day after remind you of happy memories.*

*Our thoughts are with you.*

*The staff of Samuel T. Ingram Community Hospital*

"There are no happy memories," whispered Lola. "And I don't care about tomorrow, let alone all the days that follow." Tears fell from her eyes, and Evie handed her a tissue.

"Would you like to stop now, Lola? I know it's hard, but please know that everyone at STICH is affected by this and they're all reaching out to let you know you're loved, and Sam was loved and respected tremendously."

"I'm sorry, Evie. You're so kind, and I know I'm just being a big baby about this, but . . . my world's been turned inside out and upside down and it's all gray. And I'm expected to look at a photo of some serene scene and be reminded of happiness?" She slapped the card down on the table and shook her head.

"You're not expected to do anything, Lola. Reading these cards can lesson some of the bleakness, but only when you're ready." Evie handed her another Kleenex. Lola blew her nose, sat up straighter, and chose another card from the basket.

"It's from our friends, Carol and Dan. They live in Arizona."

"Oh, how nice. Go ahead, read it."

Lola opened the card. On the front was a picture of a glistening pond with water lilies, the written caption, *In Deepest Sympathy.*

Evie listened as Lola read.

*Dear Lola,*

*Dan and I want to offer our sympathy to you on the loss of dear Sam. Our thoughts and prayers are with you. Wish we could be there to give you a hug. Let those around you encircle you with their love. We have so many wonderful memories of the four of us.*

*Always, Carol and Dan*

Lola closed her eyes and sighed. "The last time they came to visit was probably five years ago. I wonder how they knew."

"Well, news travels fast and far among people who care," said Evie. "Have you been friends for a long time?"

"Yes. For thirty years. They were in our wedding. They're such a nice couple and never passed judgment on Sam for robbing the cradle. They called me his child bride. That's the trouble with marrying a man twenty-one years older; he was bound to go first."

"Well, like she said, you've got many good memories together."

"Yeah. The three of them helped me grow up. They were golfers and pretty big drinkers, and I wasn't good at either one. I remember one summer we rented a house on a lake out by White Pine. Carol had some suntan lotion, and I smeared it all over my face and my body and laid out while they all went into town to get supplies. When they came back, Sam asked me what had happened to me, and I didn't know what he was talking about until Carol told me I was all streaked the color of rust. I had dyed myself with instant tan. It took a week to wear off. They never let me live that one down."

"That's funny. Do you wanna read another card, or is that enough for now?"

"One more." She picked up another card and opened it.

*Dear Lola,*

*Almost twenty years ago, your husband reached out to me, a neighbor and stranger, to comfort me in an hour of need. I had suffered the loss of a baby. I've never forgotten that act of kindness.*

*I reach out to you now in the same spirit of comfort. I want you to know I stand next to you, figuratively, as you, grieve, cope, and live. I am by your side as are many others, I am sure.*

*With love and strength enough to share,*

*Constance Kramer*

Lola dropped her chin and sat quietly for a moment. "That's our old neighbor. I remember when she lost her baby boy. He died at birth. Had the cord wrapped around his neck. When Sam went over to see her, I couldn't go with him. I didn't have the courage. I wanted a child for so long and was devastated when we learned . . .", her voice trailed off and she looked away. "I was angry at Sam, ashamed of myself and jealous of anyone who was able to get pregnant. Constance didn't gloat over it, of course, but she was obviously so happy and excited to be expecting a baby. I knew it was my distorted view that made me so hateful, but I couldn't help it. I watched her husband helping her into the car the morning she went into labor. She had her hands on her big belly with a grimace and a smile at the same time. Later I heard what happened, and it was as if I had lost the baby myself. I got so depressed I couldn't muster up the strength to go see her."

Evie put the card back in the envelope.

"I didn't send flowers or a card. Not even a feeble attempt to bring her a casserole. I was so selfish. I never did acknowledge that it happened. So incredibly selfish." She shook her head.

"I don't think you were selfish, Lola. You were just coping the best you could at the time. Besides, most people don't know how to deal with tragedy, especially death. They don't know how to help. People are afraid of saying the wrong thing, so they don't say anything at all. Sam was such a kind man, I'm sure he brought that girl comfort on your behalf as well as his own."

Lola sighed. "Would you mind if we read just one more?"

"Of course not." Evie picked up a large white envelope and handed it to her. The letter was written on letterhead.

*Dear Ingram Family,*

*Your gracious message in last week's Pine Tree News was my first awareness of the loss of Mr. Ingram. I am sure he was a good man. I am writing to inform you that our thirty-two-year-old son is in a residential alcohol recovery facility in Utah. This is our twelfth attempt at his rehabilitation. We are seeking donations to subsidize an obviously cost-prohibitive program. We have spent countless hours at STICH for Robbie's care. (Bleeding ulcers, facial lacerations and, most recently, esophageal varices) and find it an exceptional hospital and thank Mr. Ingram for consistently maintaining remarkably high standards. I am acutely aware that death and addiction are community issues, and the support of others is imperative.*

*We have not yet disclosed to Robbie that his sixteen-year-old cat, Maynard, has passed away. Yes, we know what sadness is. Since the day Maynard acquired juvenile-onset diabetes, Robbie only felt real life purpose when he gave Maynard the insulin injections that kept him alive for so many years. Sadly, it was renal failure that finally took the old cat, and we fear that this tragedy will send our Robbie into total despair, requiring his level of care to increase, which obviously will exhaust what resources we have left.*

*I look forward to hearing from you at your earliest convenience and thank you, in advance, for your generous donation.*

*Sincerely, Robert Friedman Sr.*

Lola put the letter on the table and looked at Evie. "I don't even know who Robert Friedman is."

"Yeah. And then there's that." Evie shrugged. "Kind of nervy, don't you think?

They stared at each other for a moment then Lola put her hand to her mouth and snorted. "Do you think he wants a donation for sick cats as well?"

Evie began to giggle, and together they laughed until tears leaked out their eyes and rolled down their cheeks.

# TEN

The next morning, the Shine On fleet was parked at Drip 'n Sip. It was payday, and Romey was handing out cash to the window washers. Max had his head out the window, barking at Ron.

"Hush, Max," said Romey. "Dude, take off your hat and sunglasses. You know that's what makes him bark at you."

"He barks at everybody, Boss." Ron took his hat off.

"Okay ladies, thanks for the hard work. My bad that I overscheduled this week, but do your best not to break any crystal vases or leave a gate open so a dog escapes. And as you know, my brother met a church girl and moved away, so say hello to Juan here. He's gonna help out for the summer. He's the nicest guy you'll ever meet."

"Hey Juan," they said, raising their paper coffee cups.

"So, Juan," said Romey. "This is Josh. He's a stud. Doesn't say much, but he's a hard worker, and so's Jake here. And this is Ron. All's I can say about him is he's super smart, reads all the time and is full of important information—so he thinks. He's quite accident prone, and he's afraid of dogs. Did I miss anything ladies?"

"No," said Ron. That pretty much sums us up.

"I'm gonna need all of you tomorrow to do STICH," said Romey. "Jake and Ron can start rappelling from the rooftop. Clip onto the main anchorage; it's a lot like the one on the school but much higher. Josh and I'll start with ladder work on the second floor. Juan, watch and learn, dude. Your squeegee is your best friend. For now, you can come with me to do Mrs. Baxter's windows. She's one crazy lady. Super picky. She'll follow us all over the house, talking the whole time about stuff we don't need to know. And she'll insist she needs to hold our ladder so we don't fall. If there's one thing you'll learn, it's that people, and especially kids, want to tell the window cleaner everything."

"Yeah, ain't that the truth," said Ron. "Yesterday I was replacing a loose screen in a teenage girl's bedroom, and her six-year-old brother comes in and tells me that his sister sneaks out the window every night to have sex with the neighbor boy."

"Well," said Romey. "That's when I would say, 'Hey kid, don't tell me your family secrets.'" Romey opened the truck door, tossed his empty cup on the floorboard, and flipped a pepperoni stick into Max's open mouth.

Later that day, after the crazy Mrs. Baxter's windows were done, she called Romey on the phone. She was hysterical because her purse was missing. She said it was because Romey had brought a Mexican to clean her windows and everyone knows they're usually poor as dirt and, of course, would steal a purse given the opportunity. She did, after all, keep a big stack of cash in her purse as well as six credit cards, which she now had to cancel, and how was she ever going to get over to Lander County DMV to get her driver's license replaced, and not to mention the purse itself was very expensive, and everything was a disaster because now she realized her keys were missing, which would mean the Mexican and his friends could come back and take anything they could get their hands on and steal the car too.

Romey slowly shook his head, as she continued to fret in his ear. How was she ever going to take her friend Lyle to the hospital in the morning for his procedure? He had that thing on his neck that needed to be removed. She couldn't remember now if they were going to cut it out or just take a biopsy, but whatever they had to do she'd promised to drive him. She was going to call the sheriff right now.

Romey held the phone away from his ear and smiled.

"My dear Mrs. Baxter. I'm sure your friend Lyle'll be okay, and I assure you we're all worthy people of this beautiful world, and everyone is doing their best. I know for sure that Juan nor any of my guys would ever steal. It's in the window cleaner's code of ethics to do your best, and to be honest and respectful. Tell you what I can do. Juan and I will come back to your house and help you find your purse."

"Don't you dare bring him back here. I'm gonna call the sheriff right now!"

"Well, if you really want to get the cops involved, I can't stop you. After all, it's your right as a citizen, and we all have free will, but remember that law enforcement has to come from Lincoln County because Pine Grove doesn't have a police station, and that could take a minimum of two to four hours. Which, in my humble opinion, would be suboptimal given your current state of mind."

She continued screaming something about jail and handcuffs and canine units that she had seen on TV.

"Mrs. Baxter, you may consider calming down slightly so they don't have to send the ambulance as well. After all, it's really a molehill not a mountain." This threw her into an uncontrollable fit. To Romey, it sounded like she was smashing the phone handle, either against the refrigerator or the floor, then the line went dead.

Romey and Juan drove back to her place. Juan and Max stayed in the truck, and Romey knocked on the front door. Mrs. Baxter entered the door with a scowl on her face. He took off his shoes and walked inside.

"Thanks for letting me take a look."

"Well, you can look, but I'm still going to call the sheriff." She glared at him with her hand on the cracked phone handle.

He said, "Fine. And if I don't find what we're looking for, then let the sirens ring!"

A moment later, Romey returned and said three things: "Mrs. Baxter, did I mention that you look lovely today?" and "These windows look great!" and "Here's your purse. It was sitting on your dresser next to your keys."

The following morning, Chrissy was in the STICH procedure room on the upper floor, scrubbed in with a head and neck surgeon. The room was freezing, and she was miserable. Her knee socks had slipped down and bunched up in the heel of her shoes, her compression socks were too short, and her legs were cold.

The patient, Lyle Bremmer, was fifty-three years old with a benign neck mass. He was awake but mildly sedated with monitored anesthesia. Slouched in his chair, the anesthesiologist had a blanket wrapped around his shoulders and was reading a boating magazine.

Chrissy rearranged the instruments on her mayo stand and shifted impatiently from foot to foot. She was agitated and irritable from erratic sugar spikes and a night of too much negativity. Frickin' Rob was always working his way into her head, and it was getting harder to ignore. After putting Dillon to bed last night, she wasted hours imbibing several glasses of wine and four banana moon pies. With an onslaught of self-sabotaging thoughts, she analyzed their breakup in blow-by-blow excruciating detail, followed by a long list of everything about her that was messed up. She fought the belief that she was a fat coward and possibly not worthy of his love. To avoid crying, she bit the inside of her cheek until she tasted blood. She reminded herself not to turn out like her mother—a self-loathing, despicable drunk. She looked at the clock on the wall, and a knot tightened in her chest. *Keep your shit together, Chrissy.*

Dana, the registered nurse, said, "Okay everyone! Let's do a time out. This is Lyle Bremmer. He is consented for excision of a benign neck mass. He has no allergies, and there are no antibiotics ordered. He takes hydrochlorothiazide for hypertension and is a smoker but claims he quit three days ago. Sequential compression device is on and running, and the warmer is on medium. The grounding pad is on the right anterior thigh and the cautery is set at twenty-five. The correct surgical site is marked. I have prepped with betadine and made sure not to remove the surgeon's marks. Do we all agree?"

"I agree."

"I agree."

"Yes, I agree. Local, please," said the surgeon.

Chrissy removed the needle cap. "One percent lidocaine plain," she said, handing him the syringe.

"No epinephrine?" he asked.

"No. Do you want epi?" Chrissy yelled, "Dana give me one percent with epi!"

"Jeez, Chrissy, I can hear you. I'm standing right here. You remind me of my sister. She literally screams at me when I'm in the same room."

"Whatever, Dana." Chrissy waved the syringe at her.

Dana pointed her finger. "They say sometimes that means a person is hard of hearing, when they talk really loud. They also say you can go deaf if you use a blow dryer without covering your ears. That happened to my cousin's wife. He actually thought she wasn't paying attention to him whenever he asked her stuff like, what's for dinner. She acted like she didn't even hear him. Well, I was the one who suggested she get her hearing checked, although she's not even as old as I am."

"Can you turn the overheads up please?" asked the surgeon.

Dana went to the wall and turned the dial. "Overhead lights on high!"

"Anyway," she continued, "sure enough, they found out she had been blow drying her hair on the high setting every day for, like twenty years. She has the kind of hair that's long and straight but super kinky at the temples, so that's where she pointed the blow dryer, right into her ears. Can you imagine that?" Chrissy looked at the surgeon and rolled her eyes. Dana said, "She shoulda put tissue in her ears, but now it's too late, poor thing. She has to wear hearing aids and that's a whole other set of problems. Not only are they super expensive, but if you don't do it right, they whistle, and my cousin says that's more annoying than being ignored. Do you really want me to get lidocaine with epi, Chrissy? I can do it, no problem."

"It's okay," said the surgeon. "I'll use this. Little poke here, Mr. Bremmer, it's just the numbing medicine going in." He injected the neck three times and set the syringe on the Mayo stand. He stepped back and crossed his arms. "We'll just let that soak in for a minute. How's your boy, Chrissy?"

Under her mask, Chrissy smiled for the first time that morning. "My little pain in the butt is having a good summer. He and his buddy, Jack, are trying to talk us into getting a donkey. They want to teach it tricks and ride it in the parade."

"Our neighbors have a donkey," said Dana.

"Of course they do," Chrissy nodded.

"Well, they call it a burro, but it's the same thing. I think burro is Spanish for donkey. They're very docile animals.

People say they're stubborn and lazy, but they're actually really smart and hard-working. I bet your son would be able to teach a donkey all kinds of cool tricks. I saw a circus once in Cabo where they had a donkey with a rooster on its back. Oh, and here's an interesting fact, a hinny is what you get when you cross a female donkey with a male horse."

"You don't say," said the surgeon.

"Yep," said Dana. "And when you cross a male donkey with a female horse, that's a mule. You know, they used donkeys in World War One for hauling ammunition and other supplies. Donkeys are so strong, they could pack huge containers of water straight up those steep hillsides to the men in the trenches. Also, and this is another interesting fact, during the war, donkeys became walking ambulances. It's kinda sad if you think about it. I guess if I was a donkey I would rather be in a parade than a war."

The surgeon interjected, "Fifteen blade." Chrissy handed him the knife and unclamped the suction. She looked out the window and wished she was outside where it was warm. It sucked to work on such a nice day. Did she really miss Rob or just the idea of him? When did they start to get on each other's nerves and why did she continue to give him the power to make her so damn mad she wanted to strangle him? She thought back to the last time he was home, of how she had grabbed the remote control out of his hand and threw it, hitting him smack dab in the middle of his handsome forehead.

Right before she kicked him out, she yelled that he was passive aggressive, and in true Rob fashion, he gave her that sincere look that melted her and said, "How can I be passive aggressive when I don't even know what that means?" She screamed that you don't have to know what something means to be it. Then they looked at each other and started laughing because the whole thing sounded so ridiculous. But, she didn't change her mind about kicking him out. She tried to convince herself that she never wanted to see him again, but it didn't help that she saw him every time she looked into Dillon's beautiful green eyes.

"Hemostat." Blood oozed out and into the suction tip. The anesthesiologist unwrapped himself, dropped the blanket on the floor, and mumbled, "Be right back."

"Where are you going?" asked Dana. "Can I get you something?"

He shook his head and went out the door.

"He's probably going to the bathroom again," said Dana. "Maybe he has a stomachache because that's like the third time this morning he's left the room. Hope he washes his hands."

"Dana, please," said Chrissy. "Spare me."

"Let's turn the suction up, please," said the surgeon.

"Suction up!" Chrissy barked.

Dana said, "Suction is on three-fifty already. I'll turn it up to four hundred. Try that and let me know if you want me to change it again. I put a new filter on right before this case. That should help because I think they were having a little problem with it yesterday. It's usually just a filter issue."

Dana adjusted the suction tubing down by Chrissy's feet. "Hey, Chrissy, I see you're wearing your clown socks today! They're so cute, although they look like they slipped down around your ankles. Do you want me to pull them up for you? I can do it, no problem."

Chrissy groaned under her breath. "No Dana, I'm good." The patient began snoring, and Chrissy thought, why can't everybody just shut up for a minute?"

"Okay," said Dana. "Suit yourself. Hey, didn't you tell me once that you got those at the Dollar Store?"

"Yeah," mumbled Chrissy. Her temples began to pound.

"Well, I think that makes them even cooler that they were only a dollar. That's only fifty cents per sock!" Dana laughed. "You're not only thrifty, but you're also fashion-fearless!"

The surgeon held out his hand. "Allis clamp," he said.

"Shit. Dana, can you grab me an Allis?"

Dana ran out of the room to retrieve the clamp and as the door slammed, the patient monitor began alarming and flashing. Chrissy and the surgeon looked at each other, the sporadic rhythm, and the empty chair. Chrissy dabbed the increasing blood flow. "You okay?" she said to the patient, but he didn't respond.

The surgeon stood with a gauze in his hand, staring at the monitor. "Mr. Bremmer?" He shook his shoulder. "Lyle! Can you hear me?"

Chrissy rapped the patient's chin with the suction tip. His face turned gray—his eyes fixed on the ceiling.

"Fuck!" She stumbled over to the wall and smacked the code button with her elbow. Overhead, the intercom sputtered and popped. The front office secretary's voice stayed calm:

"Code Blue Procedure Room Third Floor"

"Code Blue Procedure Room Third Floor"

"Code Blue Procedure Room Third Floor"

The door flew open, and the room filled with scrubs. Orderlies brought a backboard and rolled stools and hampers out of the way as nurses, materials staff, a doctor, and management rushed in.

"What's going on?"

"He's not breathing."

"Get an airway in!"

"Is there a pulse? Checking for a pulse."

"No pulse."

"Get a board under him!"

"Start CPR!"

The drapes were yanked down, the gown ripped off, exposing the patient's chest, a backboard slid under him, an airway inserted, compressions started, and a resuscitation bag near his face. Recovery room nurses came in pushing the crash cart, turning on the defibrillator, opening pads.

"Twenty-seven, twenty-eight, twenty-nine . . ."

"Switch! One two three four five six seven . . ."

Controlled chaos was everywhere. "Defibrillator on! Pads on! Is there a rhythm? Who's recording? I've got it. Open the line. Start another IV. Get a fourteen-gauge in. Antecubital. Got it. Do we have a rhythm? We've got a rhythm. It's V Fib. We're going to shock with 120 Jules. 150 Jules. 150? 150. Everyone stand back. Charging to 150 Jules. Charged. Clear? All clear. PFFFTT Shock delivered!"

When the shock hit, the torso bounced up and slammed

down on the OR table, shooting blood from his neck all over Chrissy's face shield and the front of her gown.

"Resume CPR . . . Checking at two minutes . . . pause CPR for rhythm check . . . Stand by for a second shock . . . Prepare for one milligram of epinephrine . . . Be ready for Amiodarone 300 milligrams . . ."

Chrissy felt like her mouth and ears were stuffed with cotton. She held a lap sponge over the open wound and pressed firmly. Her legs were no longer cold because she couldn't feel them, and she realized she had no suture to close the wound. But what would it matter if they lost him anyway? God, did she do something wrong? She was so preoccupied all morning, she suddenly couldn't remember if she was paying attention to the procedure or not. She had heard Dana do the time out and had agreed. Mr. Lyle Bremmer. Benign neck mass. She did push the code button, right? Where was the anesthesiologist? Everything was flashing, crackling, and beeping. Then the buzzing and thudding in her head began to fade, and as if she had been unplugged, everything went quiet.

She looked down and saw the patient's eyes flutter.

"We've got a normal sinus rhythm!"

She felt something wet slide under her mask and wondered if it was snot or blood. Staff slowly filed out, leaving the kind of quiet relief that fills every corner of a room after a Code Blue. There was only the soft beep of a normal heart rate and the suction, now laying on the floor. Chrissy and the surgeon looked into each other's eyes, immensely grateful of the outcome. Dana was quiet, preparing mentally to write up an incident report. Tomorrow Chrissy would celebrate another birthday. Lyle Bremmer had survived, and once again, life would go on.

When they heard muffled music and a series of thuds hit the window, Chrissy could barely see through her blood-splattered shield, two guys harnessed to ropes scaling down the windows like a couple of Spidermen. As if waving to a crowd, they swiped their brushes back and forth, smearing soap on the windows, totally oblivious to anything else around them. One was singing out of tune and the other was laughing, bouncing his toes off the glass.

"Oh, for Christ sakes," said Chrissy. "What are they so happy about?"

The surgeon shook his head. "Maybe I should've been a window washer."

Dana got the patient ready to transfer while Chrissy broke scrub and threw her bloody instruments in the basin. Her relief scrub came in and said, "Alice says you can take a twenty-minute break instead of ten. That was intense huh?"

"Yeah, if you call lookin' into a dead man's eyes intense, then I guess it was."

She tore off her gown and gloves, ripped her face shield off and threw it on the floor. She opened the OR door and ran down the hall to the locker room. Thank God there was no one there when she crumpled against a locker and slammed her head against the metal door several times. She went into the bathroom, locked the door, and turned the faucet on high. She kicked out of her shoes and slumped to the floor. Looking at the wad of socks around her swollen ankles, she laid her face on the toilet seat and began to bawl.

"Stupid cheery clown socks. This is all just one big happy fucking joke. You save someone's life and you get an extra ten minute break. This place sucks. This whole town sucks." The flood gates opened, and she cried like she hadn't done in years—since her worthless father left and her alcoholic mom finally died by choking on her own vomit. It was too much to wrap her head around going to work to see death looking her in the face one moment and life going on the next. Everything was so twisted and confusing. She wanted to be a better parent than the parents she had. She wanted to stop drinking and be a good wife and a good mother. She had lied to Rob about her drinking—about his drinking. When her bottle got close to empty, she would pour half of his down the drain when he wasn't looking, and the next day accuse him of drinking too much—convincing him he didn't remember—and he believed her. He believed in her when she didn't believe in herself. She was a liar and a thief, and Dillon deserved better. *How does Evie do it? I've got to get my act together. I've got to get it together and keep it together.* She lifted her head and stared into the toilet bowl.

There was a knock on the bathroom door. "Chrissy? It's Alice. Are you okay?"

She got up and turned the water off, pulled up her socks and flushed the toilet. "Yeah, I'll be out in a minute."

"Okay. Then you and Dana can go home."

Chrissy stared at the door, feeling relieved.

"The patient coded again in PACU," said Alice. "He didn't make it."

# ELEVEN

The next day was the third of July, and the Shine On boys were getting ready for the parade. They had covered the giant pine trees with patriotic lights and set up extra chairs and barbeques in the park. They decorated their work trucks with streamers and hung red, white, and blue buckets from the tailgates and the wheel wells. Juan had figured out how to attach a battery, a hose, and soap to the pressure washer and change the setting so that a constant stream of bubbles would flow out of the back of his truck.

Meanwhile, Evie was loading her truck for the Craven's backyard gala. John Craven, the school principal, was giving his wife a fiftieth birthday party. Evie would decorate the tables in purple. John Craven said the Missus would be surprised and grateful to see her favorite color instead of red, white, and blue. The Cravens were originally from Jackson, Mississippi, and loved the sprawling tables of a Southern crawfish boil. The cook was preparing fifty pounds of crawfish, thirty pounds of potatoes, and sixty ears of corn.

Stacked by the truck were six high cocktail tables, eggplant-colored linen, seven cases of bar glasses and two hundred napkins. The plates were white porcelain, with amethyst glass plates for the birthday cake. Evie had made bouquets of baby's breath and Sterling roses from Lola's garden.

Jack and Dillon ran out of the storage shed holding a long piece of PVC pipe.

"Guys, give me a hand with these tables, please. What are you doing with that pipe?"

"We're gonna make a blow dart and shoot a wild turkey."

"No, you are not going to shoot a wild turkey."

"Then can we get a donkey, pleeeeeze?" said Jack.

"You already have chickens, buddy, and remember how sad you were when Kitty died?" She thought of how sad she was when Turbo died, and that his name was really Thurman, but Ellie pronounced it Turbo.

"But donkeys live for forty years, mom, and we already have a fence and a barn for him to live in."

"We'll see," she said.

Chrissy pulled up, AC/DC blaring. She sat in the car for a minute, then turned it off and rolled out. She was wearing yellow spandex, orange eye shadow and red Christmas tree bulb earrings.

"You're going to blow your ears out with that noise, Chrissy."

"I came to pick the boys up and to remind you to come over tonight. It's my birthday and we're gonna celebrate."

*How could I not know it's your birthday. You've told me ten times already!* "I know it's your birthday. You and Mrs. Craven. I'll be over after I set up her party. It will take forty-seven minutes. What can I bring?"

"Anything is fine as long as it's alcohol. I feel like blowin' it out tonight. I just don't give a fuck about anything except what I put in my mouth."

"Language. Well, it's your birthday and your life. Just don't lose sight of the two most important things," said Evie.

"Junk food and getting loaded?"

"You and Dillon." Evie actually worried about Chrissy and Dill. Instead of mellowing, Chrissy seemed to be getting more intense and self-destructive.

"Everything alright?"

"Yeah," said Chrissy. "Why do you ask?"

"I don't know. It's almost the Fourth of July, and you're wearing Christmas earrings, for one."

"Right," said Chrissy. "Come on, guys, let's go to the Hometown Cafe and get ice cream!"

When Evie arrived at the Cravens, a Shine On truck sat in the driveway. Two washer-installers were hanging cafe lights in the backyard. Evie heard the guy with the Ron shirt explaining to John Craven that his boss, Romey, said there would be no charge because anyone who is crazy enough to oversee all the kids in Pine Grove was an absolute saint and shouldn't have to pay like a common mortal.

Evie unloaded, set up the tables, draped the cake table, and covered the food table with newspaper. As she worked, she thought of Mr. Craven and how thoughtful and romantic he was to do this for his wife. She wondered if she would ever have a husband to give her a fiftieth birthday party. She still could have had a husband if she wanted one, but what would be the point of living with someone you had no connection with? She remembered when Jon left. She had pushed him away, made herself as unattractive as possible, blaming it on post-partum blues. She stood there, holding baby Jack, thinking she should stop Jon, ask him not to leave, apologize for being who she was, brazen and cold, with a little black heart. Instead, she said nothing, and it felt comfortable to be paralyzed and mute, watching him walk out of her life like so many others had. No one really leaves without a push.

John Craven came to the backyard and asked if he could take some pictures. He said he had never seen anything so nice and that his wife was going to love it.

"Do you mind if I take a picture of you, Evie?"

"That's nice, but wouldn't you rather get a picture of your tables?"

"Let's do both. How about you stand by the cake table? I like the way your dress matches the tablecloth."

"Yes, that's a silly thing I do when I'm designing a party."

He snapped a picture of her in front of the cake table holding a sprig of baby's breath. "Great shot," he said.

"Thanks. Hey, I have to run. Lots to do today. I'll come back on the fifth to pick up, if that's alright with you."

"Yes, that'll be fine."

"Don't worry about cleaning anything. Just leave it and I'll take care of it. Enjoy your party. Happy birthday to Mrs. Craven, and Happy Fourth of July. Maybe I'll see you at the parade."

"Yes, you will. Thanks again, Evie. It's beautiful."

"You're welcome."

"Oh, I forgot, we won't be here on the fifth, so I'll pay you now. I have the invoice so let me grab you a check before you go, okay?"

Evie stood frozen. There were things that would never change and would affect her forever. Like when a customer gave her a check, she might sigh unexpectedly and deeply as her vision dimmed, or freeze in her tracks as she remembered Ellie's face—lips tight, eyes squinted, fingers grasping her pen—the first time she wrote her full name. Many years had passed since Evie had gotten their mom's checkbook and taught Ellie, at age four, how to write a check and sign her name on the line. Dear, precious, sweet baby girl. Evie stood there and hummed softly until John Craven returned and handed her the check.

Next stop, the liquor store. Inside, a guy was buying two jugs of whiskey and a carton of Camels. He was wearing baggy shorts and a ratty tank top. When Evie walked in, she saw him smile at the cashier with his mouth open. There was a gap between his front teeth wide enough to stick a quarter. *Oh my God, it's that weirdo from the lake.* She ducked into an aisle and watched him leave, swaying like he was drunk.

As she picked up a bottle of tequila, she noticed a man with a snake tattoo on his neck, pulling a six pack of Keystone

Light out of the cooler. Then he put it back and got a quart bottle instead. I know who he is, she thought, as she walked over to him.

"Why don't you get the six pack?" she asked.

"Not enough funds," he said.

"Hey, I know who you are, and I'm sorry you lost your job. I think they're hiring at the Super 8 Motel. You should check it out."

"Thanks."

"What's your name?" she asked.

"They call me P."

"P?"

"Yep. P for Preston."

"Nice to meet you, Preston. Hey, do you have kids?"

"Yes. I have a little girl. She's four."

"That's wonderful. I can imagine there is no greater blessing than to have a baby girl. I also imagine you're a good father and doing your best to give her everything you can."

"Yep. She deserves the world."

Evie pulled out a twenty-dollar bill and said, "I can buy you a twelve pack if you want, and if you still have it, I would like to buy that plastic mermaid necklace you took from a locker at STICH."

"Huh?" He raked a hand over the back of his neck.

"You may want to give it to your daughter, but as you say, she deserves the world. She deserves better than a stolen necklace."

"I don't know what you're talking about, lady."

"The necklace belongs to a friend of mine. Her niece made it for her. It means a lot to her, and today is her birthday." She held out the bill and he twitched his eyebrows and looked down at his feet. Then he put the bottle back, pulled out a twelve pack, reached into his pocket, dug out the mermaid necklace, handed it to Evie, and grabbed the twenty, all without looking her in the eye.

Evie purchased a bottle of Patrón and a bag of trail mix for Jack. She got in her truck and pulled out onto Main Street, not noticing the weirdo from the lake was parked across the street. He took a long pull of whiskey, which felt like a glowing coal in his gut, lit a cigarette, and watched her drive away.

When Evie got home, she wrapped the necklace in a small box with pink tissue paper, put a silk bow around the bottle of Patron and walked over to Chrissy's. They sat on the porch where Chrissy had her heels kicked up on the railing, exposing her lardy, pale thighs. There was a pitcher of Bud and a bowl of Ritz crackers, and they did shots while the boys rode their bikes up and down the road, followed by Rex.

"Rob called to wish me a happy birthday," said Chrissy.

"Really?"

"Yes, and he sounded good. Said he was clean and he missed me and Dillon a lot."

"Wow. Did he talk to Dill?"

"Yeah, they had a short conversation. It must be weird for both of them, not really knowing what to say. I'm not gonna get too excited about it, but he said he might be coming this way in September, before Dillon goes back to school."

"Do you believe him?" Evie asked.

"I want to believe him and, I don't know, I suppose we've had enough time apart that things might be different now. We'll see."

"Yes. One step at a time. Some things take time and effort. Forgiveness is a big one. But in the end, it's about trust. If you can't trust each other, it's not even worth trying to make it work."

Evie thought at times that trust would be a lifelong issue for her. Grief counselors had explained that because her father had left her at such a critical time in her young life, it would be very difficult for her to regain trust, especially in men. Father abandonment, they called it. She spent years trying to process why the man she loved the most, left. Later she figured out if she got rid of the men in her life first, it wouldn't hurt as badly.

Chrissy licked her hand and sprinkled salt on it.

"What's new at STICH?" asked Evie.

"It sucks. We had a Code Blue yesterday and the guy died."

"Oh no! Was it a patient?"

"Yeah. I was the last face he saw before he died and the first face he saw after he was resuscitated. Then I break scrub and leave the room and he fricking dies in the recovery room while I'm layin' on the bathroom floor blubberin' like a walrus. It pretty much put me over the edge."

"Ohhh, so sorry to hear that. Are you okay?"

"I am and I'm not. Every time something bad happens at work, it puts me closer to quitting. I mean, I'm not sure if this is really what I wanna be doing for the rest of my life. If it wasn't for Dill and if Rob was still in the picture, I'd be outta there, but I need the benefits."

"Yeah, I get it. But aren't there some things you really like about working at STICH? I've heard it's one of the best hospitals in the Inland Northwest."

"Yeah, it has a good reputation, but I'm just over the derelicts who work there."

"You mean the doctors you don't get along with?"

"It's not just doctors, or nurses, or even management. I mean, I get along okay with some of the orderlies and the girls in the front office, but like there's this one guy who makes me really sick."

"Who's that?" Evie bit a Ritz cracker. "The thief is gone."

"Oh Gawd, it's this guy named Dale. He's a "safety controller." She made air quotes. "He walks around with a binder and inspects the equipment and makes sure everyone wears a lead apron when x-rays are being used and a face shield so blood doesn't splatter in your eyes during surgery. He wears shoes that squeak and talks in a whisper, like someone with throat cancer.

"Eewww."

"We were removing a bladder tumor with a laser, and he came into the room to make sure I was wearing laser glasses. It pissed me off because I always wear my safety glasses and my x-ray badge."

"What's an x-ray badge?"

"Everyone has one. You wear it when x-ray's being used in a case, and it keeps track of how much radiation you're getting.

Dale has this shelf that holds all our badges, but that controller's such an idiot—he spelled my name Kissy."

"Sounds like an honest mistake to me."

"But the most annoying thing about him is that he whispers all this religious crap."

"What do you mean?"

"You know, like, 'I'll pray for you,' and talking about going to church every night and running a men's group and a teenage boys' Bible study. Seriously, how many teenage boys do you know who would trade playing a video game for a Bible study?"

Evie laughed. "I currently know none."

"And I heard he recruits boys by telling them 'We put the stud back in Bible study.'"

"Odd."

"He's odd and he's so self-righteous."

"I believe you mean pious."

"Whatever. Anyway, there's this medical assistant who comes on Tuesdays to assist in cataract surgery, named Cindy. She's so sweet and super smart. She has a degree in English lit, like you, and loves to read, like you. Anyway, she came in last Tuesday and looked like she'd been crying. Her eyes were all puffed up, and she wasn't wearing that big smile that you can always see even when she's wearing a mask. I went in to tie up her gown, and Dale was in the corner, checking the microscope. I asked Cindy if she was alright, and she said no, that last night she had to put her old dog, Rusty, to sleep. She had him for thirteen years. Can you imagine how sad that would be?"

Evie thought of Turbo again. He was the best dog ever.

They got him when Evie was twelve and Ellie was only one. Evie used to put Turbo in the crib so the puppy and the baby could share Ellie's blankie and Turbo's chew toy. "Yeah, that's really sad."

"I couldn't hug her because she had on a sterile gown and gloves, but then we hear Dale's shoe squeak and he whispers from across the room, 'Cindy, I'll send a prayer card to you and light a candle at church tonight. I'll pray for you and your dog for he is in purgatory until we, the followers, can pray him out.'"

"You're kidding me."

"No I'm not. Cindy and I just looked at each other like what the fuck? Cindy had tears dripping onto her mask and her safety glasses started fogging up to the point she had to break scrub and go to the bathroom. That made the eye surgeon edgy because it delayed the case and they were behind for the rest of the day."

"Unbelievable."

"When Dale slunk back behind the scope with his head down, I flipped his binder into the trash and covered it with an instrument wrapper. Then I went and got his badge off the shelf and stuffed it in the hallway waste basket."

"Jeez, Chrissy, remind me not to make you mad."

"The best part? Dale eats a tuna sandwich every single day, and when there was no one in the break room, I tossed his lunch away."

Evie thought, for her hardened exterior and all the forceful vengeance Chrissy threw at the world, she was, in her way, keeping her finger on the pulse of justice. Often it was the bitter ones who were the most sensitive. Chrissy was doing her best. She was watching another year pass and trying not to worry about getting older, losing her looks, and getting fatter. They both wondered what the future would bring. Motherhood will do that. Survival will do that. We all need a little help along the way. We all need to have a celebration on the porch, watching our children play, if we're lucky enough to have them, and enjoy the comfort of true friendship.

"Well," said Evie, raising her glass. "Here's to Rusty and Turbo. Hope they're chasing squirrels and lying in sunbeams way up there."

"Wait. Who's Turbo?"

"He was a golden retriever my little sister and I had when we were young."

"What happened to him?"

"Sad story. It was my fault. I lost him while I was at my friend's house, watching TV. I've hated TV ever since. Happy birthday Chrissy. I love you."

Chrissy burped and sat quiet for a long moment. In the distance were the moving silhouettes of Jack and Dillon as the sky turned a deeper shade of lilac and rose.

"What about Jack's dad, Jon? What happened? Did you really leave him because of the hamburger?" Her eyes were slightly out of focus.

"No, it wasn't about the hamburger. It was about his vacillating between neglect and control."

"What do you mean?" Chrissy stifled a yawn.

"Well, he would either not consider me at all or push me into doing things I didn't want to do. I used to sing all the time, little nearly inaudible mumblings to myself, not thinking anyone could hear me, just little joyful tunes. It's something I learned in therapy many years ago, just hum a little when you feel sadness looming, and it made me feel better. Occasionally Jon would catch me at it and tell me to stop."

"I work with this one doc who hates it when I sing during surgery. He says, 'Please. Do. Not. Sing. I. Am. Working. Here.' And I just smile and sing louder until he kicks me out of the room and sends in a replacement." She took a swig of beer.

"How do you have the nerve to be so defiant? I can't believe you haven't been fired yet."

"Well, if I lose my job, so what. Especially after the code yesterday. Anyway, so what finally ended your marriage?" She burped.

Evie didn't have the energy to explain that she was still incapable of trusting someone on an intimate level. Not worth it. The price was too high. "I realized I wasn't singing anymore, and Jack and I had to move on, and I had to be alone to grow." What she didn't say was that she always wanted to pin the blame on Jon, but then the real reason presented itself, clear and unavoidable. She was the reason.

"Thank you for being my friend, Evie."

"You're welcome. Here, open your present." Evie handed her the box.

Chrissy tore off the paper and looked inside. She gasped and lifted the necklace up to her face. Her lower lip pooched out, she bounced up and down in the chair and her face crumpled. Evie felt a little uneasy seeing Chrissy's rigid surface crack. It seemed powerful, yet sad.

It was the first time Evie had ever seen her cry.

# TWELVE

The Fourth of July parade was about to begin. People of Pine Grove lined the streets, standing on sidewalks, sitting in lawn chairs, and lying on blankets. Children with sacks and pillowcases jumped up and down and ran in circles with the anticipation of candy being tossed their way. There were balloons tied to cars, decorated bicycle spokes, and American flags everywhere. Evie, Chrissy, and the boys were parked near the cemetery, sitting on the tailgate of Evie's truck. Rex was panting, slobber dripping off his tongue. Chrissy sipped a rum and Coke in her coffee cup, and Evie nursed a ginger ale.

"Thanks for the birthday party last night," said Chrissy. "I hope I didn't do anything too embarrassing."

"You didn't do anything I haven't seen before. You told me Rob likes tequila because it makes your clothes come off, but you kept your clothes on."

"Well, Rob wasn't there."

"I like your necklace."

A gun went off, signifying the start of the parade. A Girl Scout troop led, followed by a vintage Jeep club, and a John Deere tractor pulling a trailer of hay bales and bleating goats. The high school Homecoming Queen waved, mounted on a steed with a glittery red, white and blue saddle. Her sequin boots flashed in the morning sun, and her long blonde braid matched her horse's tail. The silver-haired congressman had come, as he did every year, from the county seat over in Lincoln. He was wearing aviator sunglasses and drove a bright red Volkswagen convertible with two border collies in the back. A girl in the passenger seat was holding a giant flag. "Look," Evie pointed. "That's a 1971 Cabriolet. I wonder if that's his daughter or his granddaughter."

"Well, he's a politician, so it's probably neither one." Chrissy burped.

"Excuse you."

The school marching band stomped by, led by two giggling middle-schoolers crashing symbols, and a redhead gymnast doing cartwheels. They were followed by girls on skates and boys with boom boxes and squirt guns. They shot water into the crowd, clearly happy to hear squeals. Bubbles filled the air as the Shine On trucks drove by. Romey and his boys tossed candy and handfuls of fifty-cent pieces and quarters wrapped in tin foil. Kids clapped the bubbles and scooped up the coins.

"Look! Mom!" Jack screamed, "A donkey!" Mr. Murphy followed the truck, leading a donkey wearing bells around its neck and a llama with a red feather boa. Evie leaned into

Chrissy's ear. "Do you think we have a donkey in our future?"

Chrissy belched. "A donkey, my ass!"

Drums beat and the butcher from Stein's rattled by with three toddlers bawling in a shopping cart.

"Yeah," said Chrissy. "That looks painful."

Young mothers walked with babies in strollers, fathers with kids in wheelbarrows. Evie's heart quickened when she saw the gleaming Ford 350 pickup cruise by, pulling the two neon-green jet skis that had sunk Dillon at the lake. Her cheeks burned as she watched the cocky driver, behind dark glasses, honk and wave at the crowd with country music booming through his monster subwoofers. Still best not to share that fiasco with Chrissy, she thought. She shook the horrid vision from her imagination of Dillon dead and bloated on the beach with hungry gulls circling overhead.

Evie took a sip, and said, "I tried to get Lola to come with us."

"Why didn't she?" asked Chrissy.

"Suffice it to say, she's not ready. I get it."

"Look, there's Katie and Trina from the flower shop," said Chrissy.

They were smiling, big white smiles, dressed in red gingham pinafores with blue sun bonnets. They wore leis made of red, white and blue carnations. Together they pulled a decorated wicker laundry basket on a rolling cart and sprinkled rose petals and candy for the spectators.

Evie took a sip and saw Mr. and Mrs. Craven standing across the street. She waved at them and then saw a guy walking toward her. He was unshaven, wearing a brown tee shirt that said, "Bite Me," and he came way too close. His hair was tousled, and he looked like he couldn't be clean if he tried.

"Oh my God," Evie mumbled.

"So, if it isn't the girl who's got everything under control. I didn't recognize you with your top on." He smiled with his mouth open, showing that big gap.

"What the hell?" said Chrissy.

"I'm sorry we didn't get properly introduced at the lake the other day. You obviously had your hands full. I'm Marc." He put his hand out to Evie, but she sat still, feeling a rush of cold and hot at the same time.

He smiled. "It's spelled with a C, not a K."

"Hi Marc with a C. I'm Chrissy with a C. This is Evie. I like your shirt."

Evie rolled her eyes.

"I'm glad I found you, Evie," he said. "I thought about what happened, and I guess I could have been more helpful. I was a little freaked out, thinking the kid was gonna drown."

"What kid?" said Chrissy.

"I'll explain later," said Evie.

"Maybe you could get rid of these kids sometime, and we could grab a drink," he said.

His eyes made Evie think of mucky swamp water. She wasn't sure if she was more repulsed by the sight of him or the fact that he had seen her breasts.

Evie could hardly stand to look at him and didn't want to encourage him to hang around. She forced her attention onto the parade where Netty and Letty Gabilan rolled by in wheelchairs, their grandkids pushing them. Netty was sitting on her bad leg. They wore matching tiaras made of red and blue pipe cleaners and loads of costume jewelry. They each held a new Teddy bear on their lap with the tags still on the ears and grinned as they honked the rubber horns mounted to their wheelchairs.

"Those two are adorable," said Evie, as she inched closer to Chrissy, attempting to ignore Marc. "They're so attached, they think their name is NettyLetty."

Chrissy drained her cup. "I wonder if Netty knows her pants are on inside out."

"Be nice. They have every right to do whatever they want to. Can you believe how precious it is that they have never been apart? They're always smiling at each other. I love that."

Evie looked around, and Marc was gone. She felt her body ease a bit. "Good, he's gone. That Marc guy is one strange dude," she said.

"What the hell, Evie, you slept with him?"

Evie glanced at the boys sitting next to her, sucking on Jolly Ranchers.

"Shhh. No! I saw him when I took Rex and the boys to the lake. You were working. It was that really hot day, and Dill forgot his floaty things and got hit by a wake from a jet ski, and I pulled him out of the water. During the commotion, he accidentally pulled my bikini top down, but I was upset and didn't realize it until Diastema Man came over, got a good look, then disappeared."

Chrissy felt her arms go cold, realizing that Dillon had to get pulled out of the water because she had thrown his flattened floatie things in the trash. "Oh my God." She inhaled sharply. "Diastema Man?"

"A diastema is a split between your front teeth. Can you imagine how humiliating it was to be sitting there at the lake panic stricken, with my boobs sticking out?"

"Yeah, that's a cheery thought."

"I keep running into him, and it's creepy. I saw him at the liquor store yesterday and now here. I have no idea where he came from. He has Washington plates on his car, so what is he doing here? He's got a weird vibe. There's something off about him."

"Well, if you showed him your tits, you must've got him all worked up. Besides, I think he's kinda hot."

"Well, may I remind you that you're not the best judge of character. His energy's dark, I can feel it. Plus, I don't like the way he smells."

Jack crunched his candy and looked at his mom. "How do you know what he smells like?" he asked.

"I can smell him because it's hot and the air isn't moving and he was standing too close. He smells like cheap whiskey and cigarettes."

"What's wrong with that?" Chrissy smiled.

"And under no circumstances would I ever go out with a guy whose pick up line is 'Get rid of the kids and we can grab a drink'."

The parade ended, and as they were about to drive home, Jack said, "Note, Mom." He was holding a yellow Post-it that he had peeled off the window. It said, *Your the one.*

"What? Stalker! And he can't even spell." Evie shook her head. The fact that he left a note on her truck scared her. This was getting creepy.

Romey came by with a trash bag, picking up candy wrappers. "Hey Evie," he waved. "Hi Boys." He walked up to them.

"Hi, Romey," said Jack.

"Happy Independence Day. Did you guys score some candy?"

"Yeah," said Dillon, holding up a bag of candy.

"You know that'll rot your teeth, don't you." He winked. Evie looked at Chrissy and smiled.

"I saw what you did for Mrs. Craven's birthday party, Evie. That was really nice with the aubergine-colored cloths."

"Thanks, Romey. I saw what your guys did with the lights. It looked good."

"What the heck is oberjean?" asked Chrissy.

"It's the French word for eggplant," said Evie. "Mrs. Craven's favorite color. Romey, you remember my friend Chrissy."

"Yeah," said Chrissy. "Everyone knows the world's greatest window cleaner, right Romey?"

"That's right!"

Chrissy lifted her cup. "Cheers! Happy Fourth."

"Y'all enjoy each day! See ya later," he said, and walked away.

Evie said, "Bye!" waving the Post-it note in her hand.

# THIRTEEN

On the morning of July fifth, the window cleaners were leaning on their trucks at Drip 'n Sip. Romey took a drink of coffee and said, "Girrrrls, do you know why the midget got kicked out of the nudist colony?"

"No, Boss, we don't."

"He kept getting his nose in everybody's business." Romey wiggled his eyebrows and grinned. "Hey, that was a nice Fourth of July parade. It was our lucky day that we made it the whole mile. Remember last year, Ron? Your truck overheated and it was steaming and hissing and people were backing up, all scared you were gonna explode right in the middle of the parade."

"Yeah, that really sucked," said Ron. "I was better off riding with Josh this year. I just got my truck out of the shop this morning."

"Okay now, enough goofing off. Let's get back to work. You're in for a special treat. You'll be doing the Burke's windows today. It's the yellow house in the cul-de-sac on Crane Lane. I don't know the exact address, but you can't miss it. What you do need to know is that Kathleen Burke is a big shot at STICH. And I mean big shot. She runs more than one department, and if you disappoint her, it won't be pretty. And Juan, don't get distracted by her beauty because yes, she's a hottie, but man, she can burn a hole through you with her eyes if you screw up. Apparently the doctors are scared of her but she's always been nice to me. Don't worry though, she isn't as much of a challenge as her husband. Denny Burke is a man among men and you don't wanna piss him off. You have to use extreme caution on the outs because they've got all kinds of exotic plants and vines growing around the house."

"Oh, is that the guy they wrote about in the *Pine Tree*?" asked Ron.

"Yeah," said Jake. "I saw something about him growing a sunflower the size of a truck tire and a pumpkin the size of a small car. He's won a bunch of awards at the State Fair."

"No offense," said Romey, "but it seems to me like he could be a guy with a little too much time on his hands. Nonetheless, he's creating beauty, just like we are. Anyway, be careful with the ladder work, and don't let the hydro-sphere hoses knock anything over or rip out any plants. Their dogs are going to bark like a pack of wolves, but I'm almost sure they won't bite."

Ron said, "Are you sure, like really sure they won't bite?"

"Well, they've never bitten me." He winked.

"Oh great," Ron shook his head.

Romey laughed. "You know the story of the guy who sees an old man sitting on a park bench next to a Doberman Pincher and says to the old man, 'Does your dog bite?' And the old man says, "No, he doesn't bite.' So the guy bends down to pet the dog and the dog nearly tears his hand off. The guy jumps back and cries, 'I thought you said your dog doesn't bite!' and the old man says, 'That's not my dog.'"

"Okay boss, that's not funny," said Ron.

"The biggest dog's name is Hennesy. She's intimidating because she's huge, but she's actually really sweet. And Denny Burke really is the nicest guy around. In fact, I would consider him a friend, but he's a little leery of the dear window cleaners, and in his defense, he has his reasons."

"Why's that?" asked Ron.

"Well, a couple years ago, my brother was cleaning the Burke's driveway and accidentally rolled over one of their sleeping dogs with the shop vac. The dog wasn't hurt, but it upset Denny just the same. Another time, he came home to find that same brother sitting on his couch, drinking a beer and watching a football game, and he wasn't too pleased, to put it mildly."

"I'm just sure." Ron shook his head.

"There's a ton of cutups so take your time and make sure your blades are fresh and trimmed to the right size. And don't use the sponge with the green scrubber; it'll scratch the windows faster than you can blink. I know it seems counterintuitive, but if you run into water stains, pitch, or paint, and the brush doesn't get it, use steel wool. It won't scratch glass. Josh, you and I'll do the bank windows this morning, and we need to remove the Fourth of July mural from the front window at Stein's. Ron, is your truck all good now?"

"Yeah. I got the starter fixed, but now I have to go get another ladder."

"What happened to your ladder?"

"I forgot to tie it down, and it flew out on the highway when I was going to White Pine to do the Bectel house."

"Oops," said Romey. "Did you lose it around Layman's Curve?"

"Yep, never to be seen again. It's down in the ravine with everything else. That corner's a bitch."

"Oh, well. Fortunately you can always get another ladder. Oh, and before I forget, Mrs. Davidson called this morning. She said you guys did a great job on her windows, but she was very concerned that her blown glass bird collection was rearranged on the living room windowsill. Her niece is coming to visit, and apparently the niece has given her a glass bird from every corner of the world, and if the niece sees that they are not sitting exactly how she arranged them the last time she was here, well, it could be bad."

"Are you kidding me right now?" said Ron.

"I know she's crazy, but if anyone gives you grief about something like that, just remind them that arranging things differently is intentional to let the customer know we've been there and cleaned the windows. Housekeepers do it too. They leave things askew or pictures crooked to let the owners know they dusted. Josh, you good running the tucker pole?"

"Yes. My triceps are getting a good workout."

"What a stud. Stay amazing. And all of you remember to enjoy each day here on planet Earth. After all, we're creating beauty, one window at a time." He smiled.

That afternoon Romey stopped by the Burkes. Denny came out in his sweats and slippers.

"Hey, Denny, just checking in to see how the boys did with your windows."

"Kathy told me they were coming, but they never showed up. I was just gonna call you. I've been gone all day, and she's still at work."

"Wait. What? Your windows didn't get done? Are you sure?"

"Of course I'm sure!!"

"Well, J. S. M. H."

"And what the hell does that mean, Romey?"

"Just shaking my head. This is a head-shaker and a head-scratcher. But it's nothing we can't figure out. I'll find out what happened, and I'll let you know as soon as I know."

Denny stuck his hands in his pockets and shook his head.

"Don't worry, Denny, it's the world we live in, a small problem not a big one and fortunately there's a solution to every problem," he smiled.

"Oh for God sakes Romey. I don't know what you've been smokin' but you've gotta be high on something. Nobody can be that happy all the time.

"High on life, my friend. High on life."

As instructed, Jake and Ron had cleaned the windows of the

yellow house at the end of Crane Lane. They were prepared for tons of cutups, but the job was easier than they had anticipated, with only three cutups on the front door. They were relieved to see that the man among men, Denny Burke, wasn't home when they arrived, and neither were his intimidating dogs. Jake said Denny's garden was well cared for, but he didn't think it was that great—at least not good enough to be written up in the newspaper. Ron said Jake was just suffering from a lack of appreciation and that it was probable that the sunflowers and giant pumpkins had already been harvested and sent over to Lincoln to be entered in the State Fair.

"Maybe that's where Denny Burke is right now. After all," said Ron. "The Cucurbita maxima is a different species from the regular pumpkins people grow around here and for sure, Denny will win first prize again."

"Okay, Mr. Smarty Pants," said Jake. "I stand corrected."

Later that day, the whole neighborhood heard Denny Burke yelling on the phone when Romey called him to say yes, the guys cleaned the windows, but it was the wrong house. "My bad, Denny," said Romey. "I forgot your house was green, not yellow."

"You're unbelievable Romey! Where are you going right now because I think you should head straight to the looney bin."

"As a matter of fact, Denny, I'm on my way to help the church ladies set up the rummage sale. You should come by the park Saturday. There's a bunch of tools and garden stuff you might be able to use. And don't worry, take what you want. It's on me."

Denny slammed down the phone.

# FOURTEEN

It was Saturday, and there was promise of another summer scorcher. In the park, Romey and the church ladies had set up the rummage sale. There were long tables of everything from pots and pans to depression glass and collectables. Clothes hung on metal racks, a bin brimmed with toys, and books were stacked high on an antique buffet. There was an area for tools, gardening supplies, and appliances in need of repair. There were baby strollers, highchairs, and a pink bicycle. A minister's wife had made a living room display of a green plush couch and a coffee table covered with free pocket-size Pine Grove directories.

At the other end of the park, the pool was full of squealing kids playing with foam toys, splashing in the chlorine-smelling, milky-blue water, dunking each other and jumping off the side. The teenage lifeguard blew her whistle at the rule breakers.

Evie had put on a green sundress and a hat before picking up Chrissy and Dillon. She dropped them off at the park and went to Stein's to get drinks and food. Chrissy set up chairs and a blanket on the grass near the pool, where she could keep an eye on Dillon. She had bought new inflatable arm bands for Dillon, and he had fought her about having to wear his stupid floaty things. She reminded him of his trouble at the lake and told him if he kept practicing, he would be swimming very soon. She added that if he didn't wear his floaties in the pool, she would make him wear them in the bathtub until he got it through his head that she meant business. Even as she was saying it, she thought when they give the awards out at STICH for Nurse of the Year and Scrub of the Year, she would get Worst Mother of the Year. She took a long pull of vodka and Squirt from her thermos and looked for the boys. Dillon was standing in the shallow end, smiling at a girl who was slapping water and splashing him. Jack was skimming across the pool like he had motors on his feet. Chrissy couldn't tell if he was laughing or crying, his face scrunched up, water spraying in his eyes. She saw a guy emerge from underwater and stand. He had a smirk on his face and was holding onto Jack's legs. Then he let go.

"Holy crap," she said.

Evie came over, carrying a bag and stood by the chair. "I got us turkey sandwiches," she said. "Sorry, I forgot to get extra mayonnaise on yours. What are you staring at?" She looked toward the water. "Oh, my God. It's Diastema Man. What's he doing?"

"I don't know, but it looks like the creeper is the only adult in the pool and was underwater, pushing Jack. And who knows what else."

Evie dropped the bag and ran to the pool. "Jack! Come here and get to our chairs now!" Jack swam to the edge, jumped out, and ran toward the chairs.

"Hello, Evie," said Marc, hanging on the edge of the pool. She glared at him. "What do you think you're doing? You leave my son alone!" She turned around and ran toward Jack.

"What was he doing to you, baby? Did he hurt you?" she said as she ran a towel through his hair.

"He was holding onto my legs," said Jack. "He was . . . Oh no, he's coming over here."

Evie looked up and felt rage. She said, "Jack, you can go back in, buddy. I'll get rid of him. He won't be going back in. Go play with Dill for a bit, then come and eat lunch." Jack hesitated a moment and then ran past the guy and jumped into the pool but held onto the edge and kept an eye on his mother.

Marc sauntered over and stood before her. "Did you hear me? I said hello, Evie."

"What are you doing here?"

"I knew you would be here, and I wanted to see you. I haven't stopped thinking about you since the parade, and I was still hoping we could get together." He was dripping wet, his hair plastered to his face. He had a disgusting red blotchy rash on his chest.

Evie averted her eyes. "I'm not interested."

"Sure you are, Evie," he said.

"You leave me and my son alone."

"I already told you that you're the one. You can say no all you want, but we'll be together, one way or another."

Evie cringed. *What is this jerk's problem? He actually touched Jack. I'll kill him.* "Am I not being clear? Maybe you have water in your ears? Not only am I not interested, but I never want you near me or my son again."

He took a step forward and Chrissy took a quick gulp and stood up. "Hey dude, you heard what she said. She's not interested. That means she has no desire to see your face again, so keep your dick in your trunks and get lost. Now! And leave your hands off our kids."

He gave her a seething glare and stumbled away, looking at the ground and tapping his temples. Chrissy watched as he wobbled over to the rummage sale and fell, soaking wet, on the green couch.

He felt the heat begin to rise between his ears. He didn't like that fat one with the dirty mouth and the pink hair. They didn't understand that Evie was his now, for she had offered her nipples to him. *You will make her understand*, the voices drummed in his head.

"I think you're right Evie. He's more than a little off. He's totally whacked. I mean like psycho-stalker-pervert shit. Are you sure you didn't have sex with him? He's acting like a guy who got a taste of the goodies and needs some more."

"Oh, no Chrissy. No! The thought of it makes my stomach turn."

When the boys came to eat their sandwiches, Jack, with mustard on both cheeks, looked at Evie and said, "He pinched me."

"What?" Evie and Chrissy yelled in unison. Evie's eyes darted across the park, but Marc was gone.

"Yeah. On my butt under water." He lifted his shorts up and pointed at a red mark. Evie jumped up and started running toward the rummage sale. People were browsing, laughing, and talking. A church lady was wiping the wet spot off the plush couch while the others were smiling and putting money in their cash box and apron pockets. Evie spun around, her heart racing. He was gone.

The terrifying memory emerged, turning the sun down, and her vision began to fade. *Gone forever and not coming back.* She covered her eyes and gasped for air, fighting the mourning that consumed her.

Romey walked from the rummage sale and saw her with her hands over her face, and thought, Is she laughing? He stood still and watched her. *She's an artist's dream with her tawny-colored skin and honey-blonde hair, like a golden flower with a green-stemmed dress. I wish I could paint her just for the pleasure of choosing the colors.*

Evie put her hands down, blinked, and looked around. Romey stepped forward, holding a box of Legos.

"Hey, Evie."

Evie jumped. "Oh! You scared me."

"I'm sorry. I thought you saw me coming."

"It's okay. I scare easily." She covered her mouth with the back of her hand.

He held up the box of Legos. "I picked this up for Jack. It's brand new. Mrs. Crandus says her triplets don't like Legos and asked me to find a child who does. I don't want to be presumptuous, but Jack strikes me as a bright kid who might enjoy these. It's the advanced set."

"Wow, Romey. Yes, thank you." She looked behind him, then behind herself, but no sign of the pincher freak. She would kill him. She looked at Romey and had the urge to jump right into his arms and cry like a baby. She felt her eyes fill and held her breath.

Romey smiled and said, "Hey, it's not a big deal, just a little gift."

He held out the box. She took it and said, "Thank you. I'm sure he'll have hours of fun with these." Her heart was thumping like a rabbit.

# FIFTEEN

The following Monday, Evie was looking at a vine in Lola's side yard when she found the tiny tree frog in the moist dirt. "Hello, little frog, are you really a prince?" It had shiny green skin with brown specks. She thought about putting it in a jar and taking it to Jack but knew better because Rex would be curious and snuff it out with his nose or innocently maim it with his big paw. Then Dill and Jack would feel responsible for putting it out of its misery, which would lead to a science project of some sort. Besides, she had already told them "the frog stays here." It popped its eyes open and sprang away. "Off you go."

She heard a newspaper smack the front porch. Lola stepped out, bent down and picked up the paper. Evie came around the corner and said, "Hey, Lola, do you still want to go to the bank today?"

Lola felt a pinch in her chest. There it was again, that familiar sinking feeling of having to do something she wasn't ready to do. She had put off going to the bank for weeks, telling herself it wasn't necessary. It seemed that the mundane things in everyday life were still impossible, although the truth was, Lola found nothing mundane. She found everything overwhelming, realizing how effortlessly Sam had done so much.

"I'm not sure if today's the day, Evie. Do you want to come in and have some water? It's too hot out here to be working."

"Sure. I just came by for a minute to see if I need to water the lawn, but it looks good."

"You take such good care of everything. If it were up to me, the whole yard would be shriveled up."

"Well, that's my job. I can come in for a minute. Then I need to get back home to the boys. I left them in the kitchen with a giant box of Legos Romey gave us from the rummage sale."

"Oh, how nice."

"I know, super sweet. Anyway, I told them I'd be back in thirty minutes." They stepped inside the house where it was cool. Lola took the paper and went to the kitchen to get two glasses of ice water and a plate of oatmeal cookies.

"Mmm, I love oatmeal cookies." Evie smiled.

"So do I. Romey dropped them off yesterday. You know, he's left cookies for me many times since Sam passed, a lot of them I don't even remember eating. It's like time adds up, and I feel like I owe him so many thank-yous."

"Well, I'm sure he's doing it because he wants to."

"I suppose. Romey's so thoughtful. You just don't see nice guys like that anymore. Except for Sam, of course." She set the paper on the table.

"I agree." Evie remembered his smile as he handed her the Legos for Jack. She wondered what Romey would have said if she told him about Marc. Or about her past. *Everyone has a past.*

Lola looked at the front page of the *Pine Tree News.* "This is lovely, Evie, congratulations." There was a picture of Evie, standing by a table, holding a sprig of baby's breath and another of Mr. and Mrs. Craven, having a champagne toast. The headline read, "School Principal Surprises Wife with Backyard Boil!"

"Oh my gosh, that's so funny." Evie laughed. She leaned over Lola, and they read the article, which went on to say it was a fiftieth birthday with fifty guests and fifty pounds of crawfish. They mentioned it had been decorated by Evie's Tablescapes, as well as lights hung by The Shine On Washer-Installers. Lola looked at the picture and smiled. "That was nice of him to tell *The Pine Tree.*"

"Yes. John Craven is very nice. We're lucky to have him."

Evie sat down, picked up a cookie and realized it had been a long while since she had seen Lola smile. "You're right, Lola. This is better than going to the bank."

Lola stared at the floor. "I've been thinking. I don't know that I was the best wife I could be."

"What do you mean?"

"Well, being married to Sam was so easy, but in the

beginning I had my doubts about our age difference, although he was very patient and careful not to scare me away. He was wise enough to know how flighty I was. After we had been married awhile, I got antsy. It had to do with him working so much and my not being able to conceive. I began to believe his job was more important to him than I was."

"Well, for some men, work is their identity. They think they're doing what's most important which, in many cases, is providing."

"Yeah, but I didn't see it that way at the time. I invented things in my head."

"Like what?"

"Well, I remember it was my thirty-ninth birthday, and we had plans to go out to dinner, but he forgot because he was working. By the time he got home that night, I had drunk more than a bottle of wine and took a pain pill I found from his old foot surgery. I was upset, feeling sorry for myself and when he finally walked in, I turned into a crazy woman. I stood there with my head spinning, all dressed up with a run in my stocking and screamed at him that I felt unloved and that he was insensitive and didn't care about me and wouldn't even notice if I was dead or alive. I said I hated that he worked all the time and I despised golf and I hated myself, and maybe I would just get a one-way ticket to Europe and end up in Italy with a big Italian family and then boy would I be happy because I would finally be loved.

"Wow. What did he say to that?"

"He said, 'Lola, my love, you are my other half. Please tell me what I can do. I'll try to understand. I just want you to be happy. I love you, but I don't own you."

"That's unconditional love. Did you go to Italy?"

"No, because I knew it would be so easy to leave and much harder to stay and work through it. Another one of my lessons in maturity. One of the first things Sam ever told me was that most people are doing their best, and the easy road isn't always the right one."

"That's insightful, I must say."

"When I calmed down, he told me that it was Thursday the seventh, and my birthday was Friday the eighth. Can you imagine what a fool I felt like? Forgetting when my own birthday was and then getting furious at him for nothing! The next day he had tickets for a beautiful birthday getaway, champagne, flowers, and a diamond bracelet."

Lola shook her head. "That's what I mean by not being a better wife, or actually a better person. Although it did improve after that. I tried to train myself to be more grateful for all we had and stop blaming him for everything I didn't have."

"Well," said Evie, "when we blame someone else for what bothers us or for what we don't have, rarely is it their fault. Any honest woman would admit that she has stood in front of the mirror looking for something outside of herself and blaming someone else for not providing it."

"I don't even know why I'm dredging this stuff up. It's not like he's here to defend himself."

"Lola, you're processing and gradually learning to live without the man you love. Just because someone dies it doesn't end the relationship. It shifts, and you can and will have memories, even conversations with him. Has he sent you a sign yet?"

"I'm not sure if it's a sign or my own head playing tricks on me, but sometimes I see him sleeping in his chair. At three this morning, I was wide awake and came out to see him there with the newspaper on his lap." She put her hands to her face and began to shake. Evie put her arms around her, and Lola sobbed, "I saw him, but his mouth was open, like it was when he passed."

Evie held her gently as she cried. Outside the kitchen window, a hummingbird hovered in place, then lifted and flew backwards into the sky.

Dillon and Jack were in the yard when Evie pulled in. Jack stood up, chomping on gum, shading his eyes like an Indian scout, which meant they were up to something. Evie knew it well—when they were doing *that thing* that teetered between adventure and mischief. Then she saw Dillon blowing a pink bubble, bent over a piece of plywood holding a hammer. Nails were strewn about, and a bloody carving knife was lying on the grass. Rex was sitting on his haunches next to them turning his head from the board to the truck, then back to the boys, nervous, knowing full well that all three of them were in for it. Every door and window in the house was open.

Evie jumped out, trying to decipher what was happening. She knew that in a moment of hysteria, a wiser mother could possibly stay calm and be the voice of reason until the proper information was obtained. But no, she saw the mess and began to shake.

"What are you doing?" she cried.

They had been nailing a long fat snakeskin to the plywood. There were yellow globules and blood on the ground, and their clothes were wet and slimy.

"Hi Mom," said Jack. He had a bruise and a streak of blood on his chin. "Dillon stepped on a rattlesnake, and it bit his shoe so I clubbed it with a rock."

"What?" she screamed.

"Then we cut its head off behind the venom sacs."

"Oh my God! Where did you find a rattlesnake? I thought we didn't have them around here! It bit your shoe?"

"Yeah," said Dillon. "Just the rubber part though, not my foot. See?" He pointed at two puncture marks in the sole of his sneaker. "Don't worry, we dug a really deep hole and buried the head and covered it with rocks, so Rex can't dig it up."

"Mom, you shoulda seen his fangs. They were sharper than the teeth on the red fox but not as white and way longer. Here's its rattle." Jack reached in his pocket and pulled out a bloody rattle stuck on a paperclip.

"You can tell the age of a rattlesnake by the rattle, kinda like rings on a tree."

"Where did you find it?" She bit her fingers.

"By a rock up on the hill."

"What hill? Did you go up to the bluff?" She felt nauseous.

"Yeah," said Jack. "We were looking for a snake ball up by the spring. They like the muddy spots along the water. I saw a picture of it in the science adventure book you gave me for my birthday."

Evie shaded her eyes and looked up at the untraversable bluff with its seven-hundred-foot rock face. She felt her smallness and her vision began to dim.

"Oh my God, Jack! The bluff is at least a mile away. You're not allowed to go up there by yourself! I told you to stay put until I got back! I told you not to leave the house. A half hour. Thirty stinking minutes, and you boys don't listen to me! After what happened at the pool! I can't believe it. And what if you had gotten lost up there?"

"We have a compass from the explorer's kit you gave Dillon for his birthday."

She looked at the blood. "You used a knife?"

"Yeah," said Jack. "We had to use a sharp knife to skin the snake, otherwise it woulda ripped, and we want to keep it all in one piece, so we can dry it and take turns hanging it on our bedroom wall. I get to go first since I'm the one who killed it." Jack smiled.

Evie stared at him in disbelief.

"And then, we cut the snake up and put teriyaki sauce on it and baked it in the oven," Jack explained. "But it caught on fire and smoked out the house. We threw the pan out and opened the windows. Sorry Mom, it stinks really bad and there's brown stuff on the windows."

"And the walls," said Dillon.

Her heart pounded harder. *How could I have left them? What kind of mother am I to leave two innocent boys in the protection of a not-so-fierce-man-eating German Shephard and a special-edition Lego set? And with that crazy Marc out there.*

She sat on the ground and put her face in her hands. *How did this happen? What's the matter with me? Leaving them to wander off into the wilderness with a bogus compass and a pair of stupid, plastic binoculars.*

How would she ever be able to breathe again, knowing she had left them to survive in remote terrain with a magnifying glass, tweezers, and a specimen cup, while she checked on a vine and conversed with a speckled frog? Two precious boys with a love for science and the spirit of adventure—the very thing she had taught them to grasp in this life, to get off the couch, get out there and experience what nature has hidden behind every tree and under every rock. Two best buddies disappeared in broad daylight, never to be seen again except for their pictures on a milk carton, smiling back at people eating their cornflakes at the kitchen table while the TV blared bad news. She would surely be suspected of child abuse because they had bruised faces, and no one would believe that the bruises were from living the lives of real boys, doing real boy things, but . . . she gasped, a rattlesnake?

Evie pulled herself up from the ground and put her arms out. "Come here you little boogers. I need to hug you." She wrapped her arms around them and started crying. "I love you to the moon and back again."

She closed her eyes and felt Ellie's little arms around her neck. *"Sleep with me tonight Eebee. I'm gonna miss you when I go away tomorrow."* Then Evie kissed her cheek. *"You be a brave girl at camp. It'll be fun. Remember to say your prayers and don't forget I love you with every beep of my heart. I love you to the moon and back again."*

"I love you Mom," said Jack. I'm sorry."

"Do NOT go near a rattlesnake, never ever! You know they have a deadly strike!" *And you do not have permission to die! I need you Jack. Don't leave me.*

Dillon started to cry. "I'm sorry, Evie. Please don't be mad. We'll clean it up."

They were huddled together, face to face. "And once again, Dillon, if you get hurt on my watch, your mom will have my head. Probably bury it under a pile of rocks like the snake." She looked into Jack's eyes. "You know you're not allowed to use a knife. Ever. And you know better than to use the stove while I'm not here. You could have burned the house down!"

"I know, Mom. I'm sorry."

"Jack, what's my job?"

"To love me, feed me, protect me, and teach me right from wrong."

"Yes. And don't forget it. Now, let's clean this mess up, and you guys get out of those filthy clothes and take a shower."

Evie stood up and looked out across the valley. She watched a murder of crows scatter across the sky and waited for her dappled vision to clear and the nausea to pass.

# SIXTEEN

The following morning was bright and clear when Romey and his boys met at Drip 'n Sip. Max sat with his head out the window, barking at Ron.

"Hush, Max." Romey raised his cup. "Gentlemen window washers, listen up. Remember it's always business before pleasure, so if one of our lovely lady customers greets you at the door with her hair up all pretty, wearing stilettos and a see-through negligee and asks you if you want to come in and have super sex, make sure you take the soup."

"Nice," said Ron.

Romey grinned. "So, Juan has been amazing and thank you for that, Juan. Guys, keep your standards high and be proud of what you do. Like every profession, we'll continue to keep up with the necessary protocols. Although most in-services don't happen in the parking lot, we're going to do a little recap on the basics of window cleaning." He winked.

"Is it time for the inspector to come around and sniff our butts again?" asked Ron.

"Yep. It's time for the Occupational Safety and Health Administration, or OSHA, as we know it." said Romey.

"Wait, I thought that stood for Oh Shit, Here Again," said Jake.

"So," said Romey, "Over the years, I've read many pages of these standards and I still only have the first paragraph memorized, so pay attention, girls." He set a bucket full of sudsy water down in front of him. He had a squeegee, a brush, and a cloth hanging off his belt. OSHA says, "Employers shall instruct their window cleaning employees in the proper use of all equipment provided to them and shall supervise the use of equipment and safety devices to ensure that safe working practices are observed. They're coming to make sure we're doing everything legally which, I agree, it's a bunch of bullcrap, but nonetheless, do your best to keep your noses clean, stay safe, and don't finish your coffee before the end of the demonstration." He pulled out his scrub brush and pointed it at them.

"The only changes they've made in the last year is that we had to add a secondary brake, which as you know is designed to 'arrest the descent of the window cleaner in the event of an overspeed condition.' It just means, in simple terms, if you freefall so fast you don't have time to kiss your ass goodbye, a backup brake will save you from the big splat."

Ron took a sip. "Sounds reassuring."

"Yep," said Romey. "They also added one more strap to the body harness,

So, when you guys are rappelling off the rooftops, you now have a reinforced chest strap for distributing your fall arrest force. You'll still strap in over your thighs, pelvis, waist, and shoulders. All our body belts and safety lines have passed inspection. Good news is we don't need to use an outrigger beam because STICH has good sills and so does the school, and the anchorages are solid. OSHA already checked those boxes."

"Maybe by next year they'll have us wearing a parachute," said Josh.

"That sounds kinda sexy," said Ron. "Almost as kinky as a pelvis strap-on."

"Now for the basics. Jen here at Drip 'n Sip was gracious enough to lend us this very dirty window." He walked over to a side window. "We are going to cover the three golden rules of window cleaning. So, this is the brush, which is used before the squeegee. Rule number one: Brush the heck out of the windows. Some of this grime is really stuck on, so your brush is your friend, but you can't be a pussy. You really need to put muscle into it." He dunked the brush and scrubbed the glass briskly. As he took the squeegee off his belt, he saw a truck like his pull into the station. It was Evie. He watched her get out, wearing a pretty lace tank top and a white flowing skirt. He couldn't stop staring. *She looks like an angel.*

"Hey boss, you were sayin'?" said Josh.

"Yeah, I was saying this is a, um, this is a squeegee." *Stay focused.* "You may recognize it because almost everyone has a squeegee in their garage. They try to clean their own windows because how hard could it be, right? The problem's that the rubber squeegee blade could've been sitting in there for ten years. As you all know, rubber breaks down and a ratty blade will make more of a mess than Windex and paper towels or vinegar and newspaper. I change my blade every day. So, rule number two: Fresh blade. Next, you've surely noticed that everyone wants to know what's in the bucket, which brings us to rule number three: Warm water and a small amount of *Dawn*. Too much soap's gonna put you in a bubble bath before you know what hit you. Like anything, it's much harder to undo a screwup than to do it right in the first place."

"What if we can't find warm water, boss? Where do we get it?" asked Juan.

"Good question, dude. If you're outside, cold water is okay, and you use a spigot. If it's hot like it's going to be today, the water that's sitting in the hose will be plenty warm. If you're inside and the owner is home, you politely ask to fill your bucket in the kitchen sink. If no one's home, you steal it from the laundry sink if they have one, because the flow is usually better." Juan's eyes widened and he pressed his lips together.

Romey continued. "The damp cloth comes next, to remove the excess suds and water. The key here is to wring out the cloth when you're working inside. Dripping soapy water on a floor, or worse yet, a carpet, is unacceptable. Jake learned that the hard way when crazy old Mrs. Nelson had to take her dog clear over to a specialist in Rawland for a skin problem." He glanced over and watched Evie remove the gas cap and begin pumping gas. "Mrs. Nelson said the dog was covered with red bumps, and its hair was falling out. They gave it all kinds of tests, antibiotics and ointment. In the end they found out that its bed, which lies under a window, was soaked with dirty water from the window cleaner. Oops. That cost me an arm and a leg, but at least the dog's okay." Now Evie was washing her windshield. She was making a real mess with the gas station squeegee, trying to keep the dirty water from dripping on her skirt. He wanted to go help her.

"Wait, boss. Remember, that was the time we had to use the NSS?" said Jake.

"Oh, that's right, the nasty solvent stuff," said Romey.

"Yeah, I remember that job," said Jake. "Old Mr. Nelson croaked at a hundred and four years old, and it was the first time she had the windows cleaned."

"Now I remember," said Romey. "He smoked inside the house for sixty-five years, never opened a window. I had to special order the NSS to melt the nicotine off the inside windows."

"Yeah, that was a mess. I had to scrape that stuff off the ceiling fan blades, looked like old shit, and smelled just as bad," said Jake. "I guess that's how I made the mistake of getting the NSS in the dog bed, but what the hell, if the dog didn't die from breathing smoke its whole life, I'm sure a chemical wouldn't have killed it."

Romey took a sip of coffee and watched Evie get in her truck and start the engine. She looked over and saw him, smiled, and waved. He flipped his chin up and raised his cup.

"Lastly, and most importantly, gentlemen, think of window cleaning as a dance. If you think of it as work, it'll be monotonous, and the result will be just average. But like a dance, if you have grace and calmness, the windows will turn out beautifully." He smiled and his heart chirped like a little bird as he watched Evie drive away.

# SEVENTEEN

The next day was Thursday, and Chrissy was scrubbing in orthopedic surgery, where operations are performed on knees, shoulders, and an occasional broken bone. She had told Jack and Dillon that orthopedic surgeons are like carpenters because some of the instruments they use are saws, drills, screwdrivers, and mallets. Chrissy liked orthopedics. It appealed to her loud and strong personality, but she despised some of the orthopedic surgeons because of *their* loud and strong personalities. She was assisting Dr. Ned Nedson, who was known for his hot temper and short fuse. He had been written up the previous month—disciplinary action— for throwing a drill across the room, knocking a hole in the wall, and making the circulating nurse cry. He yelled at the scheduling department constantly and was known to throw a tantrum if he didn't get the parking place he wanted. When he got upset, which was nearly every case, he puffed up and his face turned molten red. Behind his back, Chrissy called him Red Ned.

This was the first surgery of the day and Chrissy was scrubbed in, hung over, and lost in her own thoughts again. As she helped drape the sleeping patient and threw off the cords and tubing for the circulator to plug into the arthroscopy tower, she knew she was in a very foul mood. Today was going to be a nightmare, having to bear the shrill sound of the power equipment and the shrieking suction that made her brain bang in her skull.

Damn that Rob. It was all his fault for making her want to drown herself in booze and pity. Bad combination—excess alcohol, self-pity, and sleep deprivation. The insides of her eyelids felt like sandpaper, and her stomach burned from too much coffee and no breakfast. Last night, after Dillon had fallen asleep, she drained the tequila bottle in less than two hours and passed out on the couch for an hour. She awoke abruptly, thinking of how she couldn't call in sick again and how screwed up she was. Her thoughts were dark, and her stealing was getting worse. It wasn't like grand theft, but insignificant things like checking her tire pressure at a gas station in Lincoln county and driving away with the station's pressure gauge in her purse, or finding and quickly grabbing a brand-new pack of bungee cords lying near the school and throwing them in her backseat. Her heart had quickened as she looked around to make sure no one saw, and she felt stupid because she wasn't really doing anything wrong, was she?

Evie, who had studied why people behaved certain ways, had explained to her that the common theme for overeating and stealing was to gain a sense of control. It was close to daylight when she rolled off the sofa and made herself a disgusting drink of gin and Mountain Dew, which wrecked her. In her stupor, she relived a huge fight she and Rob had had one afternoon, six months before over a general contractor, who she said was a big turn-on because he had his shit together enough to be a licensed contractor. She said Rob could barely hold down a job while she worked her ass off in surgery full time. She screamed that she would sleep with a general contractor before she would sleep with a doctor because most doctors were never home anyway, and most general contractors were known to please their woman. She had no proof of that but just needed to scream about something to get Rob's attention. She had told Evie about the fight and how she had kicked him out of the house. Evie explained about the spiral of negativity and how damaging it is to a relationship.

Chrissy admitted only to herself that when it happened, she actually felt possessed; once when she started yelling at him, she'd spun so out of control that it felt like her head had blown off. Of course the drinking didn't help matters, but maybe she wouldn't get so mad if he wasn't so calm about everything. Her anger escalated to dangerous heights when he suggested she "mellow out."

The contractor stuff really upset Rob, and they were both so drunk that when he stumbled out the front door and she saw him fall off the porch and pass out in the front yard, she left him lying there in broad daylight. When Evie came driving by with a truck bed full of flowers left over from one of her events, Chrissy flagged her down. She had to convince her that Rob was passed out, not dead, and it would be a good use of the left-over flowers to make a circle around his body, you know, funny. Maybe he'd wake up and think he was dead and at his own funeral! Evie went along with it reluctantly, not nearly as amused as Chrissy by the idea. Good thing Dillon wasn't around to see that.

Maybe tonight she'd take it easy on herself and try not to eat so much and drink until the bottle was gone. Although the whole idea of moderation was a bunch of bullshit. She knew she wasn't strong enough or normal enough to drink moderately. Maybe she should not keep booze in the house; although she'd tried that before and knew if she wanted to stop drinking, it could only be done if she had a bottle to talk herself out of. That's how she stopped smoking so long ago. She bought a pack of Virginia Slims and kept it, unopened, in plain sight for more than a month, then threw it in the trash. Evie suggested that Chrissy try writing her feelings instead of numbing them and that there were healthier ways to break the cycle of self-loathing. *Frickin' Evie, always holding it together. And fucking Dr. Nedson better not be a jerk today. I can't deal with it.*

The operating room was dark except for the image on the tower screen and the overhead light that illuminated Chrissy's instrument table. They were doing a knee arthroscopy and an anterior cruciate ligament repair. The procedure required visualization of the knee joint with fluid installation, a camera, light source, and scope. As usual, copious amounts of irrigation were running through the patient's knee, over the drapes, onto the floor, and into Chrissy's shoes. Lynn, the circulating nurse, was trying her best in the dim light to sop up the water with OR towels without disturbing the foot pedals or bumping the table. She was just about to tell Dr. Nedson that the new arthroscopy camera was broken and he had to use the old camera today. Lynn was pushing wet towels into the corner and saw Dr. Nedson shaking his head at the video screen.

"Take a picture," he said.

Lynn reached to the tower and pushed the button on the camera box. "Picture captured, Doctor," she said.

He scowled at the screen and moved the scope around inside the knee and said, "Why in the hell is the picture not clear?"

Lynn stepped forward. "This is the only camera we have right now, Doctor Nedson, until our other camera comes back. It's out for repair."

"I don't have time for this shit. And what do you mean it's out for repair? How long will that take?"

"I will confirm with the workroom, but I believe they'll have it fixed by next week."

"Next week? This is a goddamn hassle! Load up a ticron suture." As Chrissy was loading the suture, a nurse slipped in to give Lynn a break. Lynn whispered in her ear that they were about to prepare the graft, and things were starting to get tense, and that she could take her break later. The relief nurse told Lynn to go on break now because she had another break to give and would have to start on lunch relief right after that. Lynn reluctantly gave her report and snuck quietly out the door, knowing that Dr. Nedson hated it when staff took breaks.

"Take a picture!" he yelled. The relief nurse pushed the button, suddenly realizing that the frame had not been advanced.

"Did you just take a picture over my previous image?"

"Um, um yes, I'm sorry Dr. Nedson, but I didn't realize that . . ."

"Get the hell out of my room and get somebody in here with some brains between their ears!" The nurse stammered, ran out of the room with hot tears stinging her eyes. Water continued to roll off the drapes and splashed onto the floor.

"You don't have to be such an asshole, Nedson," said Chrissy.

"What did you just say to me?" He glared.

"You heard me. You don't have to yell at her. It was a mistake."

"I don't put up with mistakes in surgery. I want this done right, so if she's not smart enough to figure it out, then keep her the hell out of my room!"

Chrissy rapped the mayo stand with a forcep. "Seriously, you're gonna blow a gasket if you don't calm down." She could hear Rob's voice saying, *mellow out.*

"Don't tell me to calm down!" In the darkness she could see his ears and forehead turning red. Sweat beaded and glistened above his bushy eyebrows, wicking into his surgeon's cap. A wet spot, probably hot spit, grew on his mask and his eyes bulged out like a raging bull. "You better watch your mouth and your bad attitude, or you'll be next to get bounced out on your disrespectful ass."

"Go ahead and kick me out, but that's gonna screw you up good because I'm the only scrub you've got right now, and let's just see how much fun you'll have doing an ACL by yourself."

"You just lost your job. I'll make sure of it. Are we out of water? Where's the goddamn water? I can't see a thing!" With no irrigation, blood flowed in and the screen turned red. Chrissy smiled inside thinking it looked just like his big, red, fat head.

"Mark my words," she said. "Your head's gonna explode, I guarantee it."

Lynn came rushing in and hung another bag of irrigation. The screen began to clear as the fluid rinsed away the blood. They finished the case in brooding silence, and Chrissy thought about how much fun and free food she was going to have when she became a bartender at Mel's Bar and Grill.

After the surgery, Dr. Nedson made it a point to talk to Mr. Hudson, the president of STICH, to make sure he had only the best staff in his room. Mr. Hudson assured Dr. Nedson that all the staff at this hospital were hardworking and highly qualified, and that Lynn Posey, registered nurse, had been awarded nurse of the year on more than one occasion. He stated that both operating rooms almost always ran with one hundred percent efficiency. He also reminded the doctor that the reason a time out was done prior to the beginning of each case was because Dr. Nedson himself, had operated on the wrong knee five years ago, and STICH had sustained a hefty lawsuit. Dr. Nedson demanded that the fat scrub with the pink hair and the big mouth assisting him today be fired, and that pink hair should not be allowed on any medical professional. He said she'd seen the end of her career at this facility. He was an orthopedic surgeon, and one of his privileges was to decide who could be in his room, and this broad copping an attitude wasn't one of his choices.

Furthermore, he complained that the scheduling department functioned at a kindergarten level, and if he didn't get his own parking spot with his name on it, heads were going to roll!

That afternoon Chrissy was called into Alice's office and informed that she had been put on probation for six weeks. This was her second warning and if there was another surgeon complaint, she would be terminated from STICH. Alice told her she was a good scrub, but it wasn't her technical skills that were in question. It was her contrary attitude and lack of team spirit that was to be addressed. Chrissy pointed out that she was only defending Lynn Posey. She was then told that it was not her place to defend her circulating nurse.

"Well then," said Chrissy. "I guess I don't get what you mean by team spirit."

"I understand that you were looking out for Lynn's best interest, but there are more diplomatic ways to approach a situation like this. Mr. Hudson and I have decided that you will scrub in with Dr. Nedson next Thursday in an effort for you both to start fresh and maintain a professional work environment."

"Whatever." Chrissy smirked. "I hope the camera's fixed by then."

# EIGHTEEN

After lying in bed for hours, Lola twisted and turned and fitfully kicked off the covers. Insomnia is a plague, she thought. It sneaks up behind you, and when it's dark, it clamps its jaws over your sleep and flings it around, prying your eyes open and unearthing the negative thoughts you hoped to bury for the night.

Deeply disturbed, Lola stared at the wall and wondered how different life would have been had she owned up to her shameful past. Sam was the only one who knew of her humble beginnings, and now he was gone, taking her secret with him. Only yesterday Lola had nearly confided in Evie, but in a moment of insecurity, she decided to keep quiet and add deceit to her long list of Godless qualities.

Recapping her past, she fell into a deep sleep.

Lola was born in a Catholic convent in 1949, the product

of a teen pregnancy. Her birth mother was a wild, fourteen-year-old runaway, who was nine months pregnant when she was detained and sent to the convent. She passed away after a dangerous and harrowing childbirth, but the infant survived.

The nuns named the baby girl Mary and kept her under their close watch with the intention of grooming her for a life devoted to the Order. Baby Mary cut her teeth on a sterling rosary and grew to secretly regurgitate the religion she was spoon fed. Upon turning eighteen, Mary, much to the dismay of Mother Superior, changed her name to Lola and fled the convent like a Thoroughbred busting out of the starting gate. Lola didn't look back and vehemently pursued the life she had always dreamed of—a life without God as her Father, a life full of all the pleasures she would be damned for—men, sex, smoking and drinking, and speaking her mind. Never again would she live under the vows of poverty or chastity. Gone were the days of praying the Divine Office together in choir five times a day and observing hours of relentless silence.

Sister Grace, who was the most like a mother to Lola, had informed her that she was a true orphan, and one cannot and will not grieve the loss of something they never had. A few years later, when Lola met Sam, she knew his love would sustain her for an eternity. She had, as they say, put all her eggs in one basket, and Sam was all she needed.

Now, in her dream-state, Lola clearly heard Sam's voice. "Lola, my love. Thank you for the dance of life and sharing that magical part of love that few are fortunate enough to share. I can feel your warm and tender embrace and hear your laughter. I wonder how much different our lives would have been had we shared a family joy and brought our human replacements into the world. Selfishly, I have not had to share my Lola. I have seen your sorrow and have known your longing for a little girl who would look just like you, with a beautiful smile and a glorious heart to match. How could I make up for my failings, by not giving you a son, kind and sensitive like you? A boy to step into my big shoes one day and become a man like the only man you have ever loved. Lola, honey, it was our dance of life . . . Our unbreakable bond."

Lola's eyes fluttered open in the darkness. She sat up in bed, dry mouthed and edgy, thinking that something had changed in the house or in the life of the house. Oh yes, it must be between three and four o'clock, and Sam was gone and she was unable to crawl on top of him and feel the comfort of his thrumming heart. Again, night thoughts of how each would partially awaken at the same time, how she would playfully kiss his lips and breathe softly on his neck, not meant to wake him fully, but to get a little moan out of him, then roll over his warm body, caress his back, his broad shoulders and slowly slide her toes up the back of his legs and spoon, oh to spoon. They would cradle together, her breasts pressed into his back, her knees in the crook of his. Then sometime during their slumber they would switch, and he clothed her back with his soft, furry chest, wrapped his arms around her, and held her like he would never let go. Sometimes he would slip from a murmur to a groan, to a tiny snicker and they would end up in a rolling bout of laughter, void of words, just pure naked pleasure as they were overcome with love.

She fell back and sank her head into the pillow. She pinched her eyes shut and inhaled deeply, feeling his hand on the soft place between her belly button and wisp of silky hair. They had created a sacred world between these sheets. He had touched her so deftly, opening her gently, slowly, always as if they had an eternity to caress and be caressed. Magic hands, she told him. He called it treasure hunting. *My little treasure.* How he would touch her in places she didn't know existed. He whispered that he dwelled inside her, and she lived within him as well, and through his exploration and some invisible celestial guidance, this was familiar territory, for they had been here before.

*There is a before and there is a now.* She flashed back to the friends who had introduced them at a party. Ed saying that Sam needed a twenty-two-year-old girl like he needed a hole in the head, and Kay telling her to do it while her thighs were still good. She heeded Kay's advice and walked right up to Sam, an invisible force pulling her into his personal space. Without hesitation, she said, "Someday I'm going to meet a man of my caliber." Followed by, "I love sex." He took a sip of his gin and tonic, looked deeply into her eyes, and said, "That's a real ice breaker. A good way to get yourself an engagement ring."

The connection was bigger than the both of them. He would later say it was orchestrated by a higher power, that undoubtedly they had met before in another realm or another lifetime. They marveled, without question, at how they came to read one another's thoughts and finish one another's sentences. They had found Heaven on Earth. True connection—for to find the other half of oneself was to find completion. They were beyond best friends or husband and wife. They were Soulmates. Twin flames. Spiritual partners with an unbreakable bond.

Lola sat on the edge of the bed and slid her feet into Sam's slippers. Where was the daybreak and how many more sleepless nights would she have to endure? Why was this miserable arousal invading her thoughts more frequently, as if she were waiting for some impending *thing* to overtake her. Is something else going to happen? Is there more to this life than living in love and then grieving the sudden disappearance of one's other half? Disappearance? When something disappears, we make it our goal to find it, like searching for a lost cat, a missing sock, or car keys in a flour sack. The nuns would proclaim that her faith should hold her to the truth that Sam had gone to Heaven, but her faith was nil.

As a little girl she had been told that when we die, we go to Heaven, which she had imagined was up beyond a radiant sunbeam streaming down from a giant puffy cloud with a shimmering lining.

When you die you get to rise and fly somewhere over the rainbow and sit on God's lap, right? In a big chair surrounded by all that is white and bright and there are angels with calming wings, one hovering over each of your shoulders.

At some point the Great Being with the flowing white beard and an illuminated robe, signs you in with a feathered pen on a slab of gold, and lets you know this is your new home and you will be watched over and protected so that you will never again feel a flicker of pain or discomfort or fear, for pain and fear do not exist in Heaven. Lola stood up and stepped toward the bathroom. Her knees buckled and she fell to the rug, curling into the fetal position.

When the morning sun began to filter in, she sat up and rubbed her eyes. *Now I understand. Today is Sunday, the day we always made extra love.*

Going downstairs, Lola remembered this was the Sunday that Evie would take her to the cemetery. They would go at nine o'clock. They would have coffee first. Evie had invited her to go to the Hometown Cafe afterwards to have pancakes, but she couldn't bear the thought of going to a restaurant where everyone would know her and look at her like she was the sad, unfortunate widow, the freshest of Pine Grove's mourners, and whisper how it's a crying shame that she looked so frail and my, how she'd lost weight. Maybe it wasn't being pitied that concerned her as much as the idea of pancakes on a Sunday morning. She and Sam always had the best champagne and pancakes on Sunday. They laughed and kissed and watched the tiny effervescent bubbles rise in their crystal flutes. After breakfast she opened their robes and sat on his lap. Thank you for loving me and feeding me and keeping me warm, she would say. It's my pleasure, he would say, and then back to bed they would go.

She turned on the coffeemaker and went out into the warm morning sunshine. She stood before the lush dahlias, foxglove, and snapdragons. The colorful cosmos swayed in the breeze, beckoning her. Lola stepped forward and began to pick flowers. Flowers for Sam.

# NINETEEN

When they arrived at the cemetery, the flowers were shaking in Lola's hands. She felt lightheaded and overcome with mounting dread. *Sam's not here,* she thought, and a sick feeling came over her with the vision of him being buried underground. She grabbed Evie's hand.

Evie bit her lip and saw herself standing in Lori's living room. *They can't be dead. It simply isn't so. I just saw them this morning, saying come with us Eebee. They were alive and breathing, and how could it be possible that they are neither one of those things now.*

Lola breathed deeply, her face a tense mask. She was unusually quiet. Earlier she had just wanted to stay home. But she had gotten herself out the door, flowers in hand, and loaded herself into the car next to Evie. She was so confused. *How long has it been since the burial? When was it that Evie was driving the car in the funeral processional with me crushed against her shoulder?*

As they walked toward the gravesite, Evie put her hand on the small of Lola's back and said, "I'm right here Lola." The mound of soil, still slightly dark, looked hard-crusted and unnatural. The granite headstone stood perfectly erect with the inscription:

*Forever in our Hearts*

*Samuel Thomas Ingram* III

*April 16, 1926 - September 30, 1998.*

Lola placed the flowers on the grave and backed away.

"Do you want to sit on this bench for a minute, Lola?" Lola nodded. It was difficult for Evie to tell what she was feeling. Her eyes were not focused; she seemed to be looking inward. They sat on the wood bench for several minutes.

Finally, Lola spoke. "He was such an amazing, generous, understanding man."

"Yes, he was.

"I'm so . . ."

"Remember, the depth of your pain is directly correlated to the depth of your love."

"Yes, I feel it so deeply. And I'm beginning to realize that it's going to be with me forever."

"But in a different way," said Evie.

"Yes, but it's going to take a long time."

Evie saw something inside Lola shift at that moment. Was Lola coming to some form of acceptance? She tried to remember the times she felt changes inside. In the quiet, Evie felt her tragic truth nestled deep inside her and remembered how she had stayed in a catatonic stupor for one year after the accident. It was all a distant blur—the spiritual counselors and the droves of volunteers from a church youth group, there to help her with her shattered faith. Ministers supported her through her rampages against God or the Devil—whoever was responsible for destroying her life.

She put her hand on Lola's knee. Lola covered it with hers. For a moment Evie had the uncanny, dizzying feeling that Lola was comforting her and was surprised to feel her heart open the slightest bit. They breathed together. Then Lola squeezed her hand and said, "It's time to go home." The sound of Lola's voice startled Evie and pulled her back into the present from wherever she had been.

"Okay. Are you sure you don't want to go to breakfast with us? I'm meeting Chrissy and the boys there and I could bring you back right after we eat."

"Yes, I'm sure. I really need to go home."

The Hometown Cafe was full of families and the after-church crowd. The cheerful waitress, Kara, was bringing a highchair to a table, smacking her gum, and telling a young mother that Sunday was the only day that all the highchairs were usually taken. She was kindly referring to the Gabilan family at the center table, where Netty and Letty each had a highchair for their Teddy bears. They were wearing their church clothes, dark colored dresses with matching shawls, felt pillbox hats, and shiny brown shoes with compression socks.

They were celebrating their eighty-ninth birthday, sitting side by side, Letty with her hand on Netty's good leg and Netty clutching Letty's Teddy bear. They were trying to get the stuffed animals to kiss each other. Kara smiled and poured coffee for the customers, while Amanda, the pretty cook with the giant bun on the top of her head, sang in the kitchen and flipped sizzling sausage patties on the grill. She plopped heaping plates of biscuits and gravy under the heating lamp and slammed the bell. "Order up, Kara!"

Romey and Josh sat at the counter, drinking coffee and eating chicken fried steak and eggs. Romey, in his Shine On tee shirt, waved his schedule book at Amanda and said, "You can't be the only one having all the fun on a Sunday, Amanda!" Wink, wink. "Come on, toss me a berry!" He tilted his chin up and opened his mouth. She rolled her eyes and pegged him on the forehead with a plump strawberry.

Chrissy, Evie, and the boys were in a popsicle-orange booth. Chrissy's face, even under her makeup, showed signs of dehydration and internal struggle. After reliving some terrible scene last night, she had to knock herself out with a sleeping pill to get some rest. Good thing Dillon had spent the night at Jack's. She was groggy this morning, and everything felt droopy.

Jack and Dillon were lining up dominos on the table and having a contest to see who could say pancakes without smiling. Jack had a small black and blue mark on his cheek.

Evie said, "Buddy, how did you get that bruise?" She had a sick feeling seeing Jack with yet another bruise. When he was two, she had made him wear a helmet for an entire summer because he was so accident prone. Now, looking at his adorable face, she feared that she may never be able to fully protect him. The scene of him being pinched at the pool and then the boys and the rattlesnake made her heart jam in her throat, and like a crazy woman, she was considering tethering both boys to a kitchen chair just to keep an eye on them. She never should have left them alone the other day, assuming they were mature enough to follow her instructions to stay in the house and play with the new Lego set.

"We fell out of a tree," said Dillon

"You both fell out of a tree? Where was I?" said Evie.

"You were in the house, Evie, and Mom, you were at work and got into trouble that day."

"What did you do to get in trouble this time?" asked Evie.

"Oh, it was bull. We have a substitute manager named Gail, who said I wasn't being a team player, but hey, what's new? We have this sucky rule that you can't heat fish in the surgery center break room and Gail, who only comes in when Alice is off, got all bent out of shape because I put tuna salad in the microwave and stunk up the place. She said patients could smell it all the way in the lobby."

"It sounds like a reasonable rule to me," said Evie.

"It's so stupid. She says it's not good for the patients to smell any food at all because they aren't allowed to eat before surgery, and everyone's hungry." Chrissy rolled her eyes.

"That's gross," said Jack. "Why would you microwave tuna fish anyway?"

"To get rid of Calvin," she replied.

"Who's Calvin, Mom?"

"He's the scrub tech who gags when he smells fish. I wanted to eat my lunch in peace, and he was the only other person in the breakroom. He bugs me because he always takes extra-long breaks, and he turns the TV on with the volume full blast. It gives me a headache. When I eat lunch, I don't want to eat with Calvin. I can't stand being in the same room with him."

Dillon was listening intently with his tongue stuck out the side of his mouth, trying to poke a fork tine in a domino dot.

Chrissy continued, "I put the microwave on high, and the fish started popping and smelling and splatting against the glass, and Calvin jumped up, gagging, and covered his mouth and ran out. It was hilarious. I turned the TV off and started to enjoy myself 'til the boss came in and reamed me a new one. She said it was a warning, and if it happened again, I'll be written up." Chrissy clapped her hands and said, "Yay!"

She refrained from mentioning that she was already on probation for something else. As always, she thought, the punishment far exceeds the crime, and it's my right to get back at management any way I can. Fair is fair, after all.

Evie almost felt embarrassed for Chrissy. She took a sip of water and looked over at Romey, who looked happy even when he was chewing.

"But Mom, you told me you're supposed to follow the rules so you shouldna put fish in the microwave, right?" Dillon set his fork down and carefully placed the domino on the table.

"Well, you're right about that Dill, but this was a special situation. I'm being accused of not being a team player, and that's what Calvin's guilty of. I'm just trying to prove a point to my manager that if Calvin disobeys the rules, so can I."

Evie twitched in her seat, making a concerted effort not to chime in with the boys present. Chrissy was incorrigible, and it seemed to be getting worse. Evie would talk with her when they were alone, and maybe they could shine some light on why Chrissy's bad attitude was escalating. It probably had something to do with Rob, but then again, maybe she really wasn't cut out to work in a team-driven environment. It probably went deeper than just wanting to get fired so she could collect unemployment. No, there was something hidden that was beginning to surface. Evie had watched how, over the last few months, Chrissy had constantly stuffed her feelings. It's like extreme overeating, thought Evie. If you stuff too much in your body, you barf. Stuff too many problems and they'll manifest in one way or another.

Netty and Letty were squealing and clapping because Kara had put whipped cream smiley faces on their pancakes and a birthday candle nose. Amanda stepped out from the kitchen with the busboy and the other waitress and led the entire cafe in singing Happy Birthday. Netty and Letty sang louder than everyone else, and Kara helped them blow out the candles.

Chrissy looked at Evie. "Oh, give me a break, you're getting all teared up?"

"I can't help it. Like I've said before, I think they're so precious. They show everyone what love is. They're so sweet and kind to each other, and they're always smiling, like they're really enjoying life, even at eighty-nine years old."

"Maybe we'll be like that someday, Evie. We'll look at each other and say we've been friends for so long we can't remember which one of us was the bad influence."

The bell jingled at the front door, and the locals snuck a glance, pretending they weren't that interested. A stranger came in and sat at the counter, on the stool closest to the door. He was wearing dirty jeans and a long black coat. Jack looked up and said, "Look, there's that guy."

"What guy?" asked Chrissy.

"Jack, did you forget to tell?" asked Dillon.

"Tell what?" said Evie. She turned and looked at the counter.

"I'm sorry I didn't tell you, Mom. But you were so upset, and I didn't want you to get more upset." said Jack. "That guy there, who grabbed me in the pool, came to our house when we were skinning the snake. He asked for you, but we told him you weren't home. He said he has a knife like ours. He said to tell you that Marc needs to see you, and he gave us bubble gum. Please don't be mad at me, Mom."

Evie knocked her glass, spilling water over the table. "What?" she said. "Oh my God." She stood up, lightheaded, and walked over to Marc. He gave her that clown-like smile and said, "Well, hello. There's my girl."

His hands were shaking.

She was shaking from the inside. "I am not your girl. And what were you doing at my house, and how do you even know where I live, and oh, my God, you're wearing Sam's coat?"

He reached into the pea coat pocket and pulled out the note she had written and a Pine Grove pocket directory.

A sinister smile crept across his face. "I've been watching you carefully because it's my duty, and because you're my girl, Evie. I saw you hang this coat at the church and I had to have it because I know you've touched it. You left me your number because you need me too. I matched it with your name and found your address in this directory."

His thready voice, his ugly face, and the knowledge that he had been at their house sent spikes through Evie's core. The air was suddenly too thick to breathe, and the heat wafting from the kitchen stoked something already threatening to boil over inside her. Molten rage and pure, raw fear.

She shot a nervous glance toward Romey, two seats down. She didn't want him to hear what they were saying. It was just so embarrassing to be anywhere near this freak. She lowered her voice almost to a whisper. Marc had begun twisting on the stool.

"Listen to me. I have already told you to stay away from us. Do not ever come around me, my house, or my kid again or you will seriously regret it. I don't know what you're even doing in Pine Grove or what you're after, but I will have no qualms about having you arrested." She bit hard and chewed the inside of her cheek.

Kara stepped closer, eavesdropping, wiping the counter with a rag, her silver bracelets jingling.

"Everything okay, Evie?" asked Romey.

Marc stopped spinning and said, "Just a little lover's quarrel."

Romey smiled, swiped his mouth with a napkin and said, "Hey, my friend, nothing wrong with that!" He winked and shook hot sauce on his hashbrowns.

"It's hardly that," said Evie under her breath, as she turned and headed back to the booth. She was trembling, her heart banging in her chest.

Romey watched her walk away. *She looks so pretty in that skirt and those boots. Probably just been to church. But, as pretty as she looks, she sure doesn't look happy after her conversation. Maybe they really were having an argument. That guy sure doesn't look like anyone she'd be involved with, now that I think of it. What did he do to dim her beautiful bright smile?* Marc stood up and stumbled toward the door. *And why's he wearing a big coat on a warm day like this?*

Romey watched Evie slide back into the booth and put her arm around Jack. *Yup, something's not quite right there. None of my business, I guess. But...*

"What the hell," said Chrissy as she watched Marc crash out the door.

Through the window they saw him cross the street, unsteady and fumbling for a cigarette. The pressure in his head was unbearable and he needed a drink and something to turn down the voices in his head. They were laughing at him. "She is wrong," he stammered. *She doesn't understand that she belongs to me. Evie, you must help me. I need you. They're after me and I need you to save me.* "Cram, cram," yelled the voices. He slapped his cheeks hard, and screamed, "I hate you, fucking voices! Get out of my head and stop saying my name backwards!" He pulled out a pint of whiskey from his pocket and, despite the roiling protests from his bowels, he downed the bottle. *I hate that guy at the counter for questioning my girl. I hate the directory for calling her Evelyn. She is my Evie. Evelyn was the name of a horrid old woman. The devil-woman with blood in her eyes who stuck pins under my fingernails when I was small and bad. I hate Evelyn, the horrid wretch with greenish-yellow teeth who clamped a clothespin on my foreskin to keep me from wetting the bed. I hate Evelyn with a hate so strong I can taste it— rotten and bitter on my tongue.*

Chrissy and Evie stared at Marc, as he clutched the empty bottle, spread his arms out wide, and spun in circles, right in the middle of Main Street. Then he lumbered away and disappeared behind the post office.

Dillon tapped the table and the long row of dominoes fell, one after another.

"Cool," said Dillon. "It looks like a black snake with white spots."

Kara brought four plates of fluffy pancakes, smothered in wild huckleberries, whipped cream, and sprinkled with powdered sugar.

"Yummmm," said Jack and Dillon.

Evie's stomach lurched. She swallowed hard, pushing back the bile in her throat. Her vision began to dim, as it always did when she was overcome with fear. The therapists had told her she may battle with death-danger-stress-triggers for the rest of her life. They referred to it as her dimmer switch—when a trigger happened, her vision would change—a fading light, a loss of brightness and her mind became foggy and unclear of the distant past. Obscure. Shadowed. Remote. Be aware, they said. It's physiologically and biochemically more severe than the worst migraine. Get in a safe place with your head in a safe space. *Breathe, Evie. Breathe.* She looked over at the counter to see Romey was looking at her. He raised his coffee cup and smiled, which brought her comfort. She imagined he could be relied upon in this crazy world. She tried to smile back. She tapped her feet under the table but outwardly appeared calmer than she was. She had learned to do that, to keep hidden what counts.

Her thoughts switched to Marc. She would kill him if he tried anything else.

"Mom, if you're not gonna eat your whip cream, can I have it?" asked Jack.

"Sure baby. You can have anything you want."

# TWENTY

Evie startled in the middle of the night, awakened by her own soft sobs. As the world came into focus and her eyes adjusted to the darkness, she could make out her bedroom in a faint stream of moonlight, the knobs on her dresser and her shelf filled with books. She was dreaming of the hunt, but this time, the guy she was after had half of Marc's face.

Thirteen years had passed since she had become obsessed with finding the eighteen-year-old drunk driver who turned her life inside out. Visions of finding the kid just to see his face intruded upon her every thought. She spent hours planning how she would track him down, even if she had no information on who he was and why he was drinking on a Thursday morning in July. She fantasized about what she would say to him when she visited him in prison. She conjured images of what he would look like through the penitentiary bars with fluorescent lights buzzing around him. He would have pale skin that looked like death, sunken dark circles under his eyes, a zombie in threadbare stripes, hunched over with shackles around his ankles. But most importantly, he would be ridden with remorse.

Evie sat up and rubbed her eyes. It was unnerving, tinged with hope and terror when she dreamed of the hunt, then shook herself awake, back to reality. She had to absorb the truth that the hunt itself was futile, for the drunk driver had also died in the accident.

She got out of bed, wrapped a blanket around her shoulders and tiptoed through the dimness toward Jack's room. The house feels empty and cold, she thinks, but maybe she's feeling her own blood streaming through her like an ice melt.

As she approaches Jack's room, a breeze rattles the window and the curtain flutters. The old house expands here, contracts there, giving off little pops and creaks, but Jack doesn't stir. She stands quietly before him watching his angelic face in the filtered moonlight. His arms are over his head and one foot is sticking out of the covers. She leans over, tucks in his little toes, and kisses him softly on the cheek. She kneels beside the bed, folds her hands, and waits a long moment until her rapid respirations calm to match Jack's slow, even breathing. *What would I ever do without you, Jack? You are my heart, my soul, my blessed reward. Dear God, please protect my baby. I need him with everything I've got. I will no longer plead for your explanations or question the motives of the universe. I will accept the gifts I have received and continue to live in love.*

She tiptoed back to her room, crawled into bed, and pulled the covers over her. The light of the moon disappeared, swallowed up by a wall of dark clouds, heavy and brewing. She heard a far-off rumble of thunder. *Angels watch me through the night and wake me up with morning's light.*

It was just after daybreak at Drip 'n Sip, when Romey took a drink of coffee and glanced up at the persistent sky. "Hey Studs," he said. "Did any of you see that rainbow?"

"Nope."

"It was incredible. Reminds me of Bali with its beautiful rainbows almost every day."

"Nice," said Josh. "But I don't get how you saw a rainbow when it hasn't rained yet."

"Trust me, my friend, you don't need darkness to see light."

"Right," said Josh and glanced up at the sky.

Romey raised his cup. "Okay, so today we start on the school and don't stop until the bell rings on the first day of class. They say the rain's comin' this afternoon, so, if necessary, just do the innies. And remember my motto about rain: What's bad for the window cleaner is good for the flowers. Ron and Josh will do the Super 8 motel. The keys are usually at the front desk with a list of what rooms are unoccupied and what balconies you can access. I'll call ahead and have the maids unlock the doors. That way you don't have to worry about the keys. I don't even look at the list. I just turn every doorknob and go into the rooms that are open. I mean, what's the worst thing that could happen, right?"

Ron laughed. "The last time I washed the windows at the Super 8, there was a couple going at it on the balcony below me."

"Yeah, people are always asking if the window washer sees the juicy stuff," said Romey.

"Well, it wasn't that interesting. They were on their hands and knees, doing it doggie style, covered with a bath towel."

"Dude, there you go again with your mind in the gutter. It was probably a couple of kids making a fort," said Romey. "Oh, that reminds me, what starts with an F and ends with a K and if you don't have it, you have to use your hand?"

"That's pretty obvious, Boss," said Ron.

"Yep. Obvious to me too. It's a fork." Romey winked.

It was mid-morning when Evie stood at Lola's kitchen sink filling the tea kettle. She looked out the window at the high, dark cloud cover. She was spent and edgy from the impending storm and the turbulent night's sleep. "It feels like we may finally get some rain," she said.

Lola sat at the table wearing Sam's white tee shirt, boxers, and his slippers. She had the *Pine Tree News* open to the obituaries. She had begun looking to see if another person had passed away, hoping that someone else's pain might ease hers, as if dipping from the giant vat of sorrow would lighten the load. She was mad at herself for her poor coping skills and mad at life for not preparing her for such a loss. How had she made it forty-nine years without ever losing a loved one?

Evie set the kettle on the stove and turned the burner

up. She couldn't stop thinking about Marc and hoping that he would just dissolve as quickly as he had appeared. She smiled to herself as she fantasized that Romey would come riding up on a white horse and snuff Marc out. Poof. Gone. End of story.

Lola rustled the paper and read that Dr. Ned Nedson, an orthopedic surgeon at STICH, had died from a massive stroke after having a long-running dispute with the hospital. He was found in his car in the STICH parking lot last Thursday. Sam had known Dr. Nedson, and Lola wondered if they would recognize each other up there, possibly play another game of golf with pure gold clubs and balls made of miniature clouds. This is what crazy looks like, Lola thought, and pushed the paper away. She sighed and began turning her ring on her finger, groggy from another restless night. She felt like everything hurt, from the inside out.

"Rain would be nice," she said. "Maybe a sky full of angel tears will rinse away some of this fuzz and confusion." She held out her hand and looked at her wedding ring.

"Lola, I know what's on your heart, but what's on your mind this morning?" Evie took two cups from the cupboard.

"I was wondering about my wedding ring. When Sam left, I vowed I would never take it off, even to sleep. Then I started losing weight and now I keep finding the ring in our bed, which makes me nervous because I don't want to lose it."

Evie set the cups on the counter and looked at Lola.

"Did you hear what you just said?"

"Yes. I said I don't want to lose my ring in the sheets."

"You said, 'when Sam *left*.' Before, you've said, 'when Sam *died*.'"

"Yeah, I think I'm starting to get the difference between leaving and *dying*. Like he flew away to a better place instead of just being put in a box and buried in the ground." She thought how the nuns of her youth would say Sam is lying in the arms of Jesus, but Lola just couldn't picture that.

Evie stared out the window, watching the frothing clouds darken and loom above the treetops. Her thoughts shifted to her auntie, who had taken her to the ocean in Northern California when she was seventeen and explained to her that there would be no burial, no cemetery or gravesite. No one was going into the ground. There were legal instructions to sprinkle the ashes into the sea for the whales and fish. Evie remembered that day. A day as cold as stone, the sea rocking and crashing, bringing no comfort to her shattered soul.

Evie began opening cupboards and closing them again like she was looking for something, but she didn't know what. "That's right, Lola. Sam got his wings."

Lola slipped her ring off and put it back on. "Yeah, and it's not like he's sent me a clear message, but I feel like he may be telling me something about the ring."

"Well," said Evie. "What you do with your wedding ring is a very personal thing. Have you thought about wrapping some tape around the band to make it fit better, or taking it to a jeweler and having it resized?"

"No."

Evie turned the kettle off, made the tea and sat at the table. "You could put it on a chain with Sam's ring and wear it as a necklace."

Lola closed the newspaper and shook her head. "Nah."

Evie suddenly remembered that Lola had made sure Sam was buried with his wedding band on and a pair of Lola's panties in his suit pocket.

"I'm not sure what to do," said Lola. "I always told him if anything ever happened to me, he must go on. I wanted him to keep living, and since he was such a loving person, I thought he should share the rest of his days with someone else. He said he'd already had the best, and if it were the other way around, I should do the same because I probably had a lot more time left here. He said it wouldn't really matter because we would dance later, in another sphere."

"That's sweet. Remember, you're still fresh on this healing journey. You'll know if and when the time is right to remove your ring, and what that means to you."

"I hope so."

"It may mean you're healing through acceptance. It may mean you're honoring Sam's wishes, or there may come a time when Lola finds a changed Lola who may want to enjoy life again."

"Well, I don't see that happening anytime soon."

"You may choose to explore life as a new Lola with another man, or maybe a woman, or even a new puppy. The possibilities will come to you when you're ready." Evie had spent years weighing out her options, but none of the possibilities ever seemed to resonate. Sheer survival had forced her to live with her newly inherited loneliness. There was nothing she could do nor anyone who could make her feel better and fill the vast canyon inside her, until Jack came along. Lola wouldn't get that opportunity, but hopefully something else would eventually fill her void. For now, she would only be able to find comfort in the vault of her memories, reading the obituaries, unable to glimpse a future. Evie knew the painful process.

Lola held out her hand. "I remember when he gave me this ring. It seems like it was just yesterday. He was so excited about it, he pulled over on the side of the road and slipped it on my finger one hour before the ceremony. We knew each other so well. He knew I would love it, and I did. He also magically knew my ring size, my shoe size, and my dress size."

"Nice. Did you have a grand wedding? Sam was such a classy man."

"We got married high on a mountaintop on a beautiful spring day. It was just Carol and Dan and a non-traditional officiant, who happened to be nine months pregnant. Sam was running the hospital at the time, and we both thought we would have a wedding ceremony, then deliver her baby on the sacred ground, but she made it through without going into labor."

Evie laughed. "It makes me happy to hear you share these memories. This is the miracle of healing."

Lola looked at the ring again.

"He was such a generous man and gave me so many beautiful things in our time together. When he gave me my first little black dress and a pair of red spikes, he explained that a man's sensuality is different from a woman's, and if we were going to have happy hour together forever, we might as well feel delicious while we were at it."

"Hmmm. Sassy, sexy Lola."

"Yes, it does feel good when a memory springs loose.

Although, I find it impossible to ever wear a dress or heels again."

"Then don't. If that's what you want. You can wear his boxers for the rest of your life if that's what feels right."

Lola's pressed her lips together, then smiled. "I miss how much we laughed together."

A grating sensation slipped through Evie. She shifted in her chair, admitting it was envy. Although she was so blessed to be a mother, she would never have that kind of passion with anyone. Lola and Sam were incredibly fortunate to have found each other and lived together in love for as long as they had. But then again, Evie may have had a few opportunities had she been open to them. Several men were convinced that Evie was the right one for them, but Evie never felt the same, didn't feel the spark, couldn't take the plunge, or commit to the happy-ever-after. Even when she was married to Jon for a short period of time, it was like living on the outskirts of matrimony. Now, she inhaled deeply and mindfully tiptoed toward the truth. The real reason she remained disconnected was because she was immobilized by fear, once again. *Breathe Evie, Breathe.*

Lola twisted the ring around her finger, curling her toes inside Sam's slippers. She swiped the newspaper to the floor and laid her head on the table. Outside, a branch scraped against the house as the wind began to pick up.

# TWENTY-ONE

Marc stood in an alley off Main Street, trying to light a cigarette in the rising wind. *Go jump in a lake*, the voices taunted. He hated that guy at the Super 8 motel for kicking him out, forcing him to leave, just like his sister had. He wasn't planning on hurting the girl in Walla Walla, Washington; he just wanted her panties. He had watched her undress through the neighboring window, and it aroused him into a frenzy, just like Evie was doing to him now. *Leave*, his sister had said. *Go jump in a lake*. When he felt raindrops, he gave up on lighting the smoke and stumbled on to find his car.

The gunmetal-gray sky darkened, heaved, and split open, dumping fat raindrops onto the valley floor. The wind kicked up and began whipping through the trees as thunder boomed and lightning flashed over Lake Camus and beyond.

As the storm ramped up, Josh and Ron splashed through the village in the Shine On truck with their headlights on and the wipers slapping full speed. They passed a guy stumbling down Main Street, like he was impaired. Josh pointed, "That looks like that dude we saw in the café on Sunday. Weirdo's getting drenched. And he's still wearing that coat."

Lightning flashed again. Ron yelled over the noise, "Good, it's raining and that flash was pink! We don't want the lightning to be white."

"Why's that?" Josh yelled.

"White lightning is the most dangerous. It means there's a low concentration of moisture and a high concentration of dust in the air. That was the case yesterday, but with this thunder, the showers are gonna be fierce." "Frickin' Romey is probably out there dancing in the rain, catching raindrops on his tongue. He's the only one on the planet who's having a sunny day in the middle of a northern tempest." Josh smiled, stuck his headphones on, and turned up the volume.

They pulled into the Super 8 parking lot, jumped out and ran for cover with their buckets over their heads. The steamy air suddenly cooled, and a gust of crosswind shook the motel doors and windows with a violent blast, while the entire building seemed to groan down to its foundation. Josh shot Ron a nervous look. Ron said, "Come on, let's do this!"

They each opened a door and began working fervently. It took them less than an hour to divide and conquer the inside windows of the first five rooms. Josh removed his headphones and headed over to find the soda machine and take a quick break.

Ron approached room number six and turned the sticky doorknob, pushed, and felt resistance. He peered in and saw the door was blocked by a pile of wet towels and clothes. He used his bucket and his knee to wedge the door open. Inside, the dresser was turned over and the drawers were on the floor. The TV was unplugged and tipped sideways. Ripped sheets, pillows, and blankets were stuffed under the table and two chairs were lying on the bed. Ron prided himself on the fact that he had seen more booze, drugs, and women than anyone else he knew, but now he realized—not true. The floor and counters were strewn with empty whiskey jugs, rotten food, full ashtrays, trash, and prescription bottles. The drapes were partially drawn and flapping as the wind howled and whistled through a crack in the window. Outside, black clouds and driving rain hit the balcony and a flash of lightning lit up the Super 8 sign. An undefinable stench caught him and for a second he considered he may have encroached upon the first murder scene in Pine Grove.

Ron thought he should back out of the room and run and tell Josh, but instead, pushed his way further in, picked up a handful of prescription bottles and read the labels. Treatment for schizophrenia, bipolar disorder. Haldol, Zeldox, Clozapine. Antipsychotics, typical and atypical, anti-tremor, side effects include dry mouth, dizziness, blurred vision, agitation, emotional blunting. The patient's name had been mostly scraped off the label of every bottle, with Marc D left on one bottle of Seroquel.

Stuck to the mirror were several yellow Post-it notes, scribbled with *Her. E. The One. !ETAH. ETAH. ETAH.* Ripped pages from a Pine Grove directory were stuck on the curtain with duct tape. He almost bolted, but thought, in a horror movie the body would be in the bathtub, so he crept to the bathroom and peeked in. The wall was covered with notebook paper, written in blue crayon !ETAH. He looked at the reflection in the mirror, HATE! and jumped. "Too fuckin' creepy!" He dropped his bucket and tripped out the door.

Ron pulled his stocking cap over his ears and put his hoodie up. He saw Josh rushing down the corridor with his bucket over his head. "We gotta get to the office and call Romey. I just saw some strange shit in six, and I wanna make sure I don't get blamed for it."

"What kinda strange shit?" asked Josh.

"Like hair-raising psycho shit. The place is all busted up, trashed out and totally macabre."

"Macabre?"

"Yeah, like fuckin' petrifying. Come on!"

They ran to the front lobby where the manager was replacing flashlight batteries in preparation for a power outage. His nametag said Preston and he had a snake tattoo on his neck. Ron asked to use the phone to call Romey but the line was dead. He then told Preston what he had encountered in room six. The manager said he had evicted the guy earlier that day because he didn't pay for the last five days' stay.

Ron was hyped up. He shook his head and slapped the counter. "Well, the room is completely trashed."

"No kidding?" Preston put the flashlight on the counter.

"It's bad, dude. Didn't you get a credit card and driver's

license? That's totally illegal and the whacko should pay for what he's done."

Josh bounced his bucket on his knee and nodded. "It's not our policy to take a credit card. This is nineteen ninety-eight. Cash is King." There was a loud clap of thunder and the lights began to flicker, then went out.

Marc parked the car near the cemetery entrance and sat watching the water stream down the windshield, the vision of Evie still sizzling in his mind. She was waiting for him that day at the lake, lying on the blanket, reading a book, almost naked in the scorching sun. She needed him. She lusted for him; he knew it! He must make her understand. That other girl in Walla Walla didn't understand him either, but Evie would. He'd make sure this time.

He took a drag of his cigarette and groped for the pea coat. He pulled the crumpled note out of the pocket and held it in front of his hazy eyes. *If you are interested in the true love story behind this Irish pea coat, please call.*

"See? She was trying to reach me!" He slammed his fist on his leg. "Why are you torturing me, Evie?" he screamed over the raindrops beating on the roof.

*She will pay for this and I will prove to her that she purposely wrote this note for me. She needs to know that the only true love story would be ours. Marc and Evie. Together. Forever.*

His mouth began to twitch. He could taste her and feel her in his thrashing pulse.

# TWENTY-TWO

By morning the rain had stopped, the sun shone brightly, and steam rose from the valley floor. Chrissy was in the Stein's parking lot approaching Romey's truck. Max had his head out the window, barking like a banshee.

"Hush Max. Go lay down." Max curled up on the seat and let out a sigh.

"Hi Romey," said Chrissy. "I was just gonna call you."

"You were, were you?"

"Yeah. We've got a situation that needs your help."

"Opportunity to serve! Whatcha got?"

"Well, our boys made a mess of the windows and the walls at Evie's house."

"Okay, what kind of mess? Don't tell me they had a dirt clod fight in the house." He smiled.

"No, it's actually worse."

"What happened?"

"They put something in the oven and the stove caught fire so there's like smoke damage on the ceiling and the walls."

"Wow, they were lucky they didn't burn the house down. Were they baking cookies?"

"No," she looked around, then back at Romey. "They were roasting a snake."

"Whoa! Good for them. Okay. Snake-smoke-wash. This is gonna be fun! I'll come up and take a look in a bit. Will you or Evie be there, say, around noon?" His heart quickened at the thought of seeing Evie.

"Yep. I'm headed there right now. Come over when you can. And I want to pay for it since Dillon was in on it."

"No worries. Hey, I like your hair, Chrissy. Wasn't it pink when I saw you last?"

"Yep. I switched it up. Getting ready for the fall, you know, auburn for autumn."

"Cool," he said. He opened the truck door and tossed a pepperoni stick to Max.


Dillon and Jack were by the shed nailing boards together. They both had skinned knees from crashing into each other on homemade stilts. They got tripped up on a rock in a mud puddle while chasing Rex around the yard. Evie and Chrissy were trying to muscle the kitchen stove out the back door.

"Gawd, it stinks in here," Chrissy said.

"I know. It's disgusting. I love your hair."

"Thanks. I'm mixin' it up." She pressed her hip against the stove and grunted. "Okay, pull."

Chrissy pushed, Evie pulled, and the stove gave way and crashed off the steps, taking the door jamb with it.

"Good job," said Evie. "I couldn't have done that by myself. Jack and I tried last night, but we weren't quite strong enough."

"Yeah, no kidding."

"That deserves a drink. You want a glass of wine?"

"Sure, but just a half glass," said Chrissy. "Water too, please. It's only eleven o'clock."

Evie went back into the stinky kitchen and thought, that's a first. She wants water *and* she said please and since when has she cared about the time of day to start drinking? Evie's instincts had been right. Something was shifting inside Chrissy, even though she hadn't said much since she'd told her about her meltdown at the hospital. She smiled to herself as she brought out the wine, glasses, and water, and they settled on the back step in plain view of the old stove. The burners and oven racks were lying in the grass, and the door was broken off.

Evie thought of all the huckleberry pies her aunt had baked in that oven, which she had happily consumed during her childhood visits over the years. She had loved watching her roll out pie dough with the old wooden rolling pin. Her aunt had lived alone and never worried about what other people thought. Her daily attire was a housecoat and thick, beige stockings, and she kept her white hair in a braid wrapped around the top of her head that made her niece think of a crown. She was not a small woman, but her voice was surprisingly tiny to Evie's ears. It seemed to her that she would put it away and didn't use it very much. Evie often stayed with her, never imagining that the bedroom she slept in would one day be hers.

"That is a 1950 Roper stove. Irreplaceable," said Evie. "Let's raise a glass and toast yet another classic never to be seen again."

"Yes, indeedy," said Chrissy bowing to the oven parts. "We thank you for your loyal service. Out with the old, in with the new!" They clinked each other's glasses and downed the wine.

"I appreciate your help, Chrissy. And thanks for calling the Shine On guys to clean up. I don't know why it's taken me so long to take care of this mess." *Maybe because I've been preoccupied with helping Lola and a nervous wreck about protecting Jack and trying to get all my work done, while Romey's sweet smile pops up uninvited in my mind and, most of all, trying to stay sane, knowing there is a stalker after me.*

"My pleasure, honey. Dillon was as much to blame as Jack. The boys are making a ramp, so we can get it in the back of the truck. I had a talk with Romey and told him what happened. That is one cheery guy, Mr. Shine On. He said it was actually going to be fun to do something out of the ordinary. He called it a snake-smoke-wash. Then he says something like, 'Good job to those boys for getting out there and living it up!'"

"Yeah, Romey's been known to be abnormally chipper. I can't quite figure him out." *But I'd like to try.* "Did you know he cuts his own hair? He carries scissors in his truck, pulls over onto the side of the road, and snips away."

"No way. The guy has more money than anyone I know. He owns like four houses. A nurse from the hospital rents a place from him. She said that once when he stopped by to check in and make sure things were okay, her husband offered him a beer or some weed, and Romey said no. He told them that whatever it is that makes people feel high, he has it naturally in his blood. He said he's blessed and feels good all the time. Anyway, you would think he could afford a haircut from the barber."

"I guess that's part of his charm. He's apparently too busy to take the time to sit in a barber's chair for fifteen minutes or to sit at his kitchen table and eat breakfast. When I was doing the Eastons' party, he had a cereal bowl sitting on his dashboard, like he was eating and driving at the same time. Funny guy. I'm just glad they're going to come and clean up this mess."

"Yeah, he said he'll be here by noon to have a look."

"Okay."

"I'm going to take Dillon to Drip 'n Sip for a slushy, and then maybe they can have a campout tonight. They can set the tent up in our backyard."

Evie set her glass down. "So, I guess you're not going to tell me."

"Tell you what?"

"Tell me where, why, what, and how did this transformation come about? I know we haven't seen much of each other in a while, but I see a big change. I love the color of your hair, and you look so healthy."

"Thanks. I don't know," said Chrissy. "I guess it was just time for a change. I listened to what you said about writing instead of numbing my feelings."

"Did you really try journaling? I was never any good at it."

"Yeah, I tried to write stuff down but it makes me depressed. And I blame Rob for everything. Blame, blame, blame."

"Yeah, that's called blamestorming."

"Well, it's messed up, and I'm sick of being pissed off all the time."

"Yeah, resentment is bad news." Evie thought of the hunt. How dangerous it is, swallowing the pit of resentment and feeling the tendrils twist and tangle through your innermost self.

"Well, I've been workin' on it." Chrissy pushed her lips out.

"I think we have the power to make ourselves miserable or happy. I'm proud of you. It takes courage to dig deep."

"It hasn't been easy."

"But, it's part of our journey. Everyone's got stuff to deal with."

"I know, and Rob reached out to me. He called before I had the chance to tell him I was gonna get my shit together."

"That's cool. You're still connected."

"I guess so. We've been talking on the phone, and we decided to work on ourselves first and then maybe we can think about being a family again."

"Oh, Chrissy, that's fantastic. It's amazing how your world will transform when you make an internal shift."

"I was thinking about Dr. Nedson, and how we were both so mean. We got in a fight in the OR and then he went out and had a massive stroke in his car. People at work were joking that

I'm a witch and will suck the life out of anyone who's mean to me. One doctor said, 'Don't be mean to Chrissy or your hair will catch on fire!' At first it seemed funny, until I saw that Red Ned was no different than me."

"That's why you butted heads."

"And now I can't apologize because he's dead. Can you believe it? Me and Rob completely screwed up our marriage. But, like he said the other night, if we can ruin it, we can fix it."

"Right. If you can forgive, healing will begin, followed by transformation. It's a glorious thing."

"One of the reasons I dyed my hair back to its natural color was because Rob told me he loved my beautiful auburn hair. I thought about how I was trying to punish both of us by being such a weirdo, and I really let it get out of control. But the real game changer for me was when Dill and I came home a while back and there was a horrible smell in the house, almost as bad as your snake hole."

"What happened?"

"Well, I got down on my hands and knees and crawled around, sniffing like Rex, trying to figure out what was dead under the house. Finally I tracked it to a vent in the bathroom floor."

"Eww."

"I asked Dillon if he could smell it and he said he peed down the heating vent."

"What the . . ."

"Right? I was like, what the hell Dillon, why would you do that and he said, 'Because my daddy doesn't love me.' I guess some kid in the park said Dillon had a big fat mom with pink hair and a dad who didn't live with him anymore because he didn't love him."

"Oh, no." Evie shook her head.

"Before I woulda shot some tequila and marched right over to the park to find the brat and give him hell for being a bully."

"So what'd you do?"

"I bawled like a baby."

"Wow. I'm sorry."

"Yeah. Then I thought, man, change is due here. And like you said it's our job to protect our babies, to love 'em, and teach 'em what's right."

"Did you tell Rob?"

"Yeah, and he called Dillon and had a man-to-man talk with him. And now I'm sober enough to see Dillon's been really happy lately. It was like my life was going by and I was missing it. I made an appointment with our lady plastic surgeon and was thinkin' about doing something drastic. She told me I'm fine the way I am and have good skin and I'm still young enough that I could lose weight on my own if I wanted to."

"That's great."

"She also said that taking a Benadryl around six o'clock in the evening would make me more interested in sleeping than stuffing my face, and it worked. I walk to STICH when I can, which feels really good."

"Again, I'm so proud of you, Chrissy." *If more people in the world would do some introspection and have the guts to change for the better, that would dissolve a lot of problems.* "But remember, my friend. It takes commitment and work." *Really hard work.*

"Oh, yeah," said Chrissy. I forgot to mention something else that's amazing."

"What's that?"

"Rob got his contractor's license."

# TWENTY-THREE

On Tuesday, the Shine On crew stood in the Drip 'n Sip parking lot.

"Listen up girls," said Romey. "It's not windy and we're not thirsty. He winked. "Good job making it through the storm yesterday. Man, I just love catching raindrops on my tongue. Some of God's greatest work is in a late summer storm, although Max hates thunder."

"Good to know he hates something other than me," said Ron.

"Yeah," said Romey. "So today Juan and Jake will start on the remodel over in Kings Canyon. The contractor, Rob, is the nicest guy. He put new windows in the bedrooms, so be careful not to scratch the glass when you remove the labels. I told him we would haul some of the junk to the dump for him, since we have the trucks and the manpower. He just got his contractor's license, so he's not fully equipped yet. He ripped everything out of the kitchen and the bathrooms, so the rubble and the old appliances are sitting in the driveway. Also, I got a call from Rob's wife, Chrissy, up on the hill, and she has a special request for us."

"Is that the big mama with the pink hair?" asked Ron.

"Actually, I just saw her and she's not so big anymore. She looks nice. Her hair is brown now, not pink."

"Hmm, I think she and Rob are separated," Ron wiggled his eyebrows.

"Dude," said Romey. "No one is really separated. We're all together as one big human family. Anyway, whoever can guess what Chrissy wants gets a free cup of coffee. It has to do with her neighbor Evie's place at the end of the road. And I may add that Evie is probably one of the few customers we have that isn't crazy."

"Um, Boss?" said Josh.

"Yeah, stud."

"I know you've been asked this before, and I think I remember the answer, but why is it that almost everyone is crazy except you?"

"Just good luck, my friend. Anyway, back to the girls on the hill."

"Um, let me guess," said Ron, "The girls said I shouldn't go up there while they're ovulating because they won't be able to resist me?"

"Try again, stud."

"Her kid hit a hardball and snapped off the chimney cap and she needs help fixing it?" said Josh.

"Nice try, but no."

"There's a cat stuck on the roof," said Jake.

"I'll give you a hint. It involves NSS."

"Nasty solvent stuff. We give up."

"I went up there to check it out and it's nasty, alright. We're going to need goggles and gloves for sure. There's a thick coating of brown goo on the inside windows and walls, and part of the ceiling. But as I always say, there's a positive to even the greatest of disasters. It could have been much worse, but the good news is, it's only in the kitchen."

"What happened?" asked Josh.

"There was an oven fire. I'm pretty sure her stove is trashed, but the rest we can clean. This is going to be fun." Romey raised his coffee cup and smiled.

"What burned?" asked Juan.

"Teriyaki rattlesnake."

Evie and Jack were driving to the village when they passed three Shine On trucks coming up the road for the kitchen cleanup. Romey stopped and rolled his window down. Evie did the same. "Good morning," she said.

"Good morning, Evie. Hey Jack." He took his sunglasses off and smiled. "We're going to be working at your house for a couple hours. It's probably best if you can stay away until we're done because we have to use some strong cleaning stuff and it doesn't smell very good."

"We will. And I'm sure anything you use is going to be a vast improvement over how it smells now."

"Yeah. We'll take care of it. See you back around 3:30 or 4:00 okay?"

"Great. Thanks again, Romey, I really appreciate it."

"It's my pleasure," he said. "I like your top. Is that coral?"

Evie flushed. "Yeah, thanks," she said and drove away.

Jack put his hands on his cheeks and said in a high voice, "Is that coral?"

Evie poked him in the ribs. "You hush."

Jack laughed. "I think Romey likes you Mom. He's really nice."

"Well, I like him too and you're right. Romey is very nice."

"Where's his little dog?"

"Hmm, not sure, but I'm so glad we finally are getting that mess cleaned up. That reminds me, we have to go over to Newport this weekend and get a new stove."

"Sorry about the snake mess, Mom."

"We're okay buddy. Like I told you and Dillon, I'm just glad you didn't get hurt. It can always be worse. If you learned a lesson and had a fun adventure at the same time, then that's living. There are plenty of boys who aren't as brave as you two, and probably spent their summer watching TV."

"But we don't have a TV."

"I know, and the snake thing wasn't as gross as the time you found a dead skunk down by the mailbox and tried to make a skunk skin cap out of it."

"That was cool."

"That was disgusting." Evie remembered waking up to a pounding headache and looking out to see Dillon holding a flashlight and Jack poking a stick at a dead skunk that was tied to a rope, hanging off the shop door and stinking to high heaven.

"Yeah," said Jack. "The reason it smelled so bad, is because that black oil drips out of the anal sacs. It's thick and gooey, like tar."

"Yuck. Well, again, it could have been worse. I was worried that the smell would sink its way into my tablecloths, but it didn't. That was a real blessing."

They pulled into the Stein's parking lot. Evie's heart thumped when she saw the Subaru parked near the shopping carts. She thought, we have to get out of here now, but Jack had already jumped out of the car and had approached the Subaru's window. She got out immediately and ran toward him. He pointed at the dashboard.

"Look, Mom, there's my Batman sock!"

Evie looked in and every nerve in her body snapped to attention. She stared at what appeared to be a dashboard shrine. Hanging from the mirror was a Pringles lid, tied with a piece of thread. Spread across the dash was *The Pine Tree* article of John Craven's party, with the picture of Evie wearing a purple dress, smiling up through the dirty windshield. She saw her book marker of Jack and the cat, the Batman sock, now dry and crusty with old mud, and to her horror, a polaroid shot of Evie at the lake, topless and sopping wet with Dillon on her back, his arms nearly strangling her.

Her eyes darted to the back seat, covered with dirty clothes, empty cigarette cartons, and whiskey bottles. In the passenger seat she spotted the red lapels of the pea coat, and her head began to fill with air.

"Let's get out of here, Jack." She grabbed his hand and ran back to her truck, jumped in and locked the doors. "Where are my keys?" she cried.

"In your hand, Mom."

There he was, beside the truck, with a dirty palm pressed against the window. Evie gasped, feeling like a wide-winged bird was beating its way out of her chest. She started the engine, crammed it into drive and peeled out. Jack leaned his face into her shoulder and scrunched his eyes closed.

"It's okay buddy. Marc is a bad man. He's not well. He's got something wrong with his head! He's driven by an evil force called mental illness and we're going to help him."

"What are we gonna do, Mom?"

"This is Tuesday, so we can stop the sheriff when he comes through town. He'll know what to do. What Marc is doing is called stalking, and it's against the law."

"But what about my sock and the bookmark I made you?"

"We can't worry about that right now. Let's go to the cafe and wait. You can get French fries."

"I forgot to tell you that when he came to our house he said he was going to marry you. Is that true, Mom?"

"Oh my God, no! I told you he's delusional! I'm not going to marry anyone, Jack. It's just me and you, buddy."

"Good. Because I told him, she's not gonna marry you. She's gonna marry me."

"I love you so much, baby."

Marc stood in the parking lot watching Evie speed off, his hands crushing a pack of cigarettes and a frozen burrito, *Cram,*

*cram,* yelled the voices. He needed to smash them. He hated that truck for taking her away and hated that kid for sitting so close to *his* Evie. He hated the Super 8 motel for kicking him out. He hated his sister for keeping her bike and making him take her car.

He got in the car, tossed the cigarettes in the passenger seat, and stared at his dashboard. His secret prizes: The kid's sock that she left on her truck mirror. He had watched her place it there before she headed to the beach, a bag over her lovely shoulder, her dress and long blonde hair gently moving as she stepped with bare feet over hot rocks and blistering sand, like an invincible lakeside nymph. The sock was surely something she had given the punk, and he was too spoiled to take care of it.

Marc rubbed his grimy thumb on the *Pine Tree* article. There was his girl, smiling for the camera, wearing an airy summer dress, holding a flower, so pure and proud. He flicked the plastic lid she had touched with her delicate fingers and watched it twirl from the rearview mirror. He had salivated in the heat of that day as he watched her put the chips on her tongue. The bookmark, another treasure that she had held in her hand. A thrill had rippled through his groin when he saw her leaning over the blanket, searching for these items, so desperate she even asked the dog where they were. He had felt such thrilling satisfaction when he stole the items while she was distracted by panic.

Now in the Stein's parking lot, he grabbed his booze, slid the bottle neck to the back of his mouth and poured, feeling the heat of whiskey burn his throat and hit his crawling guts. *Why is she making this so difficult? She needs to know that she belongs to me. She needs to know that, like the horrid old woman said, "Don't make me mad or you'll pay."* He threw the burrito into the backseat, started the engine, and drove slowly to the lake.

Evie darted her eyes to the rearview mirror and gripped the wheel so tightly her fingers blanched and her biceps bulged. Her lip began to quiver, and her voice cracked. "We've got to find the sheriff."

"It's alright Mom. Do we still get to have French fries?"

"Yes, and ice cream too!"

"Yay!"


Marc sat squinting in the afternoon glare. Hours passed and the sky blurred with too many colors, darkened, then faded into blackness. Late into the moonless night he sat, smoking, drinking, and licking the polaroid picture. His sticky tongue on her chest aroused him, and as his blood-engorged penis grew hard in his hand, he began to thrust his pelvis against the steering wheel. He would give her what she deserved and pound her hard and fast and mean. So hard her vessels would tear and split deep inside her and bruises would erupt across her tender flesh, rich purple-red underneath his pulsating loins. He held his hot throttle and let out the guttural groan of a dying animal.

He looked down and his self-hatred deepened when he realized the steaming liquid he was sitting in was no more than his own foul urine.

# TWENTY-FOUR

When the Shine On trucks pulled into Evie's place, Romey and the boys saw the makings of a wooden ramp and the burnt-out stove lying in the grass. Donned in goggles and gloves, they set about the snake-smoke-wash project. Using NSS and an excessive amount of elbow grease, they managed to dissolve and scrape off the thick dark film.

"Looks like creosote," said Josh.

"Yeah," said Ron. "Or coal tar."

"What's that, Mr. Smarty Pants?" asked Romey.

"It's the by-product of the production of Coke and coal gas from coal. It has both medical and industrial uses."

"Where do you learn this stuff?" asked Josh.

"You mean all these relatively useless facts?"

"It's a blessing and a curse, right Ron?" said Romey.

"Yeah, Boss. Did you get that from the book you're reading? I saw it on your dash, *The Agony and the Ecstasy*. Who reads that stuff?"

"I do. Because I'm headed to Italy in February."

"Sweet." Ron peeled off his gloves and adjusted his stocking cap. "By the way, what was the crazy Mrs. Baxter screaming about this morning?"

"Oh, she claimed you missed a spot on the bathroom window, and you didn't clean the window in her garage. She said she wasn't going to pay for the job. I told her I would come and take a look at the spot and solve the problem. When I got there, I saw the bathroom window was a real mess but pointed out that it wasn't Ron's fault. She'd tried to buff out a water drop with WD-40 and a wire brush. I told her we could replace the window because now it's ruined."

"Are you kidding me right now?" said Ron. "She's such a dufus. WD-40's a penetrating oil. It does anything but remove water drops. It acts as a lubricant, rust preventative, penetrant, and moisture displacer. She's bona fide crazy." He shook his head.

Romey grinned. "That's true, but instead of telling her she's bona fide crazy, I told her she strikes me as a woman who's got great taste and very high standards. I said it was a problem the size of a water drop not a flood, and she went berserk. She said she's never going to offer to hold my ladder again."

"What did you say to that?" asked Josh.

Romey shrugged. "I told her she didn't have to pay me if she didn't want to and that I'd still like her and say hello if I saw her on the street. I also explained that after all these years in this profession, I've never allowed anyone to hold my ladder. She asked me why not, and I said that anyone who's privileged enough to hold my ladder would have to be very special. That's when she totally lost it. She started shrieking so loud that even Max was scared. Before I left, I went and cleaned the garage window."

"Okay, Boss," said Ron. "My bad for not cleaning that window, but her garage creeps me out. She's got all that dog food and crates and junk she's been saving from a dog that died like five years ago. There's a water bowl that probably attracts rats."

"You're unbelievable, Boss," said Josh. "I wouldna cleaned her stupid garage window or given her the whole job for free, especially after the way she screamed at you."

"Well, I'm not really that gracious because when she calls me in three months to do her windows, I'll smile and say, no thank you. And remember, we're the only game in town."

Juan pulled up in the driveway and honked the horn. His truck was loaded with boards and appliances from the construction site. Romey looked at the truck bed and saw the same stove as the one lying in the grass, except that it appeared to be in perfect shape.

"Hey Juan, does that stove work?"

"Yes. Rob said it's from the fifties and works great, but the owner of the remodel wants all new appliances."

"Cool," said Romey. "Maybe we can hook it up for Evie. Come and check out the masters at work. We probably won't be having teriyaki anytime soon. Max, come!"

Romey looked in his truck for Max. He called him again. "Where are you, Maxwell Smart?"

He checked near the henhouse and in Evie's shed, but no Max. "This is a real head scratcher," he said. "Max! Hey, ladies, I'm going down the road to see if he's in the bushes. I taught him to poop in anyone else's yard but ours."

Evie found the sheriff having pie and coffee at the Hometown Cafe. While Jack sat at the counter and ordered French fries and ice cream, Evie went and sat in the booth across from Sheriff Wallace. He was a large man, who smelled like cherry tobacco. He was nice-looking in an old-fashioned way, with a thatch of gray hair and a big square face with a prominent nose. Evie squirmed in her seat and began telling him about her predicament.

"I'm glad you're here, Sheriff."

"What can I help you with?"

"Well, I'm being stalked, and I'm actually afraid of this guy who's been following me. I've never seen him before. He just came out of nowhere when we were at the lake. He's incredibly creepy and possibly pathological."

"Now, where did you get a word like that?"

"Sheriff, I studied psychology with an emphasis on deviant behavior. I'm not a paranoid person, but I'm telling you, this guy's weird, and it's not me I'm worried about so much as my boy, Jack. I mean, Marc acted like a total freak with him at the park and then we just saw him again at Stein's. He came up to our truck and then I got scared, and we came to find you."

The sheriff took a sip of coffee and asked, "Mark, huh? How do you know his name?"

"He told me. He said his name is Marc with a c."

"So, you've talked with this stalker?"

"Well, not really talked, but I did ask him to leave me alone."

"You *asked* him to leave you alone or you told him, under no uncertain terms, to leave you alone?"

"I can't exactly remember, but . . ."

"You can't exactly remember? Tell me what you *do* remember, and I can call it in."

"I'm sorry, Sheriff, but I'm nervous so I'm drawing a blank."

"I understand you're a bit shook up, but I do need a description of the guy. Height, approximate weight, hair color, eye color." He took out a small pad of paper and pencil from his shirt pocket.

All Evie could think of was how bad Marc smelled and how creepy and scary he was.

"How many times has he attempted to contact you?"

"I'm not sure, three, maybe four?"

"Where did you last see him and what was he wearing?"

"In the Stein's parking lot, like I said, and I don't know what he was wearing."

"What color is his hair?"

"Brown."

"Eyes?"

"Mud."

"Excuse me?"

"Um, brown, I guess."

"Stature?"

"Do you mean height or…?"

"Yes, I mean how tall is he?"

"I don't know, average-tallish I guess.

"What about weight?"

"I don't know."

"Is he a scrawny guy or a real porker?"

"I guess somewhere in between?"

"What about anything obvious?"

"What do you mean?" She thought of the diastema.

"I mean deformities, birthmarks, handicaps, you know, like a missing finger, giant wart on his nose, a limp."

Evie thought of the rash on his chest and his dirty hand pressed on her truck window. "He walks weird, kinda off balance, and he has a split between his front teeth and a rash on his chest. And he's dirty, looks like a homeless person, but I don't know if he is."

"What is the make and model of his car, if he even has one, or is he a foot-stalker?" he smirked. "Or possibly a bicycle-stalker?"

Evie's lips began to quiver. *He doesn't believe me.* "Gray Subaru Outback with Washington plates. And there's an empty bike rack on the back." She looked over at Jack sitting at the counter. Kara was giving him a cup of maraschino cherries for his ice cream.

Panic began to grow inside her as she flashed back five years when Jack was three and they were in the city shopping at Mervyns. Standing among a sea of circular clothes racks, she suddenly saw Jack was gone. "Jack!" she cried. She looked across the department store to the automatic glass doors, opening and closing, droves of faceless shoppers going in and out. Outside, to the big scary world full of kidnappers, perverts, and child molesters.

She ran to a counter for help. "My little boy is missing!" she cried. "Do you have a security guard or someone to help me, please, please!" A male clerk calmly asked her, "What was he wearing?" Her brain went blank, and she could only scream, "I don't know what he was wearing! I can't remember!" She threw herself down on the floor to die, right there in Mervyns—a welcomed death if Jack was truly gone.

She was unaware that people began to gather around her. Everything went silent, and the old feeling of terror began to consume her. Her field of vision started to shrink. She tried to hold the queasiness and the tumult of emotions at bay, but she was defeated. She would not survive if anything happened to her baby.

Then, through the dime-size opening in her vision she saw Jack's red sneakers. He was standing inside a clothes rack, hanging onto the center pole, sneaking a piece of candy he had found on the floor.

"Evie?" the sheriff said. "Did you hear what I just asked you?" She looked at him blankly.

"License plate number? Did you get it?"

"Um, oh, yeah part of it. I remember thinking about it. 1BKR, but sorry I don't remember the rest."

"Okay, 1BKR, that's a start. Listen, take a minute to cool your head, and don't worry, we'll get him."

"Okay, thank you. I'm going to have some water and try to be more helpful.

I'm sorry, but when I get scared, which isn't often, I mean most things don't affect me anymore unless my kid or any kid is in danger or lost or, say, they get bit by a rattlesnake or almost drown in the lake, then I can't help myself, Sheriff."

"I understand." He tapped his pencil on the edge of the table. "And this isn't meant to make you feel any worse, but it's a fact that more women are stalked than we hear about. Oftentimes a stalker will keep it to himself, and the victim is completely unaware that she's being watched. Or followed. Or photographed. And when the whacko decides to shake her up a little, he proceeds in full pursuit. It's sick is what it is. If he's really a stalker, then right now is when the fun starts for him—once he sees you're scared. If you know anything about deviant behavior, you know that stalking and rape are about control."

Evie nodded and bounced her legs up and down.

"Now, if you'll excuse me for a minute, I'm gonna go to the patrol car and make a call to my brother-in-law. He's a detective in Clarkston and Eastern Washington's his jurisdiction. He may be able to pull the plate."

Evie thought about what the sheriff said about control. The day at the lake, the parade, and the rummage sale when Marc appeared out of nowhere. *Is everything under control?* And, *Well, if it isn't the girl who's got everything under control.* Her palms were clammy, and her stomach cramped.

When the sheriff left, Evie glanced over at Jack. There were three saucers, a bowl and two glasses in front of him. He was licking his fingers and twisting back and forth on the stool. She needed a minute to pull herself together, so she told Jack she'd be in the restroom and to come get her if he needed her.

Alone by the sink, she splashed cold water on her face and the back of her neck. She leaned into the mirror and didn't recognize herself. Her vision dimmed as she had a visceral flashback of standing alone at sixteen years old, staring in a mirror, looking for herself. She covered her face and began to cry. It was almost fourteen years ago when everything went black. They were sitting in the car, ready to go, Dad behind the wheel, Mom in the front seat, and Evie, Ellie, and Turbo in the back. They would drop Evie off at Lori's house and then take Ellie to summer camp close to the Canadian border.

Evie and her best friend Lori were sixteen, and Lori was the only teenager in the world who had a television in her bedroom. They would stay up until the sun rose the next morning. How many thousands of times Evie wished she had stayed in the car. "Come with us," Ellie pleaded, and Evie touched her baby sister's sweet cheek and explained, like she had the night before that she would miss her and loved her with all her heart. Selfishly, Evie just wanted to be with Lori, in her room, watching MTV because they had heard it was naughty. "Come with us," her mom had said, and Dad said, "Let her go. She's not interested in summer camp anymore." And Evie knew, as her hormones raged, that something was ending and something else was about to begin. The thrill of sharing teenage secrets with Lori was overpowering. They'd promised each other they would stay up all night. "All girls need their secrets," Dad said, "it's part of growing up." Evie had leaned over her mom's shoulder and pulled the visor mirror down. "Are you wearing eyeliner?" asked Mom. "Yes," replied the girl-almost-woman. Then, with a defiance she couldn't control, she added, "Lip gloss too."

Evie held a wet paper towel over her eyes and inhaled deeply. She would stay until her breathing became steady enough to leave the restroom.

Sheriff Wallace returned to the cafe and sat in the booth. Kara followed him with her eyes, pursed her lips, then picked up the coffee pot and walked over to him.

"More coffee, Sheriff?" she asked.

"Nah, I'm good for now."

"What's going on? Is everything okay with Evie? I asked Jack but he said he can't talk about the bad man."

"The bad man, huh. Do you know who he's referring to?"

Kara set the coffee pot on the table and hiked one knee onto the seat where Evie had been sitting. She glanced toward the restroom and said, "Probably that guy she likes. He came in here last Sunday, and I heard him say something about them being lovers."

"Lovers?"

"Yep. I heard him tell Romey they were having a lover's quarrel."

"Brown hair?"

"Uh huh."

"Medium build?"

"That's him. I remember thinking it was weird that it was warm outside, and he was wearing a long, black coat."

"Hmm," said the sheriff and jotted a note on his pad.

"He didn't order anything, and he kinda left in a hurry. Maybe they were gonna meet or somethin'. I dunno."

"Did you hear or see anything else? Anything that might lead you to believe that this could be a bad man?"

"No, not really. Evie and Chrissy were sittin' right here in this booth with their boys. They all ordered pancakes. When the guy came in and walked over to the counter, the boys were playin' with dominoes, and Evie came over to talk to him for a second. Then he left. It was the Gabilan twins' birthday, so there was an awful lot of commotion in here. All's I can say is I haven't seen him in Pine Grove before."

Kara saw Evie coming out of the restroom. She took her coffee pot and quickly went back to the counter. She smiled at Jack, who was sliding a French-fry through his ice cream. Evie came back to the booth and sat down. "Did you find out anything?"

Sheriff cleared his throat and said, "We sure did. My brother-in-law found a guy with a hell of a rap sheet who may be the guy you're talking about. He's from a mental facility in Aberdeen, Washington. Really messed up and on all kinds of psych meds. But then, out there on the west coast, they're all crazy and gettin' weirder every day."

"Well, what is he doing here in Pine Grove? Did he, um, hurt someone in Aberdeen?"

"Got a sister he'd been staying with in a trailer park outside of Walla Walla, Washington. Apparently took a bus to her place from Aberdeen about eight weeks ago. There's a prison in Walla Walla, so it attracts the bottom dwellers. Allegedly he slit the window screens of his sister's neighbor girl and stole all her gaunchies."

"Gaunchies?"

"Yeah, you know, skivvies, thongs, underwear, whatever you girls call 'em nowadays."

Evie shifted on the bench and looked around to see if anyone else had come in and could hear them talking.

"She kept buying new ones and then came home and her underwear were missing again. It happened five times."

Evie cringed.

"Well, the sister came home and found Marc overdosed but still alive, lying on the floor with panties around his neck and his arms and legs. She called the police and the neighbor girl was brought to identify her undergarments."

Evie slid her hands between her thighs to stop her legs from shaking. The lights began to dim around her. The sheriff's voice droned on in the background. She tried to listen; she had to for Jack's sake.

"But the neighbor girl got scared off and decided not to press charges. That's when the sister gave Marc some money, grabbed her bike off the car rack, threw him the car keys and told him to get out. She said, "go jump in a lake" and we suspect that's how he found Camus. He's a real piece of work"

Evie sat on her hands. She let out a long breath she didn't realize she was holding.

"He's severely ill. . ."

"Yeah, I'd say so."

". . . and the best my brother-in-law can figure, is he took her literally and spotted Lake Camus on a map and drove to it. That's where he found you. It was purely coincidental. The only missing part is, why you?"

Evie's shoulders rose up and back. She sucked in air between her teeth and patted the table edge. "He saw my breasts."

"Excuse me?"

"It was on July first, and I was at the lake with my son, and his friend Dillon got smacked by a wake and almost drowned, and Marc appeared out of nowhere. I had just pulled Dillon out of the water, and during the commotion, my bathing suit top came off. I know it sounds crazy, but I was so shook up, I didn't notice it."

"Well, it's obvious he did. This makes sense now. He believes you have offered him your, you know, self. He's obsessed with you"

"So what can we do to stop him from stalking me?"

"Between Washington and Idaho, there's a good chance we'll get him. I'm sorry to say that sometimes these stories don't end so well. I don't think I need to get graphic, but you may be in real danger."

"No. Yes, I understand."

"I'm gonna call the detective back. I'd like you to go home and lock your doors."

"I can't go home."

"Why not?"

"Well, there are window cleaners at my house, for one." Evie thought she must sound like a real nut case. The sheriff frowned. She said, "Plus, he knows where I live."

"Okay, I'll escort you wherever you need to go, but when you're ready, your home might be the safest place. We can secure you and your son there, and keep an eye on you both, and the surrounding area."

"Thank you, Sheriff."

"Unless there is somewhere else you can stay during the search. Do your parents live nearby, or any other relations you may want to call?"

"No." Evie stood up, shook her head, and walked to Jack at the counter. She tried to smile and keep her voice steady. Being a mother doesn't give you the luxury of freaking out in front of your child, she thought. "Looks like you finished your ice cream, Buddy. It's time for us to go home now."

"Do me and Dillon still get to sleep in the tent tonight?"

"Not tonight, sorry." She put a five-dollar bill on the counter without letting Jack see her hand shaking, and they walked out with the sheriff behind them. Kara waved and said, "Thanks and bye-bye!"

Sheriff Wallace followed them as they drove down Main Street in what seemed like slow motion. Evie noticed signs posted along the street that said "Max is missing. Please have him call Romey when you find him. Small white terrier with a great big bark."

"Oh no," said Evie. "I like that little dog. I hope he's okay."

It was approaching evening, and Evie hoped the sheriff

wouldn't turn on his flashing lights, or worse yet, his siren. Another "Missing Max" sign was stuck to her mailbox. Evie pulled in the driveway, and they got out. The sheriff stayed in his cruiser with the window rolled down.

"I'll go inside the house and check things out," he said. "I'll go in the back door. Stay behind me."

"Okay but watch out because the back doorknob gets jammed, and Jack may have to crawl through the window." She noticed the broken stove was gone.

The sheriff got out and walked toward the house. "You don't have a key?"

"Only to the front door, but we rarely use it. That lock isn't so great either. This is an old house, as you can see, but we've never had to worry about locking up."

The sheriff placed a hand on his holster, and Jack pressed up against his mom. They followed as the sheriff went to the back door and turned the knob with ease. "Seems fine to me."

"Hmm," said Evie, stepping in behind him. The sheriff turned on the light and proceeded into the living room. Jack walked in and said, "Wow!" The kitchen was spotless and smelled clean and fresh. Even the ceiling was shining. There was a stove that looked like her old wrecked one, but in excellent shape. On the counter was a note that said, "Hey Evie, I noticed the bulb is broken on the outdoor eave. I can take care of it tomorrow, no problem. Also, it's my policy that there's never a charge for disaster clean-up. Enjoy the stove, and please let me know if you see my dog. Stay young and happy! Romey."

Evie leaned against the counter, smiling at the note. Her heart had been racing all day, but now it was more like a little twirl in her sternum. *What a very kind guy Romey is, and he's so nice to Jack. I think I'll roast him a chicken.*

She heard the sheriff coming down the stairs. "All clear," he said. "Now, let's wedge something against the front door and keep all the lights on. I'll post some surveillance at the bottom of your road."

Jack's eyes widened, and Evie put her arm around his shoulders. "It's gonna be alright, Buddy. We're safe."

Sheriff nodded. "Yeah, not to worry Jack; give me a hand with this cabinet."

The three of them pushed the heavy pine armoire against the door, and Evie turned on the porch lights.

The sheriff jingled his keys. "You two just stay put and get a good night's sleep. I'll check back with you in the morning and most surely let you know when we get the guy." He set his card on the counter. "Call me direct if you need to."

*Breathe, Evie, Breathe.*

# TWENTY-FIVE

It was well past the midpoint of nightfall and the stars bristled like fireflies in their deep black bed. Marc was behind the wheel again but had no idea which direction he was driving, as the car seemed to float out of town. He threw his head back and howled like a wolf. His hands were sweaty and sticky on the wheel, finding it hard to perform the simple task of steering the car on the road. His head felt like a blocked drain with a taste in his mouth to match. There was a terrible stench. Reeking of himself? He knew that smell too well. He took another swig of whiskey as he drove along the highway. His lit cigarette fell out of the ashtray and rolled under the seat, but he was too blurry to reach for it. He stared at the soggy polaroid that was taped to the rearview mirror. He could barely see the breasts that were still haunting him, agitating him like a beast in a thunderstorm. *Cram, cram,* screeched the voices.

When he left his sister's house in the trailer park, he was peaking during a six-week-long manic phase and had done as the voices instructed and went in search of a lake. Then, there she was. Her. Evie. Luring him to her. He would make her understand that she was his now. How cruel she was. She knew exactly what she was doing that day at the lake. She pretended she was interested in saving that scrawny kid, when really, she was pulling off her top just to taunt him. She had openly offered him her breasts—her nubile orbs for his sucking alone. The milk of life would fix him, repair his ravaged mind, and replace the dank, fetid water they poured down his throat. They called it *medication*. His mouth was sour with hunger, needing to pin her down and lodge her erect pink nipple in the sharp trap between his front teeth. Thrilling bondage, no escape without mutilation. It was her he needed, and her he would have. He blindly accelerated.

The next morning Evie and Jack were collecting eggs in the henhouse. Evie was edgy, trying to shake off the previous restless night. She was so rattled, she had stared at the ceiling for hours with the lights on, staving off thoughts of the blocked door and all that the sheriff had said. Her mind swam with confusion and burning questions: Were they safe in their own house? Was the knob on the back door really fixed? Who was standing watch at the end of their road? And although she had told herself and God that she would no longer question the ways of the universe, she couldn't help but wonder why this was happening and what it meant karmically to have paid the dues she had and yet, still have to endure this? Why couldn't the world be graced with good men like Sam and her dear father and Romey instead of wretched, horrible tormentors like Marc who could be out there lurking in the dark.

Evie thought, I am not being paranoid. This is pure, valid, earned fear. She turned out her bedroom light and crept to the window. The lights from the house cast a twenty-foot glow across the garden with nothing but blackness beyond. Was he watching her? She dropped to the floor, cold and shaking.

When she finally fell asleep, Evie had a nightmare that Marc had slid the armoire aside and entered the house, wearing Sam's coat. He came after her, gripping a knife in one hand and the little dog, Max, in the other. There were speeding cars and flashing lights and, somewhere in the distance, she heard sirens. Then Jack disappeared. She awoke in a panic, soaked with sweat, and crawled to Jack's room to sleep on the floor beside his bed.

Now in the light of day, she was wearing the white tee shirt and shorts she had slept in. Her long hair was tied into a messy knot with a scrunchie. She still worried that Marc was coming after her, that he would appear at any moment. The sheriff said there would be surveillance, but she wasn't sure what he meant by that and was too scared to go down the road and look.

Jack was petting his big red hen and gently trying to extract the two warm eggs she was sitting on. When they heard a car coming up the road, Evie dropped an egg, and it splattered on the ground at her feet.

Romey pulled up and got out of his truck, holding a light bulb. "Good morning, Evie. Hey, Jack."

"Hey," said Jack.

"Good morning," said Evie, clutching the egg basket.

"I hope it's okay I came to replace that bulb like I said I would."

She was flooded with relief. "Oh, of course. That's so nice of you. And I really appreciate the clean-up, but the stove, what do I owe you for *that*?"

"Ah, it's all good. But if you want to cook something and test the oven out on me, I'm available." He grinned.

"That's funny. I was kinda thinking the same thing, but I've been distracted and sort of—well, I don't know—unfocused." She wanted to tell him everything. She was so stressed from keeping it all built up inside her. She hadn't even had a chance to tell Chrissy.

"I understand. I've been preoccupied myself because I can't seem to find Max. I hardly slept at all last night." He tapped the lightbulb on his palm and shook his head.

"Yeah, I read your note. And we saw the "Missing Max" signs." She looked at his furrowed brow and could see he was very concerned. It made her feel like they shared something in common.

They were both scared, for their own reasons.

"Did you walk backwards?" Jack asked.

Romey looked at him. "Sorry? Did I walk backwards?"

"Yeah. You know, when you lose something, you walk backwards."

Evie smiled. "He's referring to retracing your steps."

"Yeah," said Jack. "So, you're standing here and you go

backwards until you're at the place you last saw your dog. It works every time."

Romey scratched his head and closed his eyes for a second. He had been thinking all along that he had lost Max right here at Evie's while they were cleaning the kitchen, but now he realized he hadn't brought Max with him.

"Where were you before you came here yesterday? When we saw you driving up here, Jack noticed you didn't have Max with you."

"Right." He nibbled his lower lip and Evie saw how vulnerable he was, a little boy who had just lost his best friend.

"I was cleaning that crazy Mrs. Baxter's windows. That's right. I went back to do her garage window yesterday."

"Well then," said Jack, "if you walk backwards, you'll probably find him in her garage. I found my rooster that way."

"Wow, thanks for that Jack! I'm going to head down there right now. You two wanna come with me?"

Evie brushed the hair off her face. "Sure," she said. "Can we come back and have some eggs?"

"That sounds awesome." Romey went around and opened the truck door. "Hop in. Sorry about the coffee cups on the floor."

Evie set the basket on the front step, and they climbed in the Shine On truck. Romey handed her the lightbulb, and as they drove away with Jack seated between them, she noticed all the lights were still on in the house and on the porch—all but one—and she felt safe for the first time in weeks.

"Wow, Romey!" said Jack. "You've got a car phone."

"Yep."

"Can I call Dillon? We're gonna go right past his house."

"Sure. Just push the numbers. It's on speaker."

Jack plugged in Dillon's number, and Chrissy's voice boomed. "Hullo?"

"Hi Chrissy, it's Jack. Can you tell Dill to go out on the porch?"

"Okay."

"Bye." He pushed the button and said, "Mom, can you roll your window down."

Evie smiled and put the window down. Chrissy and Dillon were standing on the porch. Jack leaned over his mom and waved out the window. As they drove by Chrissy yelled, "What the hell."

At the bottom of the road were two highway patrol cars and a firetruck with flashing lights. Next to a huge detour sign, a fireman was redirecting traffic. There was a long line of semitrucks, trailers, and cars waiting to go through an orange roadblock. Evie was confused, thinking the "surveillance" was so conspicuous.

"What's going on?" Evie asked.

"I heard there was an accident, and they're still trying to clean it up. I know how to get around it." Romey put his right blinker on and maneuvered through the line toward the village.

"That's terrible," said Evie, as she shifted in her seat and felt a stab in her chest. She took a deep breath and held it to the count of four, something a counselor had recommended she do whenever she heard an ambulance siren. She wondered if Sheriff Wallace was at the scene and if he was going to come over this morning and tell her they caught the guy. She was so happy to be with Romey, she had temporarily forgotten about Marc.

They turned off Main Street and pulled up in front of Betty Baxter's house. Evie remembered when she was hired by Mrs. Baxter to do a fifteenth birthday party for her dog, but then the dog had died the day before the party. Poor Mrs. Baxter was inconsolable and screamed at Evie like it was all her fault. *No wonder Romey calls her crazy Mrs. Baxter.*

Romey shut the truck off. "I'll just go take a peek. Be right back. You guys good?"

"Yes," they said.

They watched as Romey got out and walked over to the old green garage and opened the rickety double door. Max sprang out and jumped right into Romey's arms. "Hey Maxwell! Boy, am I happy to see you." Max whined and wagged and licked Romey's face. "Keep your tongue outa my ear," he said and set him down. Max ran to the truck and jumped onto Jack's lap. Romey got in. "Let's get outta here before Crazy sees us." He started the engine.

When they got to Evie's house, Sheriff Wallace was standing on the front porch smoking a pipe. Evie's heart quickened. "Jack, why don't you run over to Dill's. You can invite him for breakfast if you want. I'm going to talk with the sheriff."

"Did he get the bad guy?"

"I'm not sure honey, but we're going to find out."

"Can I take Max to play with Rex?"

"Sure," said Romey. They got out, and Jack and Max ran out the driveway.

"What bad guy?" asked Romey.

Evie felt a chill and crossed her arms tightly. "Oh, there's this weird guy that's been sort of hanging around and—I guess, like following us and—he's um— he's a stalker." She didn't want Romey to see that she was scared, embarrassed, and angry at the same time, but when he looked into her eyes, it was apparent.

The sheriff puffed his pipe and watched as Romey stepped forward and put his hands on Evie's shoulders. She leaned into him and tried not to cry. His Shine On tee shirt smelled fresh and clean, like dish soap.

"Let's see what the sheriff has to say," he said. "It's going to be okay. I've got your back."

Music to her ears.

They walked toward the sheriff as he tapped his pipe on the railing and stepped off the porch. "Well," he said. "You probably heard the commotion and saw we got a big mess out there at Layman's."

Evie instinctively put her hand out and Romey took it. She leaned closer to him, which was even more comfortable the second time around. "What happened?" Romey asked.

"The sonabitch crashed out there last night." He pointed his pipe toward the west. "From what we can figure, he was grossly inebriated and driving like he was in a high-speed chase. Only problem was no one was chasin' him. Unless it was his own demons."

Evie squeezed Romey's hand. "Was he . . . were there . . . " she couldn't speak.

"Yes, it was that Marc guy we were looking for. Him and his sister's car are history. It was a fatality, but fortunately the trucker he hit was not injured badly."

A weight lifted off Evie's shoulders and took with it the panic that had absorbed her for weeks.

"Thank you, Sheriff," she said. "Thank you for everything."

"Yeah," said Romey. "Thanks. I didn't realize all this was going on."

Sheriff put out his hand. "Well, it's behind us now. I'll get you a copy of the report since we filed Evie's complaint not long before the fatality. Take care of her."

"I will," said Romey, and they shook hands. Sheriff tipped his hat and walked to the cruiser.

Evie could feel her blood coursing through her veins and pounding in her temples. Although the fear factor had lessoned slightly, an ominous cloud hung before her. Now that Marc was gone, she somehow felt responsible for taking the man's life. After all, she had threatened to kill him herself, and now he was dead.

The sheriff had said that Marc was obsessed with Evie. She honestly knew what it was like to live and breathe, completely obsessed with the one person who relentlessly torments you. Marc had hunted Evie, just as she had hunted the drunk driver who took her family. It was clear to her now, the impaired kid was young, stupid, and reckless, just as Marc was a dangerous, mentally ill, tortured soul. Both were destined for a horrifically tragic ending.

Evie inhaled deeply. *Breathe Evie, breathe.*

Romey looked at her. "Are you okay?"

"Yes, I am now. Thank you for being here. It's been kind of awful."

"Yeah, sounds like it. Was the guy really stalking you?"

"Yeah. I've tried to figure out if I did anything to make it happen, but I don't think so. I got scared and wanted him to go away, but I didn't expect him to die."

"Of course this wasn't your fault. I remember seeing him talk to you in the café and thinking it was a little strange." Evie's faced flushed remembering that day.

"Then my guys saw that he was checked into the Super 8 and destroyed the room."

"Oh, my God."

"Trust me, Evie. You are a perfectly normal person under totally abnormal circumstances."

Somehow Evie thought that was a really nice compliment.

"Thanks."

As the sheriff drove away, Jack and Dillon came running up the driveway with Max and Rex.

"Is breakfast ready?" asked Jack.

"Let's do it," said Evie.

They went inside and Evie made scrambled eggs while Romey talked to them about places like Costa Rica, where the Orb spiders were huge, but harmless and the Howler monkeys could make your ears ring. He said that in Central America they ate black beans with their scrambled eggs, so Evie opened a can of black beans, dumped them into a saucepan, and heated it on the shiny stove.

The four of them were seated at the table, each with a plate of fresh eggs. Although she was still shook up, Evie thought how nice and natural it felt, their first meal together. She brought the bubbling hot pot of beans to the table and as she spooned out a portion for Romey first, they heard a *tink* as the beans and the can lid landed on his plate. Jack looked at Dillon, and they both started giggling.

"My mom's a good cooker," said Jack.

Well, thought Evie. *I may as well add embarrassment to this gamut of emotions. Welcome to our crazy life, Romey.*

# TWENTY-SIX

The report estimated it was around midnight at Layman's Curve when the Subaru crashed head-on with a forty-ton log truck and crumpled like a tin can. The car instantly ignited in a fiery blast, glass shattered, and sprayed hundreds of feet. Hot metal and searing flames shot into the night air. The driver, wearing no seat belt, was killed on impact. The first responders' attempt at recovering the ejected carnage was futile. Among the smoldering rubble, some bagged up fragments of burned flesh and bones, while others triaged the battered trucker. "Fully loaded," he said. "Steel grill saved me. Didn't see it coming. He was doing at least a hundred, no headlights. Crazy bastard."

Forever in the ravine below, amidst years of debris, abandoned cars, and rotting carcasses, lie the remains of a wool pea coat from another time, stolen from another life.

Now charred and shredded, it had lived its glory days in love and had been worn with swagger, passion, and pride. The lovers had laughed and kissed and danced on cobblestones in the company of the peacoat, romantically personified as if it held magic within its lining. During a pelting rainstorm on the wild Atlantic coast of Ireland, drenched to the marrow, Sam had opened the coat, and Lola nudged inside and burrowed into his chest. He wrapped her up tightly, and over the howling wind, her hair around her neck like a slick scarf, he pressed his lips to her ear and said, "Tell me again my love, I didn't hear you. Did you say you are allergic to wool?" They laughed and howled with the wind and then ran for cover into a dim and lively pub where drunken Irish sang and danced in a Gaelic foot- thumping, handclapping ritual. The lovers hung the coat near the crackling fire and drank Guinness and Irish whiskey. They were fueled with joy, listening to lusty voices and ancient instruments. Smoke swirled, and pints slammed, and the thunder of laughter settled into their bones. When they were heated and flushed, they retreated to their cozy inn, and slipped into the place they knew best. They lay in bed entangled, two flames burning as one. *The dance of life . . .*

Lola sat with a cup of coffee reading the *Pine Tree News*. There was an upcoming town meeting, and they were looking for volunteers to help plan the Big Blast. I'm not going to be party to any of that, she thought. I'm barely able to fend for myself, let alone help the whole town plan a gala. She finished reading the paper. A new baby girl named Ava was born, a lost dog named Max was found, and an out-of-state car crashed in the night.

Lola pushed the paper aside and looked out the window. There were some streaks on the glass left from the last rain. Time to call Romey, she thought. It just puts me in a mood to have the windows cleaned. It was the kind of mood she needed right now. Sparkling windows with no dirt or streaks or specks of bugs. Just clean and pure and open to the world outside. She closed her eyes, remembering she didn't have that, growing up in the convent. Windows were high up on the wall, small slits with tiny iron bars, like a jailhouse or a prison where evil couldn't slip in, and piety couldn't slip out. Where only the filtered light of day periodically sifted through, as if the outdoors and the orphan girls were meant to avoid one another. She felt her throat get tight. Silly to get a tight throat over a memory that has no use, she thought. Then she admitted to herself that distant memories were percolating as Sam's one-year marker day was approaching.

# TWENTY-SEVEN

Saturday morning Chrissy read about the crash in the *Pine Tree News* and felt so weird knowing Marc had been killed. She was relieved that Evie and Jack were safe after learning from Evie how serious the whole stalking thing had become. Fortunately for Evie, the sheriff and Romey were there to help. Chrissy was also grateful that no one else was hurt, including Rob, since he and his crew were working in King's Canyon and frequently drove around the deadly Layman's Curve.

Chrissy rolled up the newspaper and whacked her thighs several times, satisfied that they were starting to feel firmer. She was anxious to organize her day. Dillon had spent the night at Jack's again, and she had a lot to get done. Bursting with energy, she set about cleaning the house. She polished the counters, swept the front porch, and vacuumed the heating ducts. She cleaned the oven, defrosted the freezer, and flipped the mattresses. All the while she was thinking of the positive changes that had taken place internally and in her immediate world, the world within her control. She no longer panicked about running out of time to become who she really wanted to be and no longer felt that she was late for her own life, standing in a fog and watching it float by.

After realizing that Rob had been gone for more than a half a year, which in Dillon's life was a good chunk of time, she was doing interpersonal work and taking charge. She had a sense that the future was bright and the year two thousand would be the best year ever. Rob was coming home for good.

Since she had completed the Drug and Alcohol Behavioral program, something in her had shifted. Evie had recommended the course that was intended to help people address their negative behavior and make positive changes. The program had promised that through hard work and commitment, a person could turn a bad situation into an opportunity. Just like Evie had told her many times, we have the power to change our behavior if we have the motivation and the tools to do so.

When she went to work on Monday morning, Chrissy's enthusiasm took a nosedive. She found herself standing in another operating room scene that was intolerable, and this time she was fed up.

As Chrissy stood, fuming and cleaning up her instrument table, she took a deep breath and tried to calm down. She thought of how the program had taught her to set priorities and be honest about what she really wanted. She had worked through half of the eighty pages of self-evaluation when she broke down and showed up on Evie's doorstep crying hysterically with the workbook in her hand. Evie had helped her get through it as they sat and finished the homework together. After perseverance and digging deep, Chrissy could honestly say she was ready for a big change and was convinced it was finally time to be a better role model to Dillon, rekindle her marriage, and reevaluate her work situation. She had learned many valuable things in the class and begrudgingly came to terms with her misuse of alcohol, which, with the amount and the frequency she was consuming, was causing depression, high blood pressure, and memory loss. She learned that she was at risk because of her family history, and was determined to avoid becoming her mother at all cost. She hadn't had a drink in more than forty days, but if she had to deal with STICH any longer, she possibly couldn't trust herself to stay sober.

She tossed the retractors in the rinse water and scowled. Although she enjoyed working with this surgeon, why did they always have to schedule her to work in the same room with the one anesthesiologist she detested? Oh yeah, she thought, in the program they said that life would keep presenting the same challenges until you figured out how to deal with them constructively. *But why is it so fricking hard?*

Earlier, the case had started out okay because Chrissy was scrubbed in with her favorite general surgeon, doing an inguinal hernia repair. The patient was a seventeen-year-old boy named Derick. He was a lifeguard at the pool and had given Dillon swimming lessons.

Everything was fine until the hernia surgery was finished. The patient was moved to a gurney, and the side rails were put up. The surgeon took the chart and, as he left the room, he said, "Thanks for your help, Chrissy." Chrissy smiled behind her mask and said, "You're welcome. Have a good day." Then she glanced at the anesthesiologist as if to say, See? I'm likable.

The patient began to shake, prompting the nurse to run out to get a blanket from the warmer. When the anesthesiologist suctioned his mouth, the kid started to buck. Chrissy was cleaning up her back table and had her hands full of bloody sponges. The anesthesiologist shoved the plastic suction tip toward her and said, "Hold this."

Before she could drop the sponges, he raised his voice, "You know, you need to help out!"

Her skin prickled. Good God, she thought. *Try and keep your mouth shut Chrissy. He's a jerk. Don't let him to get to you.* As every teenager does when they wake up from anesthesia, Derick began to thrash about, throwing punches and trying to turn on his side. He stuck his thumbs in his eye sockets and sat straight up. Chrissy leaned over the side rail and took his hands. "It's okay Derick, you're just waking up. Try not to rub your eyes sweetie. Your surgery's all done." The anesthesiologist injected medication into the IV, and Derick fell back on his pillow.

"Let's go!" the anesthesiologist said, and before Chrissy could back up, he pushed the gurney over her foot. She winced and grabbed the edge of her table. The nurse came rushing in, put the blanket on the patient and, as they rolled out of the room, Chrissy hissed, "Asshole," just loud enough for the anesthesiologist to hear.

Now, alone in the OR, her right foot was throbbing as she tore off her gown and gloves. She left the pan of instruments on the back table, stuffed the trash in the hamper, and limped out the door. The empty corridor was cast in a hazy yellow light, and she felt an odd sense of detachment, as if she would never walk this hallway again. She hobbled through two more doors and into Alice's office.

Alice turned from her computer screen and took her glasses off. Her eyes were such an intense shade of blue they almost looked unreal.

"What's up, Chrissy?"

Chrissy looked at Alice's desk covered with patient charts and a stack of employee evaluation forms. Chrissy had never gotten a good evaluation and knew she never would. The open cupboard above Alice's head exposed work manuals, policies and procedures, employee handbooks, and quality assurance binders. She would miss none of it. No more warnings and probation, no more management breathing down her back. No more plotting revenge on her co-workers or having anxiety over coming to work each day.

She raised her right knee just enough to lift her pounding foot off the floor.

"I'm done."

"Okay, if your room's done you can go. Have a good afternoon."

"No, I mean I'm really done. Like done working here. Like 'I quit' done."

Alice put a finger to her mouth and before she could say

anything, Chrissy turned around and walked out. She went into the locker room, grabbed her backpack, and left out the back door. Her toes were swelling, but she suddenly felt empowered and more confident than she had in a long time.

Out in the parking lot she took off her shoes and socks and stuck them in her backpack. Her hands were shaking and, in her excitement, she wanted to run and find Dillon. She wanted to share this moment with Rob, jump up and down and show him she was taking charge without making a mess of everything. She wanted to call Evie to tell her she was applying the principals of the program and taking control of her life. She looked around to see if anyone was watching her, a habit she had developed from being a sneak, and a twinge of fear shot through her. She chewed on her lip. What to do now?

Suddenly the voice of reason told her it was not the best idea to show up at Dillon's school barefoot and take him out early. Slow down, she thought. Take a beat. She was aware that she would continue to experience challenges and struggles. She knew the pitfalls that might lead to a relapse, including a false sense of confidence. The self-work went on for a lifetime; it wasn't anything that happened overnight. But she and Rob had worked through many of their issues, and he was very supportive of her newly found decision-making and personal change skills. She was going to help in the business, *their* construction company. She would answer the phone, do the scheduling, write up the bids, and do the accounting. She began walking quickly, ignoring the pain in her foot.

Yes. It would be okay. They would be a family again.

# TWENTY-EIGHT

Evie had promised to be with Lola this weekend, on Sam's one-year marker. But then Lola decided she wanted to be alone on that day, and Evie trusted that whatever Lola had in mind, it would be what was meant to happen.

Evie had witnessed the progress of Lola's grief journey for the last twelve months and considered it quite remarkable, given that Lola gradually had allowed the grieving process to unfold. Evie had refrained from telling Lola about her stalker or her own childhood trauma, knowing that another person's drama is the last thing a grieving person needs. Evie watched as Lola eventually opened to the possibilities of a non-fear-based existence.

There was a long passage of time when Evie was immobilized by fear. But she now knew that each moment spent on angel work—that is—helping a person with a fresh loss—is also time spent discovering a deeper layer of one's own healing journey. Being with Lola this past year had reconfirmed that we all have our individual, deeply personal ways of processing pain, and under no circumstances should we compare another's feelings to our own. Like life itself, we walk a continual path and participate daily on this spiritual playground.

Why then, thought Evie, am I still afraid, yet exhilarated to be around Romey? They had been enjoying one another's company and as they continued to spend time together, Evie wanted more than anything to open up and trust him, without fear.

She and Romey had had several conversations about life and travel, astrology, art, and the upcoming Big Blast. When he asked her about her family, she confided that she had lost a little sister. When she stopped talking and looked at him helplessly, they both knew it was a sensitive matter. Then, almost cautiously, without even realizing it, they were soon broaching the topics of loss, fear, and trust. Gradually, her trepidation lessoned, and they spoke with ease, like old friends sharing the excitement of something new.

Romey had helped Jack build a tree fort, and now he and Evie were sitting on the porch step, watching Jack twirl on the rope swing. Chrissy had stopped by earlier to tell them she had quit her job and that Rob was coming home for good. Happy as a lark, she had skipped out the driveway with Rex and Dillon behind her.

Evie looked over at Jack, then at Romey. She felt something bubble up inside her, then blurted out, "In all honesty, Romey, I like you, but I have a horrendous past, a poor track record and fear that I'm damaged goods and possibly incapable of having a healthy relationship." Her palms were sweating. *There. I've said it.*

Romey responded by saying, "One could try and bury the past, you know, dig a deep trench and cover it, lock up the awful memories in hopes they'll never resurface. But we all have a past, Evie. The point is, we also have a future . . . if we choose to embrace it."

"Wow," she said. She paused, reflected, and stared into his eyes. He gently lifted his fingertips under her chin, to close her gaping mouth.

"That's true," she said. "To think of all the time I've spent convincing Lola, and myself that life would get better and persuading Chrissy that with effort, her life could also improve."

"Well see, then you believe it too. Lola's told me how much you've helped her."

"Well, I call it angel work, and it's because of my baby sister, Ellie. She's my angel, and she guides me—if you care to believe that."

"I do."

"It works. There are good things happening all around us right now. It was only a few weeks ago Chrissy and I sat here, grinding through her self-help homework, answering each question about what she honestly wanted, and now look how happy she is. I was surprised when I did the exercise as well and discovered what I really want."

"Yeah? And what do you really want?"

Evie wiped her palms on her knees. "I want security, love, companionship, and happiness."

"That sounds very nice."

"And I think it's obvious, now that the stalker thing is over, I need safety for myself and Jack." Evie admitted that, as terrifying as Marc had been, he had guided her toward Romey and had taught her something about herself —She didn't want to do it all on her own anymore.

When Evie asked Romey about his hopes and dreams, he said that hoping and dreaming were about as useless as worrying. You could hope for something, but that wouldn't necessarily make it happen. You could worry all day long and dream your whole life away, but in the end we just have to accept who we are and what we've been dealt. He said he had no illusions of grandeur or unreachable goals, just the idea that living a good life was the basis for happiness. He added that he got the angel work thing, meaning it's good to try and help a person feel better when they're down. He said that he had spent a fair amount of time being sad, for he too had lost a brother and had to go through, as he worded it, sub-optimal experiences.

"Suboptimal?"

"Yeah, that's one of my favorite words. I tell my worker guys it's a more respectable way to say *it sucks*."

"I'm sorry to hear that," said Evie. "Do you think it's possible there is a certain number of tears we have to shed in our lifetime in order to move on?"

"Well, the way I see it is tears and good memories are the return on your investment."

Evie had never met anyone like him. Levelheaded, blunt, real. Not overly sensitive by any stretch, but he was a good listener. To Evie, he felt like a safe shoulder to lean on and when she opened up, he didn't appear to be the least bit shocked by the story of her past.

He listened intently as she told him that after her tragedy at sixteen, it had taken years before she began to see a glimmer of light. The grief counselors and her great-aunt were paramount in helping her find the strength to finish high school and get into a good college. She studied hard but carried with her a trauma that was invisible to others. She felt herself isolated in another world, a parallel universe that no one else could see.

After that fateful day when her family drove away, Evie would never fully remember the next tragic phase of her life. There would be no recollection in her adolescent mind of the doorbell ringing, the officer coming to Lori's house, Lori's mother falling to her knees, the screams, the darkness, and the silence. In the months that followed, Evie dealt with the unspeakable loss of losing both parents and her only sister. And because of the parental role she played with her baby sister, it was like losing a child. She was told that she had to work through the complexities of survivors' guilt, and her anger of unfathomable depth. Her world was uprooted, and she would never return to her family home.

That life in a family, her family, was gone forever. Experts on grieving were brought in to help. She was told that children often console their devastated parents and wait to grieve the loss of their sibling until they're sure their parents are okay, but Evie had no parents to turn to. She ached for them both and exhibited father abandonment issues; like a starving newborn, she wanted her mommy.

Finally, through it all she learned, among other things, that life is beautiful yet ruthless, and time is necessary to the long and tumultuous journey of healing.

"How did you end up here? You must have come to Pine Grove so we could meet." said Romey.

"Well, that's a sweet thought, but after a year in a half-dead state, I was finally stable enough to be placed with my only relative, my great-aunt Eleanor, who lived right here in this house."

"I don't know what to say other than I find you a remarkable person. You're a notch above most, in my opinion. A real quality woman."

"Nah, not really. I just know I have a lot to be grateful for and not a day goes by that I don't think of my angels. The whole experience has taught me that I can probably handle most difficult situations because I'm never really alone."

Romey placed his hand on hers, "No, you're not."


That night Evie dreamed of the hunt, where she was once again after the slayer of her family. She was standing in an open field. In the distance, she saw the back of him and believed if only she could see his face . . . There were flowers everywhere, bright blossoms filling all the spaces until everything was wrapped in color and light. Ellie appeared beside him and cloaked his shoulders in a flowing apricot-colored scarf, then floated away on the faint stirrings of a breeze. Evie approached him, and their eyes met. She reached out and embraced him. Forgive yourself as I have forgiven you, she said. It was an accident after all. As she held him close, the scarf blew away, and he disappeared.

Evie sat up in bed and pressed her hand to her heart. The hunt was finally over.

# TWENTY-NINE

Lola sat in her robe and slippers on the top stair step, holding a bar of soap. For twelve solid months she had been on her grief journey and had feared this day, the one-year marker of Sam's passing. Now that the time had arrived, she realized she had indeed survived and was finally able to get through an entire day without falling apart. She was taking care of herself again, washing her hair regularly, walking in the mornings, and eating well. She had even begun to listen to music that she previously found unbearable. She occasionally slept through the night and was no longer afraid of vacuuming or driving. In fact, she was no longer handicapped by fear.

Lola held the soap to her nose and smelled the pleasant lavender scent. She felt a tender shift taking place within her. She had learned that grieving took a tremendous amount of courage and that, although it never really ends, the only way you can live with it is if you fully face it.

She had come to realize that watching an ant for hours was a necessity that eventually passed. Looking up, she no longer hated the sky for being blue, but found angelic shapes in the clouds that hung over the valley—the same clouds that had darkened her days and blocked the light she truly believed was gone forever. Sam was instrumental in her healing journey. If she loved him as she knew she did, she would give him what he had asked for—to see Lola live again. She heard his whisper at night, *Enjoy what is left of your earthly journey, my love, because we know not how long we have. We know not why souls pass through our lives, connect, disconnect, and reconnect.* Sam wouldn't want her to be miserable forever and reminded her that they would dance together again. He told her that mourning is a time of new mastery over ourselves and our lives. *Lola my love, life is change. Tears are the jewels of remembrance, sad but glistening with the beauty of our past.*

It had taken Lola one year to open and read every sympathy card. Only yesterday she framed the card that many months prior had made her so upset she almost burned it. A Hopi Indian prayer. She had stood over the kitchen sink holding the card face down. *How dare someone tell me not to cry. I'll cry and I think I may die.* She lit a match and watched the match burn down to her fingertips, then dropped it in the sink and tossed the card in the junk drawer, not bothering to see who it was from.

This afternoon Lola would honor Sam by allowing herself the joy that she was once capable of feeling. The first step to letting go and coming alive was to regain a sense of pleasure—a bubble bath.

She filled the tub with warm water and luxurious bubbles, dropped her robe to the floor, and slipped in up to her ears. They used to laugh at how Sam would shave her legs much better than she could. Magic hands. There will always be those things, she thought, that are impossible without you, Sam. *There is a before and there is a now.*

After the bath she dried off and went to her closet. As she reached up to get a pair of shoes, she looked at the closet walls. It felt like they spoke to her as she stepped back ten years when she had painted the entire upstairs. She and Sam had had a little tiff the night before about her *neediness*. The next day, when Sam was golfing, she was planning to surprise him with fresh paint. A new look. A selfless act. She had ordered the paint special from Ace hardware, a trendy matt finish color series. She would do the closet first in a warm gray tone called *Wolf's Allure* and then the bedroom in a deeper saturation of *Romantic Silver Nights*. She was working in the closet, humming away, wearing short denim cutoffs and a pink halter top with one foot pressed up against the wall. She reached to the top shelf to dip the paintbrush when Sam snuck up behind her. She jumped and the pan fell on her head and slid down her back. She screeched "Jeez Sam! You scared the pants off me!" and he smiled and said, "That's my goal." She took the two-inch trim brush and poked him in the forehead, then painted his sideburns and the top of his hair. He took the brush from her hand and streaked a long piece of her hair. He dropped the brush, held her face in his hands and kissed her tenderly on the mouth. They looked into each other's eyes and began to giggle.

"Oh my God, Sam, is this what we're going to look like when we're old and gray together?"

Lola sighed, sat on the bed, and opened the shoebox with the red heels. Tucked by the strap, she found a small piece of paper folded into a square. Written in Sam's graceful handwriting, it said, *For Lola.* She held it in her palm, then unfolded the note and read:

*Long before this life began and long after we are both gone from this earth, I have loved you and will love you always.*

She folded the paper and walked to her mirror. A peaceful warmth filled her as she applied just the right amount of makeup, something she had not done in a year's time. She put on her gold anklet, the diamond pendant and beautiful earrings Sam had given her for "Just being you."

After slipping into a little black dress and the red heels, she stood before the mirror, and for the first time in a year, she liked what she saw. She and Sam standing there, his arms around her waist.

Heading for the kitchen, she descended the stairs carefully and heard Sam chuckle as she tried to walk elegantly in five-inch heels. "Swing your hips," he would say.

Looking out the kitchen window she saw a hummingbird zip back and forth across the glass, rest perfectly still on a vine, then dash away. A smile spread across her face when she looked on the sill to see the little pot of succulents Evie had given her last Spring. It seemed like an eternity ago. Next to the porcelain frog reading a book, sat the tiny, speckled tree frog. See? She thought. There is someone for everyone.

She prepared a small tray of cheese and crackers. She got out two crystal flutes and popped a special bottle of champagne. She filled both glasses, sat next to Sam's chair and propped up the framed card.

In an act of closure, she raised her glass and said, "Cheers. Thank you for loving me, feeding me, and keeping me warm." She shut her eyes and bowed her head. "This marks the day of your departure and, although I will always love you and never forget you, now I can let you go. I say goodbye to the life we had, put my yearning to rest, and know that we will continue in another realm if it is meant to be."

She inhaled deeply, took a sip, and regarded the card Evie had sent her.

*A Hopi Indian Prayer*

*Do not stand at my grave and weep.*

*I am not there. I do not sleep.*

*I am a thousand winds that blow.*

*I am the diamond glints on snow.*

*I am the sunlight on ripened grain.*

*I am the gentle autumn rain.*

*When you awaken in the morning's hush*

*I am the swift uplifting rush*

*Of quiet birds in circled flight*

*I am the soft stars that shine at night.*

*Do not stand at my grave and cry,*

*I am not there. I did not die.*

# THIRTY

On the first Friday of October, Romey awoke to the sun bursting through an oyster-colored dawn. When he and Max went out to his truck, he noticed sparkling dew lay upon everything, transforming his yard into a mystical glade. He had a song in his heart and a lilt in his step.

Last night, when Romey went to pick up Evie for a date, she had said it wasn't really a date, it was just dinner. He had brought her a bouquet of flowers from Trina's Floral Shop, and a book for Jack, called, *I Wonder Why the Dodo Is Dead and Other Questions about Extinct and Endangered Animals*. While Evie was getting ready, Romey and Jack sat in the living room and Romey gave Jack twenty-five cents for each page he read out loud. Evie smiled to herself as she heard Jack pronouncing some impressively difficult words.

Romey whistled as he got in his truck and thought of the not-really-a-date night. He had cleaned his house, finished his laundry, then prepared dinner. He had made pasta with Ragu sauce and fresh mushrooms cut in half. They had red wine, which led to good conversation. They learned that they both favored blue, and Fall was their favorite season. They both liked classical music and classic rock and enjoyed almost every kind of food, except liver and onions.

When it was time to go home, Evie was standing by his front door, admiring a painting from Honduras. In turn, Romey stood admiring Evie, and as badly as he wanted to kiss her, he wasn't sure if he should. The thought popped into his head of their first meal together, when she had served him a lid with his black beans, which to him, made her so beautifully human. Before he got tangled up in more of his own thoughts, he cleared his throat, and glanced at his clean laundry, neatly folded on a side table. In a flash of inspiration, he grabbed a Shine On tee shirt and handed it to her.

She smiled sweetly, and said, "Thank you."

On the ride home, neither one spoke. They were smitten.

Tomorrow he and Evie were going to work together on the Eastons' wedding and, afterwards he was going to show her Venus through his telescope.

Romey got a cup of coffee, then drove out to Mr. Murphy's place to wash his windows. As he approached the farm with its menagerie of grazing animals, he thought the scene was an artist's delight. Around the pond was a sea of old-fashioned hollyhocks, pampas grass, and water lilies. With the saffron-colored wildflowers spread across the meadow, it looked like one of Mrs. Easton's picturesque jigsaw puzzles.

*But wait. What's that?* He pushed his sunglasses to his forehead and looked toward the barn. He saw Mr. Murphy in a plaid shirt, denim overalls, and brown leather work gloves. He was bent over an animal that appeared to be sleeping. Max put his head out the window and started to bark.

"Hush, Max," Romey said and pulled into the driveway. He left Max in the truck and got out.

"Mornin' Mr. Murphy. Romey here to do the windows."

Mr. Murphy did not respond. As Romey got closer he could see that the old man was crying. His llama was dead.

"Oh, no. What happened?"

Mr. Murphy swiped his gloved hand across his brow and looked up at Romey.

"Tully's gone now. He had a bad bug in his innards, and it took him quick."

Romey shook his head. "Oh, man."

"Poor feller. I got him for my son Charlie when they were both just sprouts. Charlie loved him so much. Tully followed him around the place like a puppy would, right on his heels. Charlie taught him how to prance like a show horse and balance an apple on his head." He sniffed.

"I'm sorry. Can I help you? Um, do you want to bury him?"

Mr. Murphy stood up and suddenly grabbed Romey's arms, gave him a crushing hug and sobbed loudly into his neck. Romey stood frozen for a moment, not sure what to do, then awkwardly reached around and patted him on his shaking back.

"I miss my Charlie boy so much. We got the same blood, but the son-of-a-gun is so darn stubborn it just breaks my heart. Breaks my heart every single day."

"I understand," said Romey, even though he didn't know the specifics of the Murphy's father-son relationship. "It must be hard." He dropped his sunglasses and bent to pick them up, which dislodged the crying man from his chest. Mr. Murphy stepped back, took a red handkerchief out of his back pocket and blew his nose. "I'm sorry Romey. Sometimes I just can't stop myself."

"It's alright. Just let me know what you want me to do. It's an opportunity to serve." He picked up his dusty sunglasses and wiped them on his pant leg.

"I'll get a rope," Mr. Murphy mumbled. "And if you could help me pull him into the pickup, I'll take him over to the rendering plant in White Pine."

"Sure. Then I'll clean the windows, okay?"

"Yep. Thanks, Romey." He wadded up the hankie and stuffed it into his overall bib.

It was unnerving that the dead llama looked like he was smiling at them. They tied a harness around Tully's bloated belly and wrapped a piece of baling twine around his muzzle to close his bristly lips over his big yellow teeth. They maneuvered his stiff, straight legs and muscled him into the back of the truck using a two-by-four for leverage.

Romey lifted the hem of his tee shirt and wiped around his ear. This was not the first time he had a grown man's tears on his neck. His father had wept for days when his brother died. Life is just like that, he thought. But if you're lucky enough to have a son, it's shameful not to talk to each other. Although, for as long as man has inhabited the earth, there have been battles within families. Sometimes there's just something lacking—like a chemical bond—that prevents family members from loving unconditionally.

Romey picked up his bucket, stuck a squeegee in his belt, and shook his head. He watched as Mr. Murphy climbed into his truck. *Those two should be fishing and laughing and doing the things that fathers and sons do together.*

As Mr. Murphy was about to drive away, Romey walked over to him and said, "I'm not going to charge you for the windows today, sir."

Mr. Murphy shook his head. "No. You don't need to do that, Romey. I appreciate your help, and I intend to pay full price."

He put the truck into reverse and began to back out. Romey looked at the llama hoof sticking out the side of the truck bed and said, "Your son may be stubborn, but you don't have to be. Call him. It couldn't hurt any more than it already does."

The following afternoon, Romey and Evie were at the Eastons' home preparing for the wedding. Romey and his boys hung lights over the property and cleaned the windows and the poolside sculpture. Trina Adams provided stunning flowers for the centerpieces, the bridal party, and the ceremony gazebo.

The bride had requested fried chicken and waffles to be served at midnight, and a pair of Alpacas as ring bearers—something she had seen in a celebrity bridal magazine. After helping Evie load her truck, Romey and Jack had stopped by to check on Mr. Murphy and see what they could borrow in lieu of a pair of Alpacas. "Sadly," Romey told Evie, "Mr. Murphy lost his old llama to an intestinal virus. We could use the emu instead, but the bride might get upset if it pecks someone or eats the wedding cake."

Now Evie stood on the lawn, checking the table schematic and going over the seating chart, which was the hardest part of a wedding. She had explained to Romey that it took an incredible amount of time and energy to seat the ex-wife far enough away from the new girlfriend, separate the feuding cousins, and keep the meat eaters away from the one vegetarian on the guest list. Romey had shrugged and said, "Why can't we all just get along?"

Evie began setting the tables with mocha satin tablecloths and lime-green place settings. She used her rustic copper base plates and copper-handled flatware. There were floating candles on the tables and in the pool. A table, elaborately draped with swags of delicate voile and silk ribbon, would host the six-tiered cake, chocolate fountain, and fondue station. She hung a large antique picture frame from the branch of a grand pine tree as a photo booth. A dance floor and money tree were constructed, and a massive hammered-copper bar was delivered from Boise.

Beside each centerpiece, Evie nestled the tall table stands with the names of places the bride and groom had been together—Niagara Falls, Disneyland, the Laundromat—to name a few. For the finishing touch, she placed the escort cards on the entry table in alphabetical order, set all one hundred place cards according to the seating chart, and propped the *Mr. and Mrs.* place cards next to the bride and groom's Baccarat goblets.

Romey walked by carrying a tall ladder with extensions. Evie felt a dollop of something that had been brewing inside her—pure primal attraction. It was a revelation that after all this time she could still feel something so basic, biological, and pleasant. The fact that he had made her such a nice dinner and given her his work shirt lit a fire inside her. Tonight they would be stargazing together.

He took one look at her and set the ladder down. This was the first time Romey wanted to be around someone without worrying that she was half-crazy. His brothers had set him up with a girl from church and then with Patty Pinkle, the school lunch aide, but both scenarios turned out to be disastrous. Nope, no one else did it for him like Evie did. He smiled and stepped toward her. She was wearing a silky brown skirt with a jersey knit top of lime green and brown pinstripes. His heart thumped.

"This looks really nice, Evie," he said. "And I see your skirt matches the tablecloths." When he had left her house with Jack this morning, she was wearing jeans and the Shine On tee shirt.

"Yeah. Thanks." She blushed and fanned her face with her hand.

"Would you call that color coffee?"

"Very good. The bride wanted 'mocha' because that's all the rage right now. I don't have the heart to tell her it's just plain brown." Evie laughed. "Are you done with the windows?"

"Yes, but now I have to do a little magic on the sculpture in the back."

A truck with a horse trailer pulled up, and they watched as two men got out and walked toward them.

"Oh, no way!" said Romey. He looked at Evie, and she saw he had tears in his eyes.

"Who is that?" she asked.

Mr. Murphy walked up to Romey. "Hi there, Mate. As promised, we brought you something."

"Thanks, Mr. Murphy. You know my friend Evie, right?"

"Of course, I know Evie and Jack and Dillon. He put his arm around a younger man who strongly resembled him. This here's my son, Charlie."

Romey was grinning like his smiley-face logo.

"Nice to meet you, Charlie," they said.

Jack came running up. "Did you bring the donkey, Brutus?"

"Yep," said Charlie. "He's in the trailer and he can't wait to be in his first wedding. After that he's all yours, if it's okay with your folks." Evie liked the sound of that, *your folks.*

"I love Brutus! Can we keep him, please Mom?"

Evie looked at Romey and saw a tiny nod. "I suppose so, but you must take good care of him. Love him, feed him, and keep him warm."

"Yay!" Jack clapped his hands. He ran toward the trailer and the Murphy men followed him.

"That's fantastic Romey, thank you. Jack can lead him down the aisle. I'm so glad you didn't get the emu."

"Yeah, that probably wouldn't have been one of my best moves." He picked up the ladder pieces. "Can you give me a hand back there?" he asked. He looped a long strand of lights around his neck. "I have to wrap the sculpture in lights."

"Sure," said Evie. They walked to the pool and she watched as Romey attached the extensions and set the very tall ladder near the sculpture. "What do you want me to do?" she asked.

"Well," said Romey, "I forgot to mention that today is my birthday, and I was hoping you could hold my ladder."

She looked at him and thought, it's a risk, but everything in life is a risk. Loving Romey and even breathing is a risk, but love is why we breathe. He stepped on the first rung, and she placed her hands on the sides of the ladder. She held tight as he began to climb. She was nervous and didn't want to watch.

I had no idea, she thought, that Romey's birthday is on the same day as my late Auntie Eleanor's birthday, October seventh. She thought of the last time she had seen her. They were sitting on the front porch, looking out over the valley. Her old aunt gently squeezed her hand and told Evie, "God knew what he was doing when he made you. You have had to endure way too much, Honey, but remember that grief and despair and tears make you stronger, even though they are nearly impossible to bear. The Lord never promised life would be easy, but he did promise to be with us always. Love heals. Love will get you through life and make it worth living. Trust yourself, Evie, and trust God. Always be open to love."

Romey was halfway up the ladder when she called, "Please be careful. And Happy Birthday!"

She watched as he climbed higher and higher. Above him she saw the aqua sky strewn with a strand of pearl clouds. The ladder rocked slightly in her hands as he turned his head and looked down at her.

"Here we go," he chimed. "We're just getting started."

# THIRTY-ONE

The following week, Lola started the car and adjusted the rearview mirror to see her reflection. "Time for some angel work," she said.

Netty Gabilan had just passed away, and Letty was having a terribly hard time. Lola told her granddaughter she would pay a visit today and spread some love. The granddaughter had asked Lola to go through their pictures and find a photo of Netty for the memorial, but it would probably be virtually impossible to find a photo of Netty without Letty by her side.

Lola drove along a street, lined with pine trees, past little houses with freshly mowed lawns and sprinklers watering autumn flowers.

An orange-striped cat zipped across the street and Lola tapped the brakes. She passed a Shine On truck parked in Betty Baxter's driveway and saw Romey on a ladder cleaning an upstairs window. His little dog, Max, was lying next to the truck. Lola had read in the *Pine Tree News* that Max had been locked in Mrs. Baxter's garage for a whole day before he was discovered by Romey. They quoted Romey as saying, "It's a real head scratcher that he didn't bark the entire time." The article went on to say that the dog had done just fine with plenty of dog food and water and a cozy kennel to sleep in.

Lola looked at Mrs. Baxter standing, looking up at Romey. She's probably offering to hold his ladder so he won't fall, thought Lola, remembering that was one of Sam's final acts of kindness.

When Lola arrived at the Gabilan House, she saw Letty out in the garden in her wheelchair with a very large woman standing behind her. Lola parked the car, got out, and walked toward them. Letty was saying, "NettyLetty, where are you? Where are you NettyLetty?" She had two Teddy bears on her lap. She was trembling, and her fists were clenched. Before they spotted her, Lola stopped near a tree and watched them.

The big woman held a can of Coke in one hand and a doughnut in the other. She was wearing a muumuu and flip flops. She had small, rheumy eyes, a messy auburn braid, and uneven bangs. Lola could see her name tag said Marge. She was smacking, her mouth full, with frosting on her lips.

"Quit yer blubberin'," she said to Letty. "Yer sister was old, and now she's dead. My ass is gonna be grass if you don't eat yer lunch. You dint touch yer scrambled eggs so I hadda eat em."

"NettyLetty! Where are you?" she kicked her legs like a mad child.

"Yer granddaughter says yer expectin' company at noon."

Letty cried. "Nettyletty, I can't breathe! Can't breathe without you."

"Listen up, you stay put 'til I git back. I'm just goin' to the kitchen. I know. It ain't like yer gonna run away." Letty hung her head and Lola's heart lurched. She walked quickly toward them.

"Excuse me," said Lola. "Are you Marge?"

"Yeah, that's me. Irma had to go with the granddaughter to make funeral arrangements so the agency sent me. I gotta stay 'til three."

"Your agency name tag appears to be wrong," said Lola.

"No it ain't. Marge is my name." She shoved in the rest of the doughnut and packed it into her cheek with her thumb. She gulped and swiped her mouth with the back of her hand and tapped her badge.

"I don't doubt that Marge is your name, but underneath, it says *caregiver*. Someone who calls herself a caregiver surely wouldn't speak to another human being that way."

"Well, she's hollerin' senseless malarkey and it wears me out."

"I suggest you leave right now. I'll stay with Letty." Lola kneeled in front of the wheelchair. "Hi Letty, it's Lola here."

"NettyLetty, owie, owie." Tears fell down Letty's cheeks. She rocked back and forth.

"I know Letty. I'm here for you. It hurts really bad and it's okay to cry."

Marge said, "I'm gonna go git another Coke.

Lola stood and said, "I'd be willing to bet that you haven't experienced the most profound of all sorrows, Marge. Letty's been severed from her other half. She probably feels like she's lost her limbs."

Marge stuck her hand in the pocket of her muumuu and jingled some keys.

Lola continued. "She and Netty were inseparable from birth, even before birth, Marge. They were together their entire lives. They were more than just twin sisters. They were best friends. And now in her deep pain, the only thing she needs is a simple act of human kindness."

"Well then, looks like you know what yer doin. I'm gonna git a Coke and my purse and git the heck outta here." She turned and waddled away.

Lola took Letty's gnarled fists in her hands. "I love you, Letty. I'm so sorry for your broken heart. You may not believe me now, but you'll be able to breathe again. The only thing that matters right now is you. We must give Letty what Letty needs. You don't have to eat your eggs if you don't want to. You can do anything you want, except hurt yourself. What do you have in your hands?"

Letty uncurled her fists and smiled. "Netty's hair from her hairbrush."

Lola blinked. "That's really sweet, Letty. I know how much you miss her, trust me, I do. And just because Netty is gone and not here the way she was, she's still around. She's your angel now."

Letty stared into Lola's face with her wet, milky eyes and nodded slowly.

"You and Netty will walk together again in a place where there's no pain or sadness or fear. In the place where Netty lives now, her leg will never hurt again."

A red breasted robin hopped through the grass and sat next to the wheelchair. A gentle breeze blew over them. For the first time in seven years, Letty put both hands on the arms of the wheelchair and pushed herself up. As she stood, the Teddy bears fell to the ground and the breeze lifted the little balls of white hair, blowing them across the lawn and out of sight.

# THIRTY-TWO

By early November the fair autumn weather took an unexpected turn. For three solid days, rain fell in great sweeping gusts, drenching the valley, flooding the park, and bringing the banks of Lake Camus to its brink. A glut of rainwater rushed down the middle of Main Street and sloshed across sidewalks, leaching through the doors of the post office, the flower shop, and the liquor store. Power lines creaked and swayed, but held strong, as did the mammoth trees and the residents of Pine Grove.

Romey referred to this weather system as a temporary damper on his style. He and the Shine On crew had been working overtime in preparation for the holiday season and the Big Blast. Juan had left Pine Grove after Halloween, so Romey commissioned five high school boys to help hang lights as soon as the rain let up.

After three fundraisers, Trina Adams had procured enough money to subsidize the New Millennium extravaganza. In keeping with the values and traditions of Pine Grove, the message was delivered throughout the village that no one would be left behind. Every light would shine, and every living soul would be illuminated by the Big Blast.

There would be an estimated twenty thousand festive lights to be lit simultaneously just before midnight on New Year's Eve. Each week, it was printed on the front page of the *Pine Tree News*, "Get Ready! The Big Blast Is Coming Soon!"

The goal was to wrap twinkling lights around every tree, lamp post, street sign, mailbox, and school bus stop in the area. Every building in the village, including all the houses, garages, shops, and sheds would be covered with brightly- colored lights. Special care would be taken to illuminate even the highest structures — the hospital, the school, and the telephone poles. Iridescent white lights would envelope the cemetery entrances and the churches. The steeple of the white chapel would shine so brightly, it would appear to be part Heaven itself.

There were concerns, however, that computer programmers and users in other parts of the world would be devastated by computer crashes and power outages. The year 2000 problem was known as Y2K2, as well as the glitch, the scare, the Y2K2 bug, and the Y2K2 error. Jack had become an expert on it and explained to Evie and Romey that it had to do with formatting and storage of calendar data because instead of allowing four digits for the year, like there would be in 2000, many computer programs only allowed two, like in '99. Romey said, "That may be true for the rest of the world, Jack, but for the blessed village of Pine Grove, the threat doesn't exist."

Now, Evie and Chrissy were in Evie's kitchen, baking cookies for the school Fall Festival. There was an exquisite arrangement of stargazer lilies on the table. The fragrant bouquet had been sent from Romey for Evie's birthday, the previous day.

Chrissy opened the oven, took a whiff, and said, "Your house smells like a place nobody ever wants to leave."

"That's so funny, Romey said the same thing."

Chrissy took the cookies out, put another loaded baking sheet into the oven, and asked, "How was your birthday?"

"It was fantastic. Thank you for the squirrel socks. I didn't know socks came in a three pack."

"Yeah, that's in case you lose one. We're always losing socks at our house."

"And the card. Stay out of the Woods. The Squirrels are Collecting Nuts for the Winter."

"So, did Romey wine and dine you again?"

"Yes. He totally surprised me. Well, he surprised both Jack and I." Evie picked up a small wooden bowl from the table and said, "He gave me this bowl from Africa. It's carved out of ebony. And a necklace from India and a knitted hat from Bolivia."

"Holy shit. That's like a trip around the world, right there."

"I know. But then, inside the hat was a shocking little note."

"Oh my God, did he write something steamy? You've had sex, right?" Chrissy licked her knuckles, then turned on the water to rinse off her hands.

Evie ran her fingers over the bowl. "He said that I am finer than the grain of this African wood, that he needn't give me this necklace because my eyes are my real jewels, and would Jack and I like to get a passport so he can take us to the pyramids in Tikal!"

Chrissy's mouth dropped open and she leaned against the counter. "Shut up! I've totally got goosebumps. Where in the hell is Tikal?"

"Guatemala. He and Jack have been reading about it. It's an ancient Maya city from 600 AD. There's a temple that's more than 150 feet tall and we can climb up the pyramids! Can you imagine how incredible that would be?"

"Oh, my God. Are you gonna go?"

"I think so."

"What do you mean, you *think* so? You're hot for each other, right? Seems to me like you two have been spending a ton of time together."

"Yeah. We've seen each other almost every day. Either he's been here, or I've gone to his place, or the three of us have done something fun. I mean, he works harder than anyone I've ever met, but he still makes time for us, and if I don't see him, he calls."

"That's awesome, but what happened to the Evie I know, who says she needs her space?"

"Well, that's what's so good about him. I feel like he understands me and realizes that we've both been independent and self-sufficient for a long time. I feel like neither of us are going into this relationship with fear. You know what I mean? It seems natural. Plus, we're old enough to know what we want. And it's obvious he and Jack get along very well."

"That's huge. He's a Libra, right?"

"Yeah. He's a good, balanced person. And there are things I really admire about him."

"Like what?"

"Like how he doesn't worry about what he looks like. You know, doesn't care if he brushes his hair, and doesn't stress about what he's wearing. I see that as a sign of confidence, to care less about what others think."

"Yeah, I agree."

"And I also admire that he's refreshingly honest, and I think his aloofness is kinda sexy, you know, not all ego driven like so many other guys. He's got character." Evie nodded.

The phone rang in the kitchen and Evie jumped. She answered the call, and it was John Craven, the school principal. The first thing he said was not to worry, Jack was okay. There had been an incident in the lunchroom and Jack had been sent to the principal's office. Evie bit her thumbnail. "What happened?" She looked at Chrissy, who put her palms out and mouthed, "What, what?"

"Well," said John Craven, "Jack allegedly called Patty Pinkle, the lunch server, a name and threw his spoon on the floor in the cafeteria today."

"Oh, no! That doesn't sound like Jack. Do you know why? Is he there? Can I talk to him?"

"Yes, he's sitting right here. I was not present when it happened, but I'll let Jack explain."

"Okay, thank you, Mr. Craven."

Evie covered the receiver and said, "It's the principal. Jack got in trouble for something. Hold on."

Jack came on the line, and she could tell by his voice he had been crying. He told her that the lunch lady was mean to him. She yelled at him and told him he had to eat his carrots, or he'd be in big trouble. Jack told her he couldn't have carrots, or he'd throw up. She stood over him, and all the kids were watching when she squeezed his earlobe and led him to the principal's office. That's when he threw the spoon.

"Well, I thought it was in your school file that you can't eat carrots. Don't worry, buddy. Did you say something disrespectful to her?"

"Yeah. That's what got me in the most trouble, I think."

"Jack, you know that's not right. What did you call her?"

He paused for a minute, then said, "I called her a Dodo bird."

Evie covered her mouth to stop from laughing. "We'll get it straightened out. Did you apologize to her?"

"No."

"Did you get to eat your lunch?"

"Yeah, but I didn't get recess, and today recess is in the gym because of the rain. I wanted to play basketball with Dillon in the gym, Mom. It's not fair."

"It'll be okay. I'll pick you up after school. The weather is supposed to get better soon. Give the phone back to Mr. Craven. I love you, baby."

"Love you to the moon, Mom."

Mr. Craven said he had yet to consult with Miss Pinkle, and he would let Evie know if further action would be necessary, but he didn't anticipate so. Evie explained about Jack's aversion to carrots and Mr. Craven assured her it would not happen again.

"Thank you, Mr. Craven. I appreciate the call." Evie hung up the phone.

She looked at the cookies. Chrissy had gotten a turkey platter out of the pantry, and piled the maple and pumpkin-shaped cookies so high, they were sliding off the platter onto the counter.

"Don't worry," said Chrissy. I'll make sure you get your platter back after the Fall Festival.

"Thanks. It belonged to Auntie Eleanor. I'm sorry I can't make it to the festival this year, but as you know, I'm setting up for a surprise party. Romey can take Jack and Dillon if you and Rob can take the cookies. You're helping with the cake walk, right?"

"Yeah, and that'll work. Who's the surprise party for?"

"It's for Mr. Murphy. His son Charlie is giving him an eightieth birthday party at Mel's. I'm going to decorate the back room, and then I'll be home, probably by four."

Chrissy took a nibble of a cookie. "K. I think it ends at five."

Evie looked at her magnificent birthday bouquet, then out the window at the wet, glistening lawn. She thought about Jack and the lunch lady, then of Mr. Murphy and his no-longer-estranged son. "The sunshine's finally coming out."

Evie came home from setting up Mr. Murphy's surprise party, to find a white Chevy Nova sitting in her driveway. She parked her truck and got out and the driver of the Nova did the same.

Patty Pinkle stood before her holding an empty turkey platter.

"Patty?"

"Hi Evie. I came to bring you your platter. Chrissy's still helping at the festival, so I offered to return this to you." She held it out with both hands.

"Oh, thanks," Evie said, and took the platter. "Um, about the other day with Jack…"

"Don't you think you're moving a little too fast?" Patty raised her eyebrows.

"Excuse me?"

"With Romey. We are very concerned. Seems like you just met, now there's wedding bells about to ring."

"Who's *we*? And what *wedding bells*? I don't know what you're talking about."

"Look Evie, Romey used to be a member of our church group, and he and I dated. He is a nice guy, and it's obvious you're just after him for his money, you know, a gold digger."

Evie could barely comprehend what she was hearing. She looked at Patty Pinkle, with her small face and large nose. She was wearing a calico dress covering her from chin to knees, and brown loafers. She had a knot of mousy brown hair pinned above each ear and thin lips with long teeth, which reminded Evie of a rodent. *Or a Dodo bird.*

"I will refrain from saying something I'll later regret, Patty, but whatever you had with Romey was probably a long time ago? He didn't mention anything to me about you, or about your church group, and I assure you that his money is the furthest thing from my mind. We're friends."

"Did he also fail to tell you about Susan?" she sneered.

"Who's Susan?"

"His wife."

Evie felt dizzy. She stepped toward the porch, hugging the platter. "Romey is married?" she whispered.

"He *was* married to Susan until she left him. She divorced him when he decided to leave the church. We were a very close-knit group until Romey broke away and decided he no longer believed. He opted for sin, and we've all been praying for him ever since then."

"How long ago was this?"

"It doesn't matter."

"Yes, it does matter! How long ago was he married to Susan?"

Patty stepped back toward her car and put her hand on the door handle. "All I know is that you've suddenly found it real convenient to get yourself a rich husband and a stepdad for your kid." She got in the car, started the engine, and drove away.

Evie stumbled into the house and set the platter on the counter. She looked at the flower arrangement and thought she might be sick. She went back outside, and in a fog, began unloading the crates from her truck.

# THIRTY-THREE

After the Fall Festival, Romey found Evie in her garage, sitting on a box of baseplates, crying into her hands.

"There you are," he said.

"Leave me alone."

"Evie, what's the matter?"

"Where's Jack?"

"He and Dillon are in the tree fort. What's going on?" He came to her and put his hand on her shoulder. "Why are you crying?"

She pushed his hand away and stared at the floorboards. "Patty Pinkle came here to tell me that you were her boyfriend and I'm some kind of a gold digger, that I just want you for your money and…"

"Wait. What? That's not true. In fact, that's completely

ridiculous. I knew Patty Pinkle from the church I belonged to, like twenty years ago. We were barely out of high school, and we weren't *dating*."

"She said you were dating."

"Then she must be referring to the time a bunch of us went to the Hometown Café after church one Sunday, and she tried to spoon feed me oatmeal, and wipe my mouth with her napkin, which totally grossed me out. Shortly after that, the church, or the cult, as I came to know it, disbanded then regrouped. That's when I left for good."

Evie rubbed her face on her sleeve. "Why would she call me a gold digger?"

"Trust me, Evie, the churchies are all crazy. I was in it mostly because, at the time, I believed we were doing the right thing. The pastor gave me the job of driving around and picking up kids to bring them to Sunday school. That's about it. We read the bible and talked about Jesus and ate doughnuts."

Romey crossed his arms. "I think I know what this is about. Patty Pinkle's all fired up because she happened to be in the flower shop when I was ordering your birthday flowers. Trina asked me where to deliver them and what did I want to say on the card. I said, 'To Evie, Happy Birthday to the most beautiful woman in the world,' and Patty ran out of the shop and slammed the door."

Evie stood up. "You lied to me. You never told me… you were married to someone named Susan?'

"You never asked."

"That's a copout."

Romey shrugged. "I don't understand why you're upset."

Her head started to get hot, and a surge of fury overtook her. "I hate you! You just skate around the truth. You're no different than any other guy! You get what you want by pretending you care about me and Jack."

"What?" He looked lost.

"I'm not doing it Romey. I'm not going to be in another failed relationship. We're better off alone! I always knew if I need to count on someone, it can only be *me*." Her heart was slamming in her chest, but this time her vision didn't dim. She felt like she was going explode.

"Evie, please listen to me. I didn't mention Susan because it's not important…"

"Not important? You were married! Is there anything else I don't know about you Romey, Mr. Shine On? Do you have a pack of kids somewhere that you *forgot* to tell me about?"

He stared at her, shaking his head.

"Is that why you travel so much? Maybe you've got a woman in every other country? Or a whole other existence with another family?"

"No, Evie. I don't have…"

"Go away."

"Evie, I told you before, we all have a past, but if we're lucky enough and open enough to the possibilities, we can have an amazing future. Together. Life isn't perfect. You should know that better than anyone. We're part of the human condition, and humans make mistakes. Humans say stupid things and it's the misconceptions and misunderstandings that tear people apart."

"I was excited about us, Romey. It has taken me years to be able to trust someone the way I trusted you. The whole stalker-psycho thing almost put me over the edge, but then along came Romey, to the rescue. Mr. smooth talker. You convinced me that I could trust you with my heart and that we could live in love and be happy. Happy ever after."

"Evie. I do care about you. I care about you more than I've ever cared about anyone. Both you and Jack. But again, nothing is perfect. It's a beautiful sentiment, but it's not possible that all people, at all times, can live without challenges. We're not in a Hans Christian Andersen fairy tale, here. We're in an honest, real-life story. Our story."

"Well, isn't that an interesting viewpoint, coming from someone who walks around in a ray of sunshine all the time."

"I'm just saying that sometimes we need to be realistic about the way the real world works. It can be pretty bad out there. *That* is the reason I travel, to witness firsthand, that not everyone on this planet gets to live in this magical bubble of Pine Grove.

"Well, maybe I do believe in fairy tales! Maybe I do believe that life can be how we want it to be, and that evil doesn't reign. Why do you think I don't have a TV? Because I don't want to be exposed to the cruelty that exists outside of this magical bubble. I would like to think, because we are good people and have been put through the wringer of life, that we can finally have what we deserve, which is a happy, healthy, loving relationship, and be like a normal family."

"But we can, Evie."

"I was stupid enough to believe that we could actually get married and make more babies and put an addition on the house and, God, I'm such a…"

"Evie, me too. I've thought of all those things. I want to do our life together, don't you?"

There was a long, painful silence between them. He stared at her, and she stared at the floor.

"Evie, do you want to do our life together?"

*Yep, I knew it. Loving Romey was a risk, alright.* She lifted her chin, let out a big breath and shook her hands.

"Leave us alone. Take your passport and your Mayan Temple and your aloof attitude and get out of my life!" She pushed past him and ran into the house, slamming and locking the door behind her.

She threw herself, face down on her bed and screamed so loudly into her pillow, she didn't hear him drive away.

# THIRTY-FOUR

By the time school let out for Thanksgiving break, Evie had spent three days in bed. She couldn't eat and all she wanted to do was sleep. On the fourth day, Lola came to visit. She sat on Evie's bed and caressed her face. She handed her tissues when she cried and gave her broth in a coffee cup. Between Lola and Chrissy, Jack was fed and cared for, and told that his mom had a very contagious flu bug.

Evie sniveled her way through the story of Patty Pinkle, telling Lola how Romey had betrayed her. Her dreams were shattered, and she was an empty shell.

"How could I have been so stupid?" she sobbed.

"If there is one thing I've learned from you Evie, it's that we are stronger than we think. You can't let the words of an insignificant person put a dent in your armor or bruise your tender heart. Romey loves you."

"How do you know, Lola?"

"Because I know Romey. He's got you etched right into his soul. I've never seen him like this. For one thing, he quit working after only washing half my windows. He's lovesick. You think you're hurting, imagine how he feels. If you two didn't care for each other, you would both be able to carry on, unscathed. But love doesn't work that way, my dear."

"No?"

"I'll let you in on a little secret. Sam and I had been married for three years before it slipped out that he had been wed before, for a very brief time. I reacted unfairly, and later, realized if I would have given up on us just because of that, we would have never had our beautiful marriage."

"Really?"

"Really. You were the one who made me realize that although Sam passed on, he will always be with me, that the relationship with the one you love, doesn't end just because you aren't physically together. Come on, Evie. Listen to your heart, not your head. Patty Pinkle can go fly a kite. And you and Romey can take each other by the hand and live in love. Time is too precious to waste, and you are too beautiful to waste what you have left of it. Give that man a call."

It was the last night of the year and there was a gentle snow flurry flitting across the valley and through the village. It was dark and moonless except for an occasional candle burning in a window or a flashlight casting a white beam. People wrapped in warm coats, mittens and mufflers gathered on their porches and in the streets with mugs of hot cocoa and peppermint

Schnapps. Everyone had their clocks and timers set to turn on their lights at the same time.

Up on the hill overlooking the festivities, a small gathering of friends sat around a low-burning campfire. Romey and Evie snuggled together, with Max curled at their feet. Across from them, in an over-stuffed chair, Chrissy sat on Rob's lap. Jack and Dillon kneeled near the glowing coals, roasting marshmallows. Lola and Letty were each huddled under a blanket and Brutus and Rex were standing nearby with firelight dancing in their eyes.

Now, in the distance the crowds could be heard stomping, clapping, and chanting, "Big Blast! Big Blast! Big Blast!" Then the multitudes of villagers roared with enthusiasm and began shouting the countdown. Five! Four! Three! Two! One! Gunshots rang through the air and all of Pine Grove flashed in a fiery blaze of colored lights. There was a moment of silence as everyone waited for the world to blow up or go dark, but the lights glimmered and the people cheered.

"Happy New Year! Happy New Millennium! Happy Birthday Pine Grove!"

So it was that the new millennium had arrived. Another year had passed and a new century had begun. Traditions would stand strong and opportunities would arise. Old folks would pass and new babies would be born. Life would go on in the quaint village as the people vowed to honor the past and collectively celebrate the future, and as a necessity of human existence, they would continue to live in peace and love—to the best of their ability.

Romey placed his hand on Evie's slightly protruding tummy, and whispered in her ear, "It feels like a girl."

Evie's gaze wandered across the ones she loved so dearly, then from the brilliant, dazzling lights, up to the vast winter sky. From a far-off galaxy shone a single twinkling star. Its angel glow winked three times, then went out.

## Acknowledgements

I would like to thank Nina Solomita for her editorial expertise. It was her unwavering perseverance, patience, and encouragement that brought this book to completion.

A special thank you goes to Lisa Crawford Watson for her literary prowess and grammatical thoroughness. She is a Master of her craft.

I thank my first reader, Karey Demers, for her time, her suggestions, and her kind words.

I thank Nisha Zenoff for sharing her courageous book *The Unspeakable Loss*.

I am grateful for a borrowed quote from Elisabeth Kübler-Ross' book *On Death and Dying*.

A heartfelt thank you for the special ones who remained by my side through my own grief journey. You know who you are.

Finally, I wish to acknowledge Jerome Vandenbroucke for giving us a glimpse into the life of the world's greatest window washer.